PRAISED

KATE HAWTHORNE

Praised
Kate Hawthorne

Copyright © 2023 Kate Hawthorne

Edited by:
Jordan Buchanan

Cover Design:
Samantha Santana - Amai Designs

"The sweetest of all sounds is praise." - Xenophon

CHAPTER 1
FLYNN

I DIDN'T KNOW A LOT ABOUT THE EAST COAST IF IT DIDN'T HAVE TO DO with five-star hotels or three-starred restaurants, expressly limited to those existing within the very narrow margin of the New York City limits. But I knew my best friend's boyfriend's best friend—Jesus, that was a mouthful—was hotter than any man I'd ever thought that region of the country capable of producing.

Thankfully, I knew better than to shit where I ate because, on paper, Frankie was exactly the kind of man I liked to pursue. He was younger than me, he was—objectively—more attractive than me, if not in a rural Maine kind of way, and he didn't live in the same state as me.

I know one of those three qualifiers feels not like the other, but I've always believed in shooting beyond your paygrade. Or mine, in this instance. And every instance. No one ever accomplished anything of note while playing within the rules or limitations that someone else set for them. While I appreciated the foolish kind of man who only wanted to fuck someone he thought was uglier than he was, to keep them on their best behavior and coming back for more, I personally liked a good challenge.

I thrived on proving everyone around me wrong...at every possible turn and in every possible way.

It wasn't like Los Angeles had a shortage of attractive and

willing men and women for me to choose from. No, that wasn't the case at all. There was just something so quietly unpretentious about Frankie's good looks that had me wanting to take his clothes off and whisper in his ear about all sorts of inappropriate things.

Frankie had been in L.A. for four days, helping his best friend Owen relocate from the small town in Maine they'd both lived in for their whole lives. Owen was the boyfriend of one of my best friends, and if they made all men in their hometown the way they made Frankie, and honestly Owen, then I debated the merits of letting him relocate here instead of uprooting our entire friend group and moving them all across the country.

And as he unloaded the last box of Owen's hoodies into Archie's house, I knew I was running out of time to make my move.

"I see you," Owen said under his breath, bumping his shoulder into mine.

"See me what?"

"Not helping," he said. "Staring at my best friend."

"He's not bad to look at," I said.

"He deserves more than a fuck boy."

I chuckled, shaking my head. "You think so low of me? After all we've been through together?"

"I know the kind of men the whole bunch of you are."

"You domesticated Archie pretty quickly," I reminded him.

Owen's cheeks flooded with some kind of emotion that I imagined to be embarrassment. Maybe it was pride, though the two seemed potentially interchangeable at some points and that sounded complicated.

"That's different."

I didn't think it was different at all, but I wasn't in the mood to alienate my best friend's recently relocated boyfriend so early on in their relationship.

"I'm just saying, I've heard the story, Owen. I know Val had your cock in his mouth the first time Archie laid his eyes on you after the grand breakup of your teenage years. I don't really think there's harm in getting your dick wet, and I'd be more than happy to help your friend out with it."

"What is this?" Archie asked, coming out of the house with an air fryer in his arms.

"An air fryer?" Owen answered him with a question, and it was impossible to not laugh at both of them.

"I'm not sure if you noticed or not, but unless you count spraying cheese onto crackers, our mutual acquaintance here hasn't ever prepared an actual meal in his kitchen." I slapped Owen on the back, hoping he took the entire conversation for the joke I wanted him to believe it was.

Because I was very serious about taking Frankie to bed.

Or at least to the bathroom.

A parking lot maybe.

Even an alley. I heard that worked out well for Owen and Archie, at least.

"It doesn't count," Owen said, taking the fryer from a confused Archie's hands.

"Have fun with that one." I turned to head into the house in pursuit of Frankie.

"You too," Owen said, resignation over my intent with his friend splashed across his face.

"Are you sure?" I asked, wanting to pursue him for fun, but not if it was a real issue for Owen. I might have been a fuck boy —his words, not mine—but I wasn't callous and I was never cruel.

"It's up to him."

"What are the two of you talking about?" Archie asked, looking back and forth between the both of us.

"Nothing," I said, brushing him off and heading inside to find the subject of our conversation.

Frankie was easy enough to locate, standing in the middle of the dining room with his hands bracketed against the narrow dip of his waist while he stared at a pile of boxes with a frown on his face.

"Were the boxes talking shit?" I asked, coming to stand in front of him. "Want me to kick their ass?"

Frankie looked up at me and huffed an unamused laugh. "Do lines like that work on men out here?"

"Who said it was a line?"

He rolled his eyes. "I know your type."

"Do tell." I gestured for him to go on. I was curious how the man saw me, and his answer would undoubtedly give me insight about how best to make it happen with him before his trip back to the east coast.

"You think you can buy whatever you want," he started.

"For the most part, I can."

My bank account wasn't anything to laugh at, but I didn't think I oozed pretentiousness the way my other friends Barclay and Rob did. I'd have to take that one back to the drawing board. Not to say my money didn't help me seal a deal if I couldn't quite get it across the finish line with my looks and personality alone, but I didn't ever intend to leverage it right off the bat.

Good to know.

"You're too attractive for your own good," he went on.

I grinned, plucking at the collar of my shirt with a sense of satisfaction that proved I knew myself better than I thought after all. "That sounds like a compliment."

"I didn't mean it that way."

I rubbed the front of my chest with a pretend grimace. "You wound me."

"You could use some of that, I think."

I let out a breath, not interested in fighting for a meal.

"You know that after you pack your suitcase up and go back home, that I'm going to be the one here still, right? That I'm one of Archie's best friends, and I'm honestly rather fond of Owen already, as well."

"What does that have to do with anything?" Frankie asked.

"When you're gone, we'll be who he has left."

Frankie laughed, shoving his hair away from his face, revealing two sparkling green eyes that hadn't yet stopped taking my breath away.

"I'll never be gone, Flynn."

"Hey, hey!" Owen came inside finally, air fryer tucked beneath one of his arms like a sack of potatoes. "Archie was saying we should go grab a drink. You in?"

Frankie's eyes were locked on mine.

"I'm always in to hang out with you," I answered.

Frankie's lip twitched, but he didn't break my stare. "I'm happy to see a little of the city."

"Where did you have in mind?" I asked, looking away from Owen and catching Archie's eye.

"Nothing fancy." He shrugged. "Grayson says there's a bar in Manhattan Beach that has turtle races."

"What now?" I asked.

"We used to do that for free at the pond back home," Frankie said, smacking Owen in the chest fondly. "You remember that?"

I knew what he was doing. Frankie was posturing, trying to swing his dick and assert his claim over Owen. But the joke was on him. He could have Owen all he wanted. Archie's boyfriend was not where my interests lay. The fact that Frankie looked like he would have kicked me into traffic on the 405 only served to make me want him more. Because then I'd be able to prove him wrong across the board.

I wasn't too rich or too good-looking. And even if I were, I only used my powers for good. There wasn't anything wrong with liking sex and having sex. There wasn't anything wrong with the kind of sex I liked to have either. In fact, I found most people enjoyed it beyond measure, and I was always more than happy to open their eyes to all the exciting and very verbal ways you could bring someone off.

"We can all fit in my car," Archie said, giving his house a quick scan and counting off on his fingers.

There were five of us handling the last of the unpacking.

Between the three of them, me, and Grayson, we'd gotten it finished pretty quickly.

"Tight squeeze in the back seat," I said, earning a glare from Frankie.

Grayson appeared from the bathroom then, dusting his hands off on the front of his chinos.

"For someone who looks like he's never met a washcloth he likes, you have a surprising amount of toiletries," he said.

"Are you sure you want to live here?" Frankie asked, tone half serious and half teasing. "They're all kind of horrible."

"You haven't even met Barclay yet," Grayson said with a casual raise of his left shoulder.

"They're not horrible," Owen interjected. "They're just…who they are."

"That doesn't sound much better," I said.

"Trust me, it is."

"But wherever we go, I'm taking my own car because I'm supposed to meet Rob at Rapture later tonight, and that sounds a lot more fun than hanging out with you guys. No offense."

"I want to go to Rapture," I pouted. "Why didn't anyone invite me?"

Pulling my phone out of my pocket, I swiped through my messages until I got to the Trophy Doms group text.

Me: I want to go to Rapture tonight.
Me: Why didn't anyone invite me to Rapture?

Archie's phone vibrated in his pocket and he sighed, ignoring it.

Dalton: Who's going to Rapture?
Rob: Grayson and I.
Dalton: And us?
Barclay: I'm taking a pass tonight.

Barclay: I also still want the record to reflect I'd like to take a pass from this group chat too.
Me: Just put your phone on silent if you don't want your romantic dates with Val to get interrupted.
Dalton: So are we going to Rapture?
Archie: I'm down if you are.

I looked up with a wicked smile.

Me: Let's bring Owen's friend. Really show him the sights.
Rob: You're a menace.
Me: Is that a yes?
Rob: It's a public club. I can't stop you.

I didn't bother to read anything after that, sliding my phone back into my pocket with a victorious smile.

"Hey, Frankie, you want to go to church tonight?"

"Not especially."

Owen chuckled and scratched the back of his neck, turning to his friend. "It's not really a church, it's a…shit."

"Don't be shy, Owen. Frankie was just telling me how close the two of you were."

"Sex club," Archie said, taking the air fryer out of Owen's hands and carrying it into the kitchen. "And considering the history between you two, if we go, all of the dicks are staying in the pants."

"Speak for yourself," I muttered.

"I'm just…you know what I mean."

"I assure you, Archie, my interest in sleeping with Owen has been gone for longer than it ever existed." He made an X across his heart. "Boy scout's honor."

"Dicks in the pants is fine," Owen said, sliding his arm around Frankie's shoulder and pulling him toward the guest room. "Let's find you something to wear."

"No turtles then?" I asked.

"I love the turtles." Grayson smiled at something on his phone, then looked to me and Archie. "But if that's the last of it, I'm taking off. I want to go home and freshen up before Rob's off work."

Archie stretched out his arms and gave Grayson a quick hug. The two of them had gotten close since Grayson and Rob became involved, which I really loved. Archie was the youngest of our friends and I worried that sometimes he was too alienated from us because of life and experience, but Grayson, for as outlandish as he could be sometimes, had been a surprisingly steady anchor for Archie.

Or maybe it was the other way around.

Either way.

———

Five hours later, I found myself at Rapture, elbows resting on a cocktail table on the main floor. It was a change from the comfort and quiet of the loft, but Frankie hadn't even bothered to dial down his patronization in the slightest from the afternoon and I didn't want to say something I'd later regret.

But the tables had turned, and Frankie apparently derived some sick pleasure in pushing my buttons because he found himself at the table beside me, warm shoulder pressed against mine.

"I didn't peg you as a quitter," he said, taking a sip of his gin.

"You didn't peg me at all."

That earned a low laugh, and he turned toward me, mouth twisted into a challenging smile.

"I have a deal for you."

"That's not going to end well for you." I shifted so we faced each other. "I make deals for a living."

"Good thing you don't know what winning looks like for me."

"Touché." I took a swallow of my scotch. "By all means then, go on."

"Kiss me," he said.

"Or what?"

"No or." Frankie shook his head, and I noticed his eyes were the same shade of green as the stained glass on the wall behind him. "Kiss me, and if you do it good enough to make me change my mind about sleeping with you…"

He trailed off, leaving the win unsaid.

"This sounds like a trap," I said.

"This sounds like you're a horrible kisser."

That was a bridge too far for me. With a haughty laugh, I slid my hand around the back of his head and pulled him toward me, stopping with his mouth less than an inch from mine. His pupils dilated and he rolled his neck, testing the hold I had on the back of his head.

"Are you scared you'll lose, Flynn?"

I didn't even offer him a reply, instead crashing our mouths together without another word. Frankie didn't fight when my tongue slicked across the seam of his mouth, and he didn't protest when I changed the angle of my head to deepen the kiss. He kissed me back, with his hands settled gently on my hips, but it didn't take long for me to realize there wasn't any fire in it.

From either end.

Pulling back, I let my hand fall from his hair, and I touched the corner of my mouth, the mix of our spit still present on my lips. Frankie let go of my hips and reached for his drink, taking a reasonably-sized swallow. I grabbed my scotch and finished the rest of it off with a grunt.

"Flynn."

"Don't."

"Flynn, is that…is that really how you kiss people?" he asked.

"Is that really how *you* kiss people?"

He scoffed. "I'm a great kisser. You're the one who…"

"Kissing you was like making out with one of those life-size cardboard standees," I said, wishing I had more liquor in my glass.

I was pressed to remember a kiss as bad as that one, and I'd done a lot of kissing in my life. My first kiss hadn't even been as boring and bland as my last one.

"I've never kissed a fish." Frankie laughed. "But that's what I've always thought it would be like if I did."

"Fuck off."

My ego and pride were more wounded than anything else, and the soft cock between my legs was proof that Frankie was the one at fault, not me. I was a good kisser. I knew how to kiss. I'd made people come just from kissing before, just from my tongue, and it felt important to tell him that.

"This mouth"—I pointed at my mouth, drawing a furious circle in the air above my lips—"knows how to kiss."

"I'm a fair kind of guy," Frankie said, his stupid useless mouth tipping up into a smirk. "I'll give you another chance to prove it."

"I'm not kissing you again."

How had I been so wrong about him? Going off looks and attitude alone, Frankie had all the markers that should have made him a great once-off, and yet…there we both stood.

Flaccid and unimpressed.

"I'm not kissing you again either, Casanova." He looked over his shoulder scanning the dance floor before obviously finding his target. "You're kissing him."

CHAPTER 2
ROSE

THE ONLY THING WORSE THAN DATING A CHEATING FUCK BOY WAS getting dumped by a cheating fuck boy.

In hindsight, I should have expected it. A leopard can't change its spots or however the saying goes.

But Cody had always been really good with his tongue, whether he used it for telling me lies or eating my ass until I forgot my own name. Unfortunately, the latter made me forget the former and, well...

"Rosey!" My friend Drake shouted my name. "You need a shot!"

I threw an exhausted glance at him because he'd been the one with the horrible idea of dragging me out to a sex club that looked like it was going to send me straight to hell just for stepping over the threshold. Rapture was in Pasadena, tucked inside an old church and nestled against a grove of trees, and while I loved the idea, the timing was less than ideal. I wanted to drown my sorrows in ice cream and baked goods, not tequila and the sounds of other people getting off.

Not that I hated the sound of other people getting off. I was, in fact, a fan of anyone and everyone getting off. Myself included. I liked to hear it, hear about it, even see it if the situation allowed. Cody said that made me a voyeur, but I'd never thought that seriously about it. He must have, though, because he made sure I got an eyeful when I walked in on him with that lying, cheating, tongue of his shoved up his roommate's asshole.

I always had a weird feeling about their relationship, but I'd listened to his assurances and believed him for months. The worst part was, I was sure they'd been sleeping together the whole time. Probably from before Cody and I even got involved, and that was just embarrassing. My imagination ran rampant, thinking of the two of them jacking each other off after Cody and I had been together, or who knew what they got up to.

Fuck.

I needed to go get tested.

Again.

"I don't need a shot," I told him, but he had already left me. I watched his shock of dyed pink hair disappear as he made his way through the crowd and toward the bar.

Taking advantage of his momentary absence, I pulled my cell phone out of my pocket and scrolled down to my text messages, finding at least half a dozen apologies from Cody sitting unread. With a sigh, I tapped the icon next to his name, a picture of us both, our heads angled together, on our very first date when he'd taken me to the Santa Monica pier.

Cody: It's not what you're thinking, Rose.
Cody: Adam and I are just friends.
Cody: I love you.
Cody: The thing with Adam isn't anything serious. It's just fun. I thought maybe one day we could all play around.
Cody: He thinks you're really hot, and he's not wrong.
Cody: Please give me another chance, sugar. I'm sorry.

He wasn't sorry, though.

Rather, he was only sorry because he'd gotten caught. Otherwise, he wouldn't have let me walk out and stew in my anger for three hours before finding the balls to reach out to me. I'd ignored him for a day, then caved in and responded, but everything he'd said had been a whole lot of the same. A lot of nothing.

I'd caught them together four days earlier, and I knew sooner or later I was going to have to get over my wounded ego and talk to him in a meaningful way because my favorite lingerie was still at his house and a matching La Perla set wasn't something I was willing to walk away from without a fight. I just needed to let my emotions—and my sex drive—calm down.

Because for as much as I didn't want to date a fuck boy, I did want to date a boy who fucked. Or a man would probably be better. I liked to play, I liked to have sex, and more than that, I liked to get off. I liked to get *other* people off. It wasn't even a self-esteem issue or anything like that either. I knew I was good-looking and I knew I was a catch. I honestly just liked fucking, and I liked people who liked to fuck.

I liked people who liked to fuck me, more specifically.

Not people who liked to fuck everyone.

But, unfortunately, they were often one and the same.

Maybe it would be good to take a break for a little while, let everything after Cody settle and then hit the ground running to see if I could find myself another man who could live up to my borderline insatiable sex drive.

"Shots!" Drake shouted in my ear, returning with two whipped cream-topped shot glasses.

"We're too old for this shit," I reminded him, tossing back the Blow Job before he could insist that I did it the traditional way with no hands. When I swallowed and used the back of my hand to swipe the residual whipped cream off the corner of my mouth, his glare was proof enough that I'd foiled his plan.

"You're just getting boring."

Drake made quite the show of tangling his fingers behind his back before taking the shot glass between his lips and throwing the whole thing back.

"Would a boring friend bring you to a place like this?" he asked.

I looked around, finally allowing myself to notice the couples on the dance floor that were pressed a little too close together for things to look decent, the spattering of men who were shirtless, only wearing the soft and buttery-looking leather harnesses with jeans or leather pants on the bottom. I glanced around and looked up, finding what I assumed to be an organ loft that had been converted into something much less holy…or more, depending on how you looked at it.

"I love you, but I think you have ulterior motives," I said.

"I've heard there's good cruising in the bathroom."

I allowed myself a glance toward the hallway behind the bar that led toward the restrooms before turning my attention back to Drake. "I don't think it's all that clandestine here. Pretty sure you could get it wherever you wanted."

"What I want is upstairs," he said.

I sighed. "Did you already set your sights on someone for the night?"

Drake was like me in some ways, but polar opposite in others. He was fully motivated by sex, but if our places had been swapped, he wouldn't have cared one way or the other if he'd walked in on Cody and Adam. He would have joined in before Cody even had time to worry if he'd made a mistake. I loved him for that, the ease with which he played around with non-monogamy, because while there were lots of things I could get my head around, sharing my partner was not one of them.

"There's someone over by the bar," Drake admitted, cheeks so flushed I could see the color under the stained glass disco ball reflections. "Do you want to watch?"

Groaning, I closed my eyes, hating the way my cock did spark the slightest bit of interest at the request. Cody had called me a voyeur, and my body proved him right.

"Don't use that against me," I grumbled.

"I think it's hot." Drake grabbed my arm and pulled our faces close together. I could still smell the sugary whipped cream on his breath. "There's nothing wrong with watching. Or being watched."

"I know. I'm just still upset about Cody."

"You can be upset *and* horny. The two feelings don't exist in a vacuum, Rose."

I hated that he was right, but being upset with Cody and turned on about being around so many people with erections was a complicated set of emotions to manage, especially considering how sober I was.

"Go get me a drink first and then go," I said, finally giving in.

My response brought a megawatt smile to his face, and half the fight went out of me as he practically ran back to the bar. There wasn't any harm in watching, and from the table I'd probably not be able to see much anyway. I could observe and sulk, and hopefully work up a little bit of a buzz. Not enough to call Cody, but a little bit, just so I didn't want to cry. It was a little selfish of Drake to bring me out under the ruse of distracting me from being sullen about Cody just so he could go pick up a guy for himself, but it wasn't like I was out there trying to get anything for myself either.

I really needed to get over my shit.

Shoving my hand into my pants, I adjusted my cock and balls in the soft, lace pocket of my underwear, then waited for Drake to return. The bartenders at Rapture were nothing if not efficient, because it felt like mere seconds before he was back with a salt-rimmed margarita for me to sip on.

"What's he look like?" I asked.

Drake pointed toward the L-shaped corner of the bar. "Long and dark hair, olive skin. You see him?"

The man he was referencing was impossible to miss.

"I see him," I said. Drake gave me a smile and returned to the crowd, heading for the bar yet again.

Taking my drink, I decided the middle of the room wasn't the place for me. One, I was alone, and two, I didn't want to look like a weirdo lurker. Carefully navigating through the crowd, I came to stop near the emergency exit door on the far wall. It felt like a secret little bubble, safe from the lights of the dance floor and the thrum of the other patrons dancing and laughing.

I watched as Drake made his way to the man in question, who looked like he was all long limbs and silken hair. Drake's mark definitely wasn't my type, but I knew Drake well enough to know all of his tells. He leaned in and smiled. He walked his fingers up the front of the other man's chest, right to his throat and around the side of his neck. He took control without being dominant about it, but it was in the blink of an eye before the man switched the power play and turned, pressing Drake against the bar and leaning down to whisper something into his ear.

Of course, I couldn't hear, but I didn't need to. The fantasy of it was enough and my brain was quick to supply me with a fictional narrative to feed my own interests. I hated to admit that Drake *had* been right. Getting out of the house was exactly what I needed. Even if I'd at first thought watching wouldn't be enough to distract me, the quick downward flow of blood to my dick proved otherwise.

I allowed myself a sip of margarita, the tart mixture burning as it slid down my throat. Drake's lashes fluttered and I watched the back of the other man's arm move in a familiar up and down motion, his hand obscured. If he wasn't jerking Drake off, he was getting close. With my free hand, I adjusted myself again, fighting back embarrassment over how quickly the scene had gotten me hard.

It was proof that my emotions had made me a walking disaster, so I forced myself to look away from Drake as to avoid coming in my underwear without so much as a hand from a stranger, let alone myself. But I didn't find any solace in the other views the club provided because everywhere I looked, there was something good to see.

Half-dressed men in various states of arousal, women in leather skirts and tight-laced corsets that sucked their waists to nothing and pushed their soft tits skyward, couples and singles, and everyone in between. When I closed my eyes, the sounds from the loft filtered down over the music, leather against skin, laughter, the softest melody of someone's moans.

I raised the little cocktail straws to my mouth for another drink. I needed more tequila, and then I needed fresh air. But first, I had to give Drake one more check-in before heading out front to get myself back under control. When I swallowed the last of my drink, I opened my eyes, searching out Drake and his raven-haired conquest. They were nowhere to be found, which wasn't surprising, but the man heading toward me, dressed in tight black slacks and a crisp white button-up, sleeves rolled past his elbows and an expression on his face like he had something to prove, stopped me in my tracks.

I FOLLOWED THE DIRECTION FRANKIE POINTED, SCOFFING AT HIS selection. "I've kissed him before, and if you're trying to prove that I'm not good at it, he's not the one to try."

"Him then." Frankie pointed at Val's old roommate, who was dancing away without a care in the world on the middle of the dance floor.

"I've done a lot more than kiss him," I said, leaning in close. "I can tell you all about it if you want."

"What about her?" Frankie was getting exasperated, clearly trying to change tactics by switching genders. While it was a fair guess I'd spent less time in bed with the female patrons of Rapture, there were always exceptions to the rules.

"Women are much easier to please than men," I said with a shrug. "I'm happy to illustrate the point if she's your final answer."

"No, wait." Frankie stopped me with a tight squeeze around my bicep.

I hid my grin before throwing a look over my shoulder at him.

"Him, then."

That time, he didn't point. He jerked his head toward a man who leaned against the wall by the fire exit, an almost empty drink clutched loosely in his hand. On the top of his head sat a shock of yellow-blond curls weighed down by the warmth and humidity of the air in the club. He had a round face with a wide mouth and bright blue eyes that sparkled like tumbled aquamarine even through the dark of the dance floor. He was short and he looked delicate, with long fingers and a curious tongue that darted out to lick at the corner of his mouth. He was scanning the room, looking for someone, but he found me instead, those unmistakable blue eyes locking onto me and holding steady.

"Alright," I agreed, but I was already on my way across the room.

The man, who was definitely younger and considerably smaller than me, held my stare with rapt focus as I closed the space between us, and when I came to stand in front of him, almost toe to toe, he tipped his head back and grinned up at me like he was looking for trouble.

"You look like a man on a mission," he said, his voice as soft as the rest of him.

"My friend over there…" I pointed over my shoulder toward the table I'd left Frankie at, not bothering to look away from my pending challenge. "He thinks I'm a bad kisser."

"That's not as strong of an opening as you think it is."

"Well, it's stronger than you think, because he's wrong."

The man beneath me arched a well-shaped brow in doubt. Raising his glass to his mouth, he sucked the last of his drink out until the straw rattled around the ice.

"Am I meant to be the judge?" he asked, handing me his empty glass.

I took it.

I didn't have anywhere to put it, but I took it because he offered it to me, and although I'd never been one to cater to another person outside of the bedroom, it had almost felt like second nature. We both looked down at the glass in my hand and his shock at me taking it seemed to match my own for the same act.

"You're meant to prove me right," I said.

He let out a little laugh that sounded like a song.

"I think *you're* meant to prove yourself right," he wagered. "I don't have anyone in this room doubting my kissing skills."

"Can I, then?"

His luscious mouth twitched up in the corner and he cocked his head from one side to the other. "You're asking?"

"I always ask," I rasped.

"Ask me in detail."

I bit back a groan, swallowing down the supreme amounts of enjoyment the back and forth with this gorgeous—and still nameless—man was bringing me. After the rough jabs with Frankie, it was nice to be engaged by someone who had a sense of humor and an interest in having a little fun.

"I'm not the one who takes instructions…" I trailed off, tipping the word up at the end in question, hoping he'd pick up the ask.

"Ambrose," he answered. "You can call me Rose."

"Is that your nickname?" I asked.

"That's what my friends call me."

"I'm a stranger," I said.

His nostrils flared, pupils dilating as he sucked in a breath.

"What do your lovers call you?" I asked, shuffling an inch closer. There was already hardly any room between us and the air was thick enough without all the sexual tension. Just being around him was enough to make me hard, and if I kissed him like shit, I was likely to climb to the roof of the club and throw myself over the edge.

"All sorts of things," he said teasingly, voice low as be batted his lashes, sending a thousand ideas and endearments through my mind.

Gorgeous boy.

Pet.

Slut.

Mine.

"Ambrose," I repeated his name, barely more than a whisper.

"Never that one," he countered.

"There's a first time for everything."

He made a rough sound in the back of his throat. "Are you gonna kiss me or not?"

I was going to kiss him.

Hard and deep and long.

I snaked my hand around the back of his neck and met him in the middle, crashing our mouths together a little harder than I'd intended, but I hadn't expected him to come up onto his toes to close the space.

His lips tasted like lime and honey, a little sticky from what had to have been lip gloss at some point. Rose reached out and braced his hands around my waist, moaning into my mouth as my tongue dipped inside to explore. I took another step, walking him against the wall and my chest against his. He was firm in all of the right places, and I was hard in the one that mattered most. He must have felt my erection because he pressed his stomach against me, applying a sinful amount of pressure against my already constrained dick.

I wanted to kiss him better, touch him more, but his damn margarita was in my hand and there wasn't a table in sight. I cracked one eye open and caught sight of the fire alarm beside the door. It was risky, but it would have to do. I set the drink on the mechanism, watching as it teetered in a precarious balance. One of Rose's hands slid around my belt, fingers grasping at the leather and giving it a tug.

I grabbed him, my fingers wrapping all of the way around his wrist and bringing him to a stop. He nipped at my lower lip, his cock pressing against my thigh. Slowly, with our mouths still fused together, tongues still dancing, Rose's golden lashes began to flutter. His eyes rolled back a little as he tried to bring me into focus, and his lips curled into a smile against my mouth.

"That definitely wasn't bad," he murmured.

No, it wasn't, but I was nowhere near ready to be finished kissing him. "I can do better."

I shifted the angle of my head and kissed him again, licking past the surprised seam of his lips. He let go of my belt and I let go of him, bending at the knee and dragging my hands down to the backs of his thighs until he got the memo and pushed off the floor. Rose wrapped his legs around my waist and I pushed him back against the wall, one hand against his face and the other underneath his ass.

He swirled his hips against mine, drawing a low growl from the depths of my throat, then he broke the connection and tilted his head up, giving me access to his neck. I peppered kisses over his Adam's apple and toward the hollow between his collarbones, then worked my way back up the side of his neck until I reached his ear. Rose turned his face into me, and I searched out his lips for a third time, licking the taste of his drink out of his mouth until the only thing left for him to taste was me.

"That was definitely better," he teased after coming up for air.

"That was nothing," I whispered the promise against his ear, slowly unwinding his legs from around my waist and easing him back to the floor. I bent down with him, not ready to break away from the heat of him or the feel of him.

"Talk me through it then, big guy."

"Flynn," I told him.

"Do you not like big guy?" He settled his hands back on my hips and I leaned back enough to see his face.

"There are things I prefer."

"Like what?"

"Like Sir," I said.

Heat flared up Rose's face, coloring his cheeks a red so bright it looked like it came right out of one of the stained glass window panes above our heads.

"Well, okay then." He cleared his throat and tried to square his slim shoulders. "Talk me through it, Sir."

"Nuh-uh." I wagged a finger at him, shaking my head to double up on the no. "That one is earned, Ambrose."

"I'm quickly forgetting how good that kiss was, and I don't think you want me to give a bad report to your little friend."

Rose was an absolute spitfire of a man—I had to give him that.

He more than made up for his slim build and short statute with an attitude big enough to knock even the most confident Dom back on his feet.

The problem was I didn't know why I cared. I didn't know why I entertained his attitude or his unsolicited demands. I'd wanted to kiss him and he'd allowed it, that should have been the end of the transaction. I had no place to even be thinking about more with him. Rose was a stranger to me, save for the two things about him I'd learned since our first exchange. He took absolutely no shit from anyone, and he lit a fire under me like no one ever had.

"Here," I said, pressing the tip of my finger against the spot where his neck sloped into his clavicle. Hoping to infuse as much sternness into my tone as I could manage, considering how positively unraveled he already had me, I took a deep breath before continuing. "I would kiss you here. Bite you and suck a bruise so right into that thin skin."

"A good start," he whimpered, grabbing my wrist like I'd earlier done to him. I didn't get the impression it was to stop me, though. He wanted to go along for the ride, so I traced my way down over his chest until I felt out a nipple, which I took between my fingers with a gentle twist.

"Then down to here. Another kiss, and then lower still." I dragged both our hands down to his surprisingly substantial bulge. Rose was clearly not slight all over, and I tried to not let him see the look that crossed my face when I felt his dick against my hand.

"Would you kiss my cock?" he asked, pressing into my hand.

"I would suck it," I told him. "Suck this cock and these balls. But I would kiss your hole until it was wet and sloppy—"

I cut myself off. I was taking it too far.

Sure, he'd asked me to tell him what I would do, but I only had consent for a kiss and we were in public. While exhibitionism was fine and dandy, it wasn't something we'd discussed. There were a lot of things we hadn't discussed. He'd just barely learned my name.

"Don't stop there, Flynn."

How did he make my name sound like sin?

I'd forgotten where we were. Who he was. Who *I* was. I'd all but erased Frankie's existence from my mind, but I knew he was across the room and he was watching. And while we'd all agreed on a kiss, I wasn't quite ready for either of these strangers to see me unmanned.

"That's enough for tonight," I said. "I'm sorry."

"For what?"

I cleared my throat, untangling our hands and bodies so I could take a step back. Air rushed between us, hot and sticky, smelling like sweat and a hundred different kinds of cologne. My nose twitched in disgust, and Rose eyed me cautiously, like I was some kind of predator.

And in a way I was.

It was good he understood that before we talked ourselves into something neither of us really wanted. See, I didn't have a problem with casual things. Casual sex, casual friends, casual whatever. It was honestly what I preferred, but something about Rose sent all of those long-held beliefs right out the window.

And that was dangerous.

"I like things a certain way," I said.

"The Sir way." He rolled his eyes at me. "I figured."

"It's more than that."

"It always is." Rose plucked at his tight shirt until it settled back into place, giving me the chance to make out both of his hard nipples under the fabric. "Well, let's go tell your friend that you're the best kiss I've ever had."

He took my hand and gave me a tug toward Frankie, who eyed us like someone had shit in his Cheerios. I tried to school my features and settle back into the smug kind of protection I generally wore, but Rose's palm against mine made it impossibly hard to not be affected.

"You don't have to lie," I said as we got closer.

Frankie wouldn't believe it if the answer was too over the top.

Rose gave my arm a rough tug and I looked down at him, his cheeks still pink and his lips still shiny, but now swollen from our kiss.

"I'm many things, Flynn, but I'm not a liar."

CHAPTER 4
ROSE

If that was a fair representation of how Flynn kissed, I didn't even want to imagine what it would be like to fuck him, but I'd asked anyway and he'd talked me through enough of it to know that I shouldn't even *think* about it.

Flynn wasn't like Cody, but Cody was enough like Flynn that I knew to stay away. Men who approached random strangers at the club for a kiss were only a hop, skip, and a jump away from men who slept with their roommates behind your back for months. There was a level of discretion that some people just didn't seem to have. I knew where Cody stood, and I wagered Flynn wasn't too far away.

Even with all the talk he'd done about asking for consent and not wanting to take things too far, he was just too good to be true. Too tall and too broad, too handsome, and too willing to cater to silly little whims like holding an empty margarita glass so I could get a better angle on the kiss. Flynn said he liked to be called Sir, but I wagered I could have him calling me all kinds of things if I played my cards right.

But I was going to fold before the hand even got dealt.

"You don't even need to say a word." Flynn's friend waved me off before I could get my mouth open.

"Come on, Frankie," Flynn teased, tightening his hold on my hand when I tried to let go. "Hear him out."

"He's a good kisser," I said.

"I feel like we're an even split," Frankie said. "One for and one against."

"I can pull a sampling from the dance floor if you want to take a poll," Flynn offered and a shock of unexpected jealousy flared up the base of my spine. I tried again to shake my hand free, but he refused to let go.

"I give up." Frankie raised his hands in surrender. "I'm going to go find Owen and Archie and leave the two of you to it."

"There's nothing to leave us to," I said, but Frankie was already gone and Flynn was already looking down at me again, his eyes dark and telling.

I swallowed, blinking slowly.

"I should go and find my friend," I managed, gesturing with my free hand toward where I'd last seen Drake.

"Is that what you want to do or just what you think you *should* do?"

"Do you have a better offer?"

The question was out of my mouth before I realized the words had formed, and I cursed under my breath. Flynn laughed softly and I caught sight of Drake's bright hair on the other side of the room. He was still with the dark-haired man he'd chased after before Flynn had set his sights on me, leaning against the bar in conversation.

"About a thousand," Flynn whispered.

"I shouldn't."

"Neither should I," he agreed, taking a step toward me. "But I want to anyway."

"I get the impression you don't get told no very often."

Flynn smelled expensive, like a soap or cologne that was meant to make sure you remembered the fragrance without even realizing it. Just being in his space conjured up some kind of vague memory that made me want to strip my clothes off and roll around in money for no discernible reason. The erection between my legs was probably the reason, and that had nothing to do with his smell, though, and everything to do with his mouth.

"Not really, no," he agreed.

"I've got bad news."

"Don't say that." Flynn raised our joined hands toward his mouth and dusted a kiss across the top of my knuckles.

His lips burned my fingers.

"I don't do casual encounters."

"I do," he said. "But I don't think I could with you."

"Also not as strong of an opening as you meant that to be, I don't think."

"You know what?" Flynn let go of my hand and I hated it. "I don't even know what I'm doing with you."

I scoffed, the sound catching in the back of my throat. I wanted to argue with him because when he had my back against the wall and one of those huge hands of his groping my ass, I was fairly certain he knew exactly what to do with me.

"Thank you for letting me prove my friend wrong," he said, dipping his chin toward his chest. "Can I buy you a drink?"

"This feels like a consolation prize."

"I assure you, it's better than the other option." Flynn sidestepped away from the table and held his arm out toward the bar. I shrugged and tried not to show any kind of physical response when he settled his hand against the small of my back to guide me toward the other side of the room.

I was still a little sweaty from the club and a lot flustered from the kiss, and while his constant back and forth was giving me whiplash, it also gave me the impression I wasn't the only one under some sort of aroused and confusing duress.

"You don't have to buy me a drink," I said.

"You didn't have to kiss me."

We reached the bar and I rolled my eyes, flattening my hands against the sticky bar top so I didn't do something stupid like grab him by the lapels and go for another round. Not that he was wearing a jacket—he wasn't. It was that damn dress shirt, all crisp and clean without being starchy and the ridiculous veins in his forearm that peeked out from beneath the rolled cuffs that got me going. Hands on the bar so I didn't do something stupid like grab him by the shirt sleeves and go another round.

"I enjoyed it," he whispered in my ear, one arm coming around me so his hand could land just beside mine. He boxed me in and I should have hated it, but it only served to stir the arousal we'd both been fighting since the kiss broke.

"So did I."

"But we can't do it again." As those words left his mouth, the bartender appeared and Flynn ordered a whiskey for himself and a margarita for me.

"How did you know what I was drinking?" I turned around so my back was against the bar. I wanted to see his face, which was a bad idea because it brought half our chests together, his thigh pressing right in all of the most sensitive spots between my own legs.

"I could taste it on you when we kissed. Salt and tequila."

"And you're a whiskey drinker?" I asked.

"Scotch, but whiskey will do."

"Do you have any idea how bougie you sound?" The question came out weak, like a deflating balloon.

"Absolutely."

Our drinks appeared on the bar and I swiveled away from him, grateful for the reprieve from his intense stare. Flynn had eyes that reminded me of caramel chocolate and they made me want to do all sorts of things that I'd regret in the morning.

"Well," I said weakly, sliding my drink into his until the glasses clinked. "Thanks for the drink."

"Thanks for the kiss."

He didn't move and neither did I, though it would have been much easier for him to be the one to dislodge our bodies. I would've had to squat down and slide out from underneath his arm, which felt almost comical, when all he would have to do is lift his arm and step out of the way.

"Are you going to go?" I asked, raising my drink to my lips.

His breath burned hot against the top of my head with every exhale.

"That feels reasonable."

"But?"

"*I'm* not feeling reasonable," he said.

"Has anyone told you that being with you is about as easy on the stomach as a ride on a tilt-a-whirl?" I turned again to face him, dropping my head back so I could see his face.

Bad idea.

All of the lust he'd made me feel during the kiss was painted across his features, clear enough even under the rainbow-colored disco lights to take my breath away.

Again.

"It's your fault," he murmured, eyes half closed and mouth half open.

"As much as I'd like to believe that..." I trailed off as Flynn angled his face toward mine, whiskey and want all over his breath.

"Tell me I can kiss you again."

He was practically already there, but I managed a nod and he sealed his lips against mine one more time.

What was it about this man that had me absolutely upside down over him?

Drake had dragged me out to Rapture to distract me from my cheating fuck boy of an ex and I'd tripped and fallen right into the mouth of another one. Sure, Flynn was better dressed and definitely had more money and more expensive taste in alcohol, but I knew the type.

I was actively trying to remind myself I knew his type when the hard rod of his erection flexed against my stomach and I immediately forgot absolutely everything in my brain besides my own name and the word *please*.

Flynn's tongue invaded my mouth, his hands groping their

way down my sides and pulling our bodies flush. He was such a big man and his fingers trembled against my waist, the tension coiled through his whole body like a snake, and for as much as I didn't…I really wanted to know what he would be like when he let loose.

In the pocket of my shorts, my phone started to vibrate, a sharp and unexpected splash of cold water. I leaned into the kiss a little longer, ignoring the insistent buzz against my thigh, but eventually Flynn smiled against my mouth and pulled away for a breath.

"I don't think I've ever activated a vibrate feature with just my mouth," he said, kissing the corner of mine.

"He's got jokes," I muttered, because it was positively insane that he could crack a joke when I was less than a minute from crawling out of my clothes—and my skin—for how much I wanted him in bed.

"Is someone looking for you?" he asked, glancing down at the outline of my phone against my leg. "Do I need to be jealous?"

"It's either my best friend or my ex." I wiggled my phone free and found Drake's name across the screen, a single text message followed by enough eggplant and peach emoji's to start a fruit stand.

Drake: The best way to get over someone is to get under HIM.

Heat burned my cheeks and I shoved my phone back into my pocket, hopefully before Flynn could read the message.

"The ex then?" he asked.

"The friend."

"Is this your emergency out?"

I rubbed at the bridge of my nose, giving him a quick shake of my head.

"Not at all."

As if he could sense my distress, Flynn placed my drink into my hand.

"How much have you had to drink tonight?" he asked.

"This is my second. Why?"

The icy tequila was refreshing and did enough to calm my nerves that the need to crawl out of my skin had finally started to subside.

"Are you drunk?"

"Not even close."

"Are you buzzed?"

I set my drink on the bar, the glass almost still entirely full.

"Why the twenty questions?" I asked, letting my hand fall away from my face.

"I don't play with people under the influence," he said, so matter of fact.

"That's presumptuous." But even as I countered him, my palm landed against his stomach, feeling out the shape of his muscles beneath his shirt. "How much have *you* had to drink?"

"This is my second." He grinned, ignoring my hand against his stomach as he raised the glass to his mouth. Taking the smallest sip, he set his drink on the bar beside mine. "Who's being presumptuous now?"

"I was just making conversation," I lied.

Every word out of his mouth unraveled my willpower a little bit more, and Drake's message flashed behind eyelids like a neon sign, obscuring the mental picture of Cody in bed with another man.

"Earlier you said you didn't do casual encounters." Flynn leaned back enough that his whole gorgeous face was in focus, so when he licked the taste of me off his lips and let loose a little groan, I saw the whole thing.

"I try to not."

"I have a proposition for you."

"Oh?" My voice came out weak and raspy, like a breath between us. "Don't keep me in suspense then."

"How about we get out of here, Rose. You let me take you back to my place, or yours, whichever you prefer. Hell, I'll even book a hotel room if that would make you feel better. And then we go wherever you want and then I take you to bed in a very…" He was back in my space again, lips dragging their way up my cheekbone until they reached my ear. His mouth were hot, his tongue wet, and he kissed my earlobe in the messiest and most indecent way I think I'd ever been kissed on any part of my body.

My cock fucking leaked all over my panties and I leaned away from him so he could have more room to do it again.

"In a what?" I managed, bringing us both back to the club, back to the moment.

He hummed, smiling against his handiwork.

"Then," he said, teeth sharp against my skin. "I take you to bed in a very, very serious and definitely not casual kind of way."

CHAPTER 5
FLYNN

What was the saying?

In for a penny, in for a pound?

That's what I kept reminding myself on the drive to The Roosevelt. I didn't even bother saying goodbye to Archie or the rest of them, every cell in my body focused on getting Rose out of the club and someplace private before either of us changed our minds. He regarded me like I was a predator, but little did he know that I offered him the same kind of wariness.

Since I hadn't driven to Rapture, I had to call a car, but Rose had insisted on meeting me at the hotel instead of coming along. It felt like self-preservation, which I couldn't begrudge. I'd gotten his phone number out of the deal, and after I checked into a suite, I sent him the floor and room number, then went up and waited.

He wasn't far behind me, but thankfully I'd had enough time to stop for lube and condoms at the pharmacy, and after arriving at the hotel, still had enough time to take in the suite. The bedroom offered a four poster bed, which had me lamenting the fact I wasn't prepared, a velvet couch at the foot of the bed that faced toward the rest of the room. I left the lube and condoms on one of the dark wood nightstands beside a green-shaded lamp and a notepad and pen.

A wood dining table separated the space and a long leather

couch flanked one of the walls beneath the window. It wasn't the fanciest hotel I'd ever stayed at, but it had a touch of old Hollywood glamor that reminded me of Rob's library.

All in all, the only thing I didn't like about the room was how nervous being alone in it made me.

I didn't know what it was about Rose that had me absolutely out of my mind, entertaining all kinds of fantasies that should have never entered my mind. He was too hot for me for one, too young for another. I was pushing past thirty and he looked like he was still too far from twenty-five for it to even count. He wanted things I didn't, someone to hold his drinks and be serious about him, which he deserved. I'd never argue that point, but I didn't hold drinks and I didn't do serious.

I mean, I was serious about the way I fucked, which was casual and unattached.

I hoped he understood that.

I hoped he knew this was for now, not forever.

A self-assured knock on the door was enough to drag me back to the present, and I popped open the top two buttons of my shirt while I went to let him in.

Even in the golden brightness of the hallway, Rose was as gorgeous as I thought he was the whole time. His skin was a little paler, and his hair maybe a little blonder than I'd first thought, but still...

"Not too late to change your mind," he said with a shrug.

I shook my head, stepping out of the way to let him into the suite. The out was well intended, and I probably should have taken it, but just the sight of him was enough to have me salivating.

After he closed the door behind him and gave the room a onceover, he blinked up at me. "You didn't have to go to all this trouble."

"It's no trouble," I assured him.

"It makes me feel a little bought."

"Do you think you don't deserve any of this?" I asked, giving a quick gesture toward the room behind us.

"It's not that."

"It's exactly that." I tugged the tails of my shirt out from behind my waistband, happy to get some relief from the tightness of my clothes. My muscles were still sore from helping Owen move earlier in the day and I was eager to get off my feet...for more reasons than one. "Why shouldn't you have a room like this for anything you wanted? If you wanted to come watch TV in a hotel room like this, why wouldn't you deserve that?"

"It's extravagant," he said.

"Not for me."

"It's unnecessary," he tried again, eyes lingering on the soft leather couch against the wall behind my back.

"If you want it," I said, taking a step toward him, "it's necessary."

Rose huffed out a quiet noise and tilted his head back to look up at me as I closed the space between us.

"You're beautiful." I brushed the side of my fingers over the curve of his forehead and down the side of his face. He leaned into me like his cheek was meant to fit against my palm, lashes fluttering. "You're gorgeous. You should have all of the things you want at all times."

"I want you to stop talking," he murmured, looking up at me with eyes bright enough to take my breath away, "and kiss me."

"I will," I promised, hooking my thumb over his chin. He let his mouth fall open with the slightest hint of pressure, and I bit back a groan at the simple show of obedience. "But we need some ground rules first."

"I didn't know it was gonna be like that."

"If you couldn't tell, I like things a certain way."

I walked us back to the couch, expecting him to sit beside me. It took work to stifle a pleased sigh when he climbed on top of me, his knees sinking into the distressed leather on either side of my thighs.

"I suppose all the best games have rules," he conceded.

"Condoms," I said, and he held up a finger between us.

He definitely had gotten a manicure recently, I noticed.

"Just for penetration," he added. "Not blow jobs."

Instinctively, my hips lifted off the couch. The mental image of his mouth around my cock was enough to get me hard. Rose gave a seductive swivel of his hips and raising a second finger.

"No face slapping."

I licked my lips and let out a low hum. "That's a shame. I'm certain you'd like it."

Rose gave me a small smile, a slight flush up his throat. "Maybe another time."

I uncurled his middle finger, bringing it up to speak the next, and in my opinion, most important rule. "If you want me to stop, say stop."

"Not red?"

"Not yet."

There were plenty of times where stop didn't really mean stop, but not on a first time and not with a man like Rose.

"Don't pee on me," he said with a chuckle.

"What about in you?"

That turned the chuckle into a full-on laugh, and he smacked my chest playfully. I grabbed his wrists and held him there, adjusting us both so the length of my cock rested better against his ass.

"No piss," he said, giving another wiggle. "But you said you liked things a certain way? I'd rather hear about the things you want to do instead of the things you don't."

I was like my friends in a lot of ways, but in some we were very, very different. Over the years of my life, I'd learned that kink took many different forms and it meant all kinds of things for all kinds of people. Rob liked control, and Archie liked to play with his food, and me…

"Praise," I whispered, sliding his hands down the front of my chest until we reached one of the buttons I'd yet to undo.

"You like to be told you're a good boy?" Rose flicked open the button and spread his fingers wide against my skin. "That you have the biggest and best cock I've ever seen?"

I bit the tip of my tongue, shaking my head. "No. Not like that at all." On my lap, he shivered, working his way to the next button.

"I might have the biggest and best cock you've ever seen, but I'll be the one doing the talking."

"Oh?"

I crooked a finger and beckoned him closer, until his ear was flush with my mouth so I could tell him what he was in for without raising my voice over a whisper.

"Just like that," I rasped, my words turning into a low growl as I spoke. "You're doing so good. Taking this cock like you deserve it. You do deserve it, don't you, Rose?"

"M...maybe."

He slid his hands to my belt, hesitating until I raised my hips off the couch in encouragement.

"There's a good boy," I whispered, transfixed as he worked my belt out of the loops and tugged my zipper down. "There's my pretty little thing."

"I'm not...not yours." Rose reached behind him and tugged his shirt over his head, discarding it on the floor. His jeans were impossibly tight, though, and there was no way he was going to get them off without getting up.

"And you don't do casual, so here we both are being very serious for the night."

I gave his jeans a tug, pulling the button and then reaching for his zipper. I'd expected many things when the fly of his jeans opened. I knew from our encounter on the dance floor that he was far more hung than his slender stature would have let on, but what I wasn't prepared for was the black lace that came into view as the denim spread open.

"Are you wearing panties?" I pressed my fingertip against the small black bow that decorated the waistline of his undergarment.

"I like nice things," he murmured, climbing off of me and shimmying his jeans down an inch to reveal more of the decorative fabric that did little to hide the golden hair of his happy trail or the thick swell of his erection. "Are you a nice thing?"

"I can be."

Rose took a step toward the bedroom, beckoning me after him with a curl of his fingers and the darkening of his eyes. I stood, loving the way he didn't cower when I towered over him.

"There's one thing we didn't talk about." He pushed his pants down a little bit more, the backs of his knees hitting the velvet couch at the foot of the bed.

"Tell me."

I encroached on his space and he sidestepped out of the way until I was the one with my back to the bed. He looked good enough to eat. The light hadn't done a single thing to change that. Just gazing at him, spit pooled in my mouth, and I circled my shoulders, letting my shirt fall to the floor. My belt was already open and I shoved my pants to my ankles with one quick motion. Stepping out of my slacks, I pulled off my socks and straightened back to my normal height, dick doing some massive stress testing against the cotton of my boxer briefs.

"We talked about condoms," he murmured, "but we didn't talk about which one of us was going to wear it."

I'd never been a fan of stereotypes, but there were some that did play out in my life. I was a dominant man who preferred to top. That didn't mean dominant people couldn't—or didn't—receive, but I could count the number of times I'd bottomed on one hand. While I didn't hate it the way some people did, it wasn't something that I often sought out. It was a lot of action for little reward, but as I worked my way through formulating an answer, Rose was busy working out of his pants, proving just how little his lace panties left to the imagination.

To call his cock massive would have been an understatement. It was bigger than mine in both length and girth, and I was already pushing eight inches. A quick look at his face confirmed he knew he was packing, and it honestly would have been a waste to *not* let him top.

At least once.

"What's your preference, Flynn?"

"I like to top."

"I figured you would."

"But I…I don't…" I didn't even know what I was trying to say.

Was I asking to bottom or was I asking to flip? It wasn't often that another man's cock made me speechless and yet here we were. Rose in his black lace with his giant erection waving around like it didn't have anywhere better to be than buried inside of me. My feelings about his cock were anything but casual, and again, I tried to remind myself this was just supposed to be for the night because I didn't do serious and he didn't do casual, and this was all just an elaborate game of pretend so we could get our rocks off.

"I'm vers," Rose offered, clearly sensing my confusion. "So, if you change your mind…"

"Duly noted." I cleared my throat, desperate to get my head back on straight and regain control of the situation. I sat down on the couch and spread my legs, patting the top of my thigh with one hand. "Now come over here, Ambrose, and get on your knees."

FOR SOMEONE WHO LIKED TO BE CALLED SIR, FLYNN SURE WAS EASY TO push around, but I stepped in between his spread legs and went down to my knees. The hotel carpet was ridiculously luxurious, offering more padding than I would have anticipated. The other decadent indulgence in the room was, of course, Flynn himself, and the absolutely unexpected way my stomach fluttered when he called me by my full name.

No one called me Ambrose, not even my parents, and they were the ones who'd burdened me with the ridiculous moniker in the first place. A name like Ambrose should have come with a trust fund, but all I had was a huge cock and a limited gag reflex.

"Did you want me to suck you off?" I asked, batting my lashes up at Flynn, pretending to be coy when we both knew I was anything but. I had the impression we were both breaking our own rules to be with each other, but he was hot enough to lean into the fib for a few more hours before I let the guilt take over.

"Very much," he answered with a low rumble. He still wore a pair of tight, black boxer briefs, and what looked to be an substantial dick tested the durability of the fabric with every flicker of his heartbeat. "I'm not trying to sound arrogant, but—"

"It comes naturally," I said, reaching for the waistband of his underwear and pulling them down to expose his length. Like the rest of him, his dick *was* impressive.

"Not what I was going to say."

"It's well deserved," I assured him.

Making a tight grip around the base of his cock, I flattened my tongue against his shaft and licked my way up and over the tip. Precum had already gathered in the slit of his dick, a little warm and barely salty, a promise of what I knew was to come. Before I got started on him, I'd have to decide where I wanted him to come —in my mouth, in a condom buried inside my ass, or all over his own stomach.

Honestly, I wanted all three.

"How old are you?" I asked.

"Does it matter?"

"Just trying to decide how I want you to come," I answered. "Ranking the options so I don't miss out."

Flynn chuckled, leaning back and spreading his legs a little bit wider. My hand still held his cock and my lips hovered over the tip, waiting.

He arched a brow. "How many choices do I have?"

"I'm thinking three."

"And you're deciding?" he asked.

"I'm prioritizing." I swirled my tongue along the flared underside of his crown, ready to get a better taste of him.

I could pick later, I decided, sealing my mouth around the head of his dick and hollowing my cheeks. Flynn immediately groaned, arching off the seat and threading his fingers through my hair. He cursed under his breath and I swallowed him down to the base of his dick, my fingers connected with my lips. Pressing my tongue against the underside of his shaft to take the last half an inch, I flattened my hands against his thigh and hummed in delight at the feel of him prodding against the roof of my mouth.

"Jesus."

I pulled all the way off, using the tip of my finger to swipe some spit from the corner of my mouth.

"I haven't decided on my ranking yet, so don't get any ideas," I said.

Before he could answer that, I was back between his legs, absolutely loving the way my jaw ached as my mouth stretched around him.

"Fucking Christ, Ambrose," he murmured, fingers flexing against the back of my head as I bobbed up and down his cock. "Just like that. That's so good."

I raised up, taking him back into my hand and slapping his dick against my tongue. The wet squelch made my own cock hard, precum slicking down the head of my cock and saturating the lace.

"If you come in my mouth, I want to top you," I decided.

"What if I don't?"

"Then I suppose we'll have to flip a coin."

"You're—"

I took whatever words Flynn was about to say out of his mouth, sucking them right into the back of my throat instead.

With my balls in one hand and his in the other, I set a slower pace than I'd started with, really giving myself the opportunity to enjoy the thickness of him inside of my throat and my mouth.

The no-gag reflex thing hadn't been natural. I'd trained myself over time because I loved sucking cock and I hated being annoyed, and not being able to suck as much of someone's cock as I wanted was *very* annoying to me. So I'd started in college, practicing on dildos and perfecting the skill on actual boyfriends. Plastic was fine; using a real cock was like going from the lab to a field practice. Not to imply I'd been promiscuous with it, because that had never been me. I preferred monogamy and the trust and intimacy that came with it.

"Hold on," Flynn whispered, tightening his fingers against my scalp. "Hold on."

I went as still as I could manage with his balls resting against my chin. Doing my best to tilt my face up, I blinked through the tears I'd never been able to shake and waited for him to say his piece.

"It's good, Ambrose. Your mouth is so good, but your throat…"

He trailed off, head dropping back with a groan.

I swallowed, letting the muscles of my throat flex and grip against the head of his cock. He fucked his hips against my face, burying himself deeper.

"Your throat is the best thing I've ever fucked."

I smiled, laughing as much as I could manage with a mouthful of cock. I jerked my head against his hand and he let me up, long trails of spit connecting my lips to his shaft.

"I'm pretty sure I'm fucking *you*," I corrected, lip twitching into a smirk. "But you're more than welcome to try, if you want. I can clearly handle it."

Flynn pushed me onto my feet and stood, hooking his hands under my armpits and throwing me onto the bed.

"Over the side," he said, coming around in front of one of the nightstands.

The bed was nice, elevated off the ground with four posters on the corner, and I took the position change as an opportunity to get my own cock into my hand. Situating myself with my knees bent and my dick poking out from the lace, I hung my head over the side of the bed and obediently opened my mouth.

Flynn settled his hand over the curve of my throat and slowly eased himself into my mouth. Even with the height of the bed, he had to bend at the knees to reach my mouth. I worried he wouldn't be able to hold the pose for long, but he was more than welcome to climb onto the bed and ride me if the mood struck him right.

"Is this okay?" he asked, drumming his fingers against my skin and I nodded, breathing out through my nose as he slid deeper.

The position was a good one, giving him more access than we'd had on the couch. Tears leaked from the inner corners of my eyes on their own accord, and I made the smallest gagging noise when he bottomed out in my throat.

"Still good?" he asked.

I motioned for him to get on with it, and he let out a devilish-sounding laugh before pulling almost the entire length of his cock out of my mouth. He snapped his hips and slid back in, drawing another surprised choke out of me. Flynn cradled my throat with both of his hands, the pressure of his fingers against my windpipe and his dick making me hard enough to come with little to no intervention.

I pulled back the side of the lace panties so I could reach myself easier. Palming my dick through the soft material wasn't going to be enough. The sound of his shaft sliding in and out of my throat while he fucked me like that was one of the sexiest things I'd ever heard. It was wet and messy, and sounded absolutely pornographic. I moaned, my hand flying up and down my length, the pace far more aggressive than the one Flynn set in my mouth. Even for as hot as the sounds were, it was frustrating how easy he was going on me, so I decided the way I wanted him to come the most was all over that firm and tanned stomach of his.

I tensed my throat and sucked him, giving him a couple more minutes on the best blow job of his life, then I slid across the bed disconnecting our bodies. The lube and condoms were on the nightstand, and I tore a condom open with my mouth, spitting the wrapper onto the sheets.

"You said you *like* to top?" I set my attention to the bottle of lube, hoping that the signals hadn't been mixed and I understood the stuttering message he'd tried to send me earlier in the night.

"Yes."

"Not a pre-requisite?"

Flynn licked his lips, taking time to let his stare trace over every inch of my body, from my toes up to my thighs, down the length of my dick and back up again, then toward my stomach, my sternum, my throat, before settling on my face.

"No," he rasped.

Relief washed through me, working like a wave to push all the rest of my blood right into my dick.

"Good. Then I've made my decision."

"Oh?" He sounded a little bit stunned, if not somewhat

amused, eyes flickering from his exposed cock to my sheathed one.

"I want you to come on your stomach," I told him. "All over my hand, with my cock buried so deep inside of your ass you don't even remember why you ever liked topping in the first place."

He dragged his tongue back and forth across his upper teeth, then he sat on the edge of the bed and arranged himself against the pillows with his knees bent and his legs spread. His balls were heavy, hanging low enough that I couldn't see his hole, and I took the time to wonder if it would be smooth like the rest of him or if there'd be an unexpected dark whorl of hair around his rim.

"That's definitely not casual," he muttered under his breath, and that earned a laugh.

Nothing about what was happening between us felt casual, so I had to take him at his earlier word, that it would be seriously casual…

Whatever that meant.

"It's whatever it is. For right now," I said.

He gave me a *casual* shrug and reached between his legs to raise his balls, revealing the shadow of his smooth and hairless asshole. I fought back a groan, eyes rolling back as I situated myself between his legs.

I knew I was well endowed, and I knew it had probably been awhile since Flynn had taken a dick. Even as I teased his hole with my latex sheathed tip, I poured lube over us both, not giving a fuck about the sheets or anything else beyond making good on my word.

Drake was right.

I didn't even remember my stupid ex's name.

I replaced the tip of my cock with two of my fingers, pushing in and spreading him open.

"I'm not…" The muscles in Flynn's jaw were tense and he squinted before letting his head fall back into the pillows. "I wasn't prepared for all of this."

"For me?" I laughed. "No one ever is."

"That's not what I meant."

I knew exactly what he meant.

"I'm a big boy, Flynn. I can handle it." I scissored my fingers apart inside of him, then added a third.

It was almost unfair that my fingers were so proportionate to my body when my cock looked almost out of place for how big it was. Fisting Flynn would have been closer to a fair amount of prep, but I didn't think either of us was up for that conversation. I prepped him until his balls were high enough to give me the view of the prize on their own, then I positioned myself at his entrance and fell forward, bracing one hand on either side of his head.

"Are you sure this is okay?" I asked.

He'd been so good about asking for permission and consent, I owed him the same in return. Briefly, I wondered if I should call him Sir, if there was something he would have liked more than my dick in his ass or my throat around his cock. But I also didn't know why it should matter. Flynn was a rebound, a distraction to help me forget about a man who'd never deserved my attention in the first place.

We were different people who wanted different things, and we were coming together one night so we could, in theory, come together.

A new goal.

"I can take it," he promised.

So, before he could change his mind and ruin both our nights, I gave it to him.

CHAPTER 7
FLYNN

I DIDN'T RECOGNIZE THE NOISE THAT LEFT MY THROAT WHEN ROSE'S massive cock pushed into me. Tipping my head back, I clenched my jaw, trying to call up every smooth-talking line I'd ever whispered to somebody else when their body proved too tight for me to get inside of.

"Flynn," Rose's voice was strained.

"Hmn?"

"If you don't relax, you're going to snap my dick off."

His honesty made me laugh and eased enough of my tension that another inch of him slipped in.

"I know how it works."

"Then act accordingly."

I scoffed, wincing when he pulled almost all the way out.

Had it always been such a burn and stretch or was it just him?

"It's not my fault you're hung," I told him.

"You're right." Rose grinned, a flop of curls falling down over his eye. "It's your privilege."

"So modest."

He bottomed out and went still, giving me time to acclimate to the feel of his thickness and length up my ass. I suspected it was a power move, but since this was a one-time thing, I was happy enough to let it slide.

"So modest," he mocked, wiggling his head side to side like a bobblehead. "Just like you were on your great kissing quest earlier tonight?"

"It got you here, didn't it?"

He adjusted himself at my comment, changing the angle of penetration and dragging his tip across my prostate. He fucked me like that, with short and shallow thrusts, enough to send goose-flesh up the back of my neck and into my hairline.

"You don't strike me as the kind of man to end up on his back often," Rose murmured, hiking one of my legs up onto his shoulder to bury himself deeper inside of me.

I moaned, my hips coming up off the bed to give him an assist. "I'm not."

"That's a shame because you look so fucking hot with my dick in your ass." He braced his hands against my waist and snapped his hips forward.

"Don't get used to it," I grunted.

"I wouldn't dare." Rose rolled his eyes. "We're seriously casual for one night only. I haven't forgotten."

Funny that he mentioned it—because I had.

"Less talking," I murmured, bringing a finger to his mouth. My words were getting ready to leave me whether he stopped talking or not.

Normally I was the one who did the talking. I was the one who gave the instruction, the commands, the *praise*. But with Rose's cock stretching me open, there wasn't much for me to do besides chase after the orgasm he'd already told me he expected.

And who was he to expect anything of me?

"More fucking?" He raised a brow, those glossy lips of his twisted into a wry smirk.

I managed a nod and reached up, hooking my hand around the back of his neck and pulling him down. The ache in my thigh from being stretched between us was miserable, but the taste of him when he crashed our mouths back together made it tolerable.

How Rose managed to keep our mouths connected while

pistoning his cock into me was a mystery I didn't think I'd ever have the answer for, but in less than five minutes, he'd gotten it down to a science. Fucking me with a hard and steady pace, his tongue swirled around my mouth, exploring and tasting me like he had any right to my body.

Time blurred and swirled into darkness, and when he curled his hand around the base of my cock, it took less than five pumps of his wrist to send me over the edge. Rose went still when I came, putting enough space between our mouths that my noises weren't muffled. With every groan and sigh that left me, he shivered, and when he followed after me into his own release, I felt him thicken and pulse inside of me.

Rose was almost silent through the duration of his own orgasm, save for the quietest whimper when he dropped his forehead against mine at the end. I wiggled my leg to stretch it out, and he re-settled himself between my legs with a content sigh. Wrapping my arms around him, I petted my hands down the sweaty curve of his back, dragging my fingers over the swell of his ass and giving it a squeeze.

He huffed a laugh and reached between us to pull out, which had us both wincing and gasping for breath. Rose flopped onto his back beside me and let out a long and trembling breath. I closed my eyes and searched out his thigh, resuming my gentle petting. I loved the noises he made, the soft whimpers in response to my touch. He'd be so perfect to play with properly, so eager and receptive.

Very nearly everything I could have ever asked for.

A breath turned into a minute, and a minute turned into a moment, and I was so close to sleep when Rose cleared his throat. The bed shifted as he stood up, and I rolled my head to the side in time to watch him unroll the condom and tie it off with a snap. He padded out of the bedroom, wandering through the sitting room area until he found the bathroom on the other end of the suite. Rose flipped on the light and closed the door behind him. The whirring bathroom fan sent a low him through the whole room and I forced myself out of bed.

I needed to do something to regain my hold on the situation, even though I didn't know why. It was habit, at best. The water in the bathroom started to run, and I stepped back into my boxer briefs, grimacing at the stickiness of the cum all over my stomach and the precum smeared in my underwear. A trip to the bathroom would help clean me up and clear my mind.

Rose was still in the bathroom, and I headed that way, quietly rapping my knuckles against the wood.

"You good?" I asked.

"I'm almost done."

It was a non-answer, but I wasn't going to push him one way or the other.

Almost immediately, Rose opened the door. The bright fluorescent was surprisingly blinding, and I stepped back, shielding myself from the light.

"It's all yours," he said, standing proud and naked, gesturing like he was allowing me into his castle. His pale skin was flushed, blue eyes bright, and his hair all askew like a tornado on top of his head.

He looked like he could have been an angel.

He looked like he would have been my downfall.

Given the chance.

"Do you want to order up some room service?" I asked as I passed him, trading places and stepping into the unforgiving brightness of the bathroom.

He gave me an exhausted smile.

"I could eat," he said softly, pushing the door closed on me and effectively ending the conversation.

With space between us, I took a deep breath in what felt like the first time in hours. What a cliché, meeting a man on a whim who took my breath away. I'd originally intended on rinsing off in the sink, but if Rose was ordering food, I had time for a shower.

Happy to get out of my soiled and sticky underwear, I turned on the shower and stepped under the hot spray.

Even in the silence, it was impossible to find a moment of peace because my mind raced with thoughts of Rose, the things we'd done, and all of the things I *wanted* to do. But as I gently soaped between my legs, I reminded myself that we wanted different things. I tried to forget the way my cock throbbed when he called me Sir at the club, even though it had been in jest. Even though he didn't understand what kind of man I was or what that word meant to me.

Too much time passed, and I hadn't fully convinced myself of anything besides the fact that I wanted to take him to bed again. Turning off the water and grabbing one of the hotel robes, I was ready to tell him as much, but when I walked back into the room, the sight of him naked on the couch wearing nothing but that lace underwear of his, zapped every thread of common sense out of my mind.

"I didn't know what you wanted to eat," he said, looking down at the array of food spread across the low table in front of him.

"Honestly?" I adjusted the knot on the robe, making sure my cock was still tucked away. "Just you."

"Am I the best you've ever had, Flynn?" Rose chuckled, brushing his hair back from his face and sitting up straight. He tucked himself into the corner of the couch and crossed his legs at the knee.

He was, but I wasn't sure how I felt about it yet, and I didn't want to tell him that either. I'd been having kinky sex my entire adult life, so to be knocked into another galaxy by an otherwise vanilla twink was a lot for me to try and digest.

"You weren't the worst," I hedged, which earned me a grin so broad I knew for sure he saw straight through my game.

"I figured you were going to say that. Which is why we need to talk."

He patted the cushion beside him, and I took a seat, ready to lay a decent amount of my wants onto the table.

"We do need to talk," I agreed.

"We need to talk about all the reasons we aren't ever going to do that—" He paused and pointed at the bed. "Again."

"I'm sorry, what?"

Of all the things I'd expected out of this terribly unexpected man, that wasn't anywhere near the top of the list.

"We can't do that again," he said.

"And why not?"

Rose pointed at himself. "Serious." Then me. "Casual."

"Seriously casual," I repeated the lie from earlier. The ruse I'd spun to get him into bed in the first place. "But why not casually serious?"

He rolled his eyes at me. "What does that even mean?"

I didn't have an answer, but I wasn't ready to give up on the fight. I had talked my way into and out of more serious deals and situations than a stranger's bed. There was no reason I couldn't talk my way into his life now. My interest in Rose was giving me whiplash, but only because I kept trying to convince myself I *didn't* want him. When I quietly admitted the truth to myself, everything felt easier. Like it made more sense. There were a lot of pieces of it that I didn't understand, but I was a smart man.

I could learn.

"It means you make things that I thought were hard limits feel not so rigid."

He swallowed, watching me thoughtfully.

"I've never had a boyfriend," I admitted. "Never done anything serious in my life, to be honest."

"That's probably the least surprising thing about you," he said.

"But not because the situation never presented itself. Just because I've never wanted to."

"What are you saying?"

"I'm saying that…saying…I could see myself maybe trying with you. For you."

"That's oddly touching," he said, angling himself toward me more. "But I don't want you to change on my account."

"So, we can't be together because I don't want anything serious, and when I tell you I would be willing to give serious a try for you, you tell me no?"

"I'm telling you that I don't want to be serious with a man who changes *for* me."

"I would have thought that could be the biggest compliment someone could give you."

"I want to be with a man who changes himself because he wants to be a better person whether or not I'm in the picture. If you change for me and things don't work out between us, what was the point of it in the first place?"

Now it was my turn to gesture to the bed. "More of that."

"That was casual." Rose stood and sighed. "That was some of the best sex I've ever had too, for what it's worth. And I think that you could be a real special person for me, but I just got cheated on by a man I thought loved me, and I'm done settling for less than I deserve."

"That's why I'm asking you for a chance."

"I know and, for some reason, I believe you're being sincere, and that's why I'm not going to walk out of this hotel room and turn my back on you forever."

"No?" A spark of hope flared at the base of my spine and I stood too, reaching for him.

Rose took a step back, holding up a hand to stop me and shaking his head.

"You have my number in your phone already," he said. "And if you figure out how to be the kind of man I deserve, then I hope you use it."

CHAPTER 8

ROSE

FIVE DAYS AFTER THE BEST SEX OF MY LIFE, AND I'D YET TO JERK OFF without closing my eyes and picturing my cock buried up Flynn's ass. And I didn't know much, but I was pretty certain that most men who said they liked to be called Sir didn't make a habit of getting on their back for other men, especially men like me. But he had, and he'd done it so well, and I hadn't been able to stop thinking about coming inside of him again or what kinds of things I would have to do to earn the right to call him Sir.

Variety was the spice of life, after all.

But there were some things I refused to budge on, like the whole casual versus serious situation we'd found ourselves in. And half a week later, I didn't know what had possessed me to leave him my phone number. Maybe it had been in the hope he'd change or maybe it had been wishful thinking. Probably a little bit of both. I'd meant what I told him—I didn't want him to change just to get me back into bed. That wasn't fair to either of us, and it wasn't sustainable either.

Just because he wasn't on my body didn't mean I had to keep him off my mind.

After I'd put my number into his phone on Saturday night, or Sunday morning, whenever it had been, I stopped myself from sending a message to my phone from him. Having his number would only get me into trouble, and Cody had proved to bring more than enough of it to my life these days.

My microwave counted down toward zero and I stabbed at the button to open the door when it ticked down to one second remaining. My frozen macaroni and cheese smelled delicious, and my stomach gave a confirming growl at the first whiff of the cheesy, goopy goodness. I had to work later that night and knew getting dinner between tables would be a rough chance, so I'd planned to enjoy my afternoon with some melted cheese and a quick binge of my favorite murder documentary.

Unfortunately, the chime of my doorbell immediately turned any excitement sour because only one person used the doorbell, and it was Cody.

"Go away!" I shouted toward the door, carrying my food into the living room.

The doorbell rang a second time.

And then a third.

"Cody!" I hollered his name. "No!"

"I just want to talk," he pleaded through the door. "Just let me in and hear me out, and if you don't like what I have to say, I'll go."

I knew enough about the man—who up until a week ago I thought I loved—to know he wouldn't leave without getting his way, so with a quickly growing sense of dread in the pit of my stomach, I abandoned my meal and shuffled over to the front door.

I secured the chain and unlatched the deadbolt, pulling the door back a couple of inches until the chain went taut. Cody immediately shouldered into the door, his expression twisting from tiredness to anger.

"Let me in, Rose," he said.

I shook my head, hand still on the doorknob. I used my body to block his view into my apartment, even though he could easily see right over my head. Sometimes I hated how small I was, but more often than that, I hated how being small made me feel. I was the smallest person in my family and I'd always been the smallest kid in all of my classes, and oftentimes it made me feel powerless, and that left me scared.

It wasn't so much that I needed control as I hated the way I felt without it. Weak, and small, and scared in a way that manifested like sludge in my veins, slowing my thoughts and my movements until I didn't know up from down. I'd spent a long time trying to work around those feelings or through them, but they weren't gone completely. Things that made me feel powerful had helped, the lingerie and the lace, for one. The teasing ease of leaning into non-traditional femininity, another.

And it was the prickling unease that registered in my body during Cody's onceover that reminded me I was in a pair of pink lace boy shorts, the edge of them peeking out over the waistband of the sweats I'd not yet bothered to change out of. I didn't have on any makeup, and I definitely wasn't wearing a shirt. I knew what I looked like, and I knew what he thought about it.

"You can't come in," I said, squaring my shoulders.

"You haven't been answering my calls."

"Because I don't want to talk to you."

I tried to push the door closed, but his foot was in the way.

"You're overreacting," he said, brows knitting together like he meant the insult as an apology.

"You may think that, but either way…"

"Sugar, come on." Cody tried to reach into the apartment, fingers dusting across my stomach before I jumped back, out of reach.

"You don't get to touch me anymore," I warned. "I'm done talking to you, and I'd like you to go."

As he sputtered a protest at me, I wondered what I'd ever seen in him in the first place. Sure, he was attractive enough, but he was bossy, and not in a fun way. Not in the way Flynn wanted to be.

Flynn.

There he was again.

Fresh in the forefront of my head, all naked and writhing with my cock shoved so far up his ass he could have probably tasted it if he'd tried hard enough. Flynn, with his rules and his casual games, and his honorifics that I hadn't earned the right to use. Not that I even wanted to use them. Not that I wanted to give him anything more from me than he'd already had. But I'd be lying if I didn't say the whole idea of it had at least piqued my interest a little bit.

"I'm not going to stand here all day with you," I told Cody, giving the toe of his sneaker a kick with my bare foot. "So you can stand here as long as you want, but I'm done."

I knew the chain would hold him and I knew he wasn't crazy enough to try and break the door down, so I walked away. I went back to my macaroni and my TV, and I flipped on Netflix and clicked onto the next episode of the series. From outside of the apartment, Cody continued to protest, his voice growing louder before sliding down into a hushed tone that almost sounded sincere.

But he'd sounded pretty sincere with his dick in his room-mate's ass too.

The macaroni and cheese had already started to congeal, and I swallowed down a goopy bite of it, not anywhere close enough to giving Cody the ability to get another look at me by heading back into the kitchen to get something else to eat. I suffered through the quickly cooling meal and ten minutes later, before the first real scene break in the show, he'd given up and shuffled off.

Finishing off my lunch, I got up and closed the door, latching the deadbolt and the door lock. The episode ended and my apart-ment lapsed into a painfully loud silence. I didn't do my best work when I was left to my own thoughts for too long, which was why Drake had come over and dragged me out to Rapture the weekend before. When I was alone, I tended to overthink things, and without anyone to talk to, I oftentimes talked myself in circles.

Circles that turned into spirals.

Drake had ended up going home with that dark-haired man the night I'd gone back to the hotel with Flynn. They'd spent two days in bed together and then the man had departed without so much as leaving a phone number. Or a name, I later found out. After Drake shared the story with me, I'd been absolutely horrified at the idea. I wouldn't ever judge him—or anyone else for that matter—on the things they wanted to do sexually, but it just felt so impersonal to me.

I wasn't a romantic or anything. I didn't go into relationships thinking they would all last forever. Statistically, every relationship had a one out of two chance of ending, and those weren't the best odds. But I'd always figured the more you made things count, the less likely an ending would be. If you put in the work and learned about a person, understood their likes and their dislikes, their goals, their dreams. Even their fantasies. That was the key to beating the odds.

Drake didn't share an interest in doing that kind of work, and I loved him for that. Sometimes, I was envious of the way other people were able to move from partner to partner. And on the tail of my most recent breakup, I'd really started to see the appeal. Good sex and no drama…

What wasn't to like about that?

Again my thoughts went to Flynn.

And like most other times I'd thought of him over the week, my dick took notice, pushing up insistently against my underwear and my sweats.

I didn't have to work for another couple hours, so there wasn't any harm in having another wank about him before I started to get ready.

Lifting my hips, I pushed my sweats down and cupped my hand over the lacy bulge between my legs. A moan tumbled out of my mouth, and I reached around the material to get more direct skin against skin. I tipped my head back against the wall, and almost immediately I was fully hard. With my free hand, I covered my throat, calling back the memory of how Flynn had held me there while he tested my gag reflex over the edge of the bed in the hotel room.

My balls ached for release, even though I'd come in the shower earlier in the day. I licked my palm and made a tight fist around my dick, not interested in dragging out the session like I sometimes enjoyed. I wanted to come fast and hard, and it was thoughts of Flynn fucking *me* that sent me over the edge this time.

He was a conundrum of a man, that I knew.

Clearly more money than sense, if the hotel room he'd reserved for us was any indicator, and if he didn't think I recognized the red soles of his shiny black dress shoes, he was mistaken. I'd found in my life there were only two kinds of rich men in the world—the ones who wanted you to know and the ones who didn't care if you did. Flynn was easily the latter, and I wasn't a gold digger, but there was something really fucking hot about that.

I called up the memory of the first time he kissed me at Rapture. The way he'd lifted me against the wall and claimed my mouth like he had a right to it. The way the swirl of his tongue and the heat of his body had convinced me in under a minute that he might be worth breaking some of my own rules for. That if it had been another time, maybe *before* Cody, the night and the morning after could have gone very differently.

But there were his lips and his fingers and his gorgeous and smooth asshole, and that was enough for me then and enough for me again.

My orgasm came on quick, but it wasn't rough or hard. It was soft, like a slowly rising tide. Up over the ankles, then the calves, and the knees, and then cum pooled in the webs of my fingers, a few stray splatters against my stomach. The wave of pleasure left me breathless, and for the first time all week, I cursed myself for not taking his phone number for myself.

I'd labeled him a rebound, and I didn't think one taste of him would be enough, but I'd spent a handful of hours with him and I was already obsessively attached. I couldn't go to bed with him a second time without more understanding of who I was and what I wanted from a partner. I wanted to believe what he'd said to me at the hotel was more than lip service, but...

There it was again.

The doubt that always snuck in after the orgasms. The insecurities and the worry that wrapped around me when my brain got quiet.

"You're an idiot," I muttered to myself, swiping my quickly drying cum against the thigh of my sweat pants. "At this rate, I'm going to need another rebound to get over my rebound."

I stripped out of my clothes and took another shower, hoping the water would be enough to clear my mind. It wasn't, but I got ready for work anyway, finally checking my phone as I pulled it off the charger on my nightstand when I was ready to leave for work.

I had one unread message, and it was enough to catch all of my breath—and my hope—in my throat.

Unknown: I haven't been able to stop thinking about you and I'm not sure how to be the kind of man you want me to be, but whenever I figure it out, I promise you'll be the first to know.

CHAPTER 9
FLYNN

I HAVEN'T BEEN ABLE TO STOP THINKING ABOUT YOU AND I'M NOT SURE how to be the kind of man you want me to be, but whenever I figure it out, I promise you'll be the first to know.

I read and re-read the message I'd sent Rose earlier in the day until the words didn't mean anything anymore. I'd read it about twice as many times before sending it, changing the words and the sentence structure, even though by the time I was done writing it, I had no idea what I'd wanted to say in the first place.

It felt disingenuous to say he made me want to be a better man, but it was also the opposite of what he wanted to hear. He didn't want me to change for him, he wanted me to change because it was the right thing to do, but it almost felt unfair because he didn't know a single thing about me. He had ideas and assumptions about me based on my looks and my money, and some of them were probably right, but I wasn't a bad person.

I wasn't a bad man.

But I didn't date, and that was clear. And so I understood what he meant, what he wanted. And I didn't see any harm in sitting with myself for a couple of weeks and trying to see if it was maybe time for me to grow up a little bit. Rob and Archie had both fallen in love and it wasn't the worst thing in the world for them. Maybe letting someone get close to me wouldn't be horrible either.

I'd spent my adult life avoiding serious relationships because I'd watched them go so wrong for so long. Barclay, for example, with his ex-fiancé and the disaster that their whole relationship had been was enough to sour me for at least two years, and after that it was basically muscle memory. But none of that was a drastic change. I would be the same man whether I was fucking people casually or fucking one person seriously. I wasn't scared of monogamy or commitment. I knew what I could bring to the table, and the longer I sat with Rose's words and unspoken assumptions about me, the more frustrated I found myself.

I relaxed against the familiar and soft leather of the oversized chairs at Cunningham's, stretching my legs out with a groan and tucking my phone back into my pocket. The status of the message to Rose sat on *read*, and that was better than nothing. I hadn't sent it expecting a reply. I had sent it because I meant it, because for whatever reason, I wanted another taste of him. I wanted to take my time and talk him through it, and really show him how good sex with me could be.

But that would take time, which I didn't have anywhere near enough of. It had been almost a week since I met Rose. Days and days of sensitivity between my legs, being forced to remember the thick stretch from when he'd settled between my legs and pushed into me. Days on top of that when I'd been left to think about the way my chest flooded with heat when he kissed me. And I would have been happy to stay home and do nothing beside relive those hours, but it was Thursday, my standing drink night with all of my friends, and for the first time in the history of ever, I was the first to arrive. Staying home any longer would have driven me wild, and there was something to be said for the potency of whiskey that didn't live in your own liquor cabinet. It wasn't long before one of our regular waiters spotted me. He was quick to get me a drink while I waited for Rob, Archie, Dalton, and Barclay to arrive.

For years, we'd met on Thursdays for drinks. It was a chance to decompress from the week without interfering with any weekend-based escapades. But the timing and the frequency had turned a little more sporadic, with Rob falling in love with Grayson, and Archie moving Owen across the country, and all of that. I was happy for my friends, truly. But I wasn't a huge fan of change and the shifts happening in our circle made me a little less than comfortable.

It was a spiral of thoughts earlier in the day about all of my friends falling in love and splitting off into their own little worlds that had me texting Rose about changes I had no right promising him. But I hadn't been able to get him off my mind, and it wasn't just about the sex either. It was the way he looked on the couch when I'd gotten out of the shower, and the way he'd squared his shoulders when he told me I didn't deserve him.

No one had ever talked to me that way.

I mean, sure, Frankie had implied it, but everything with him had been in jest, it had been fun. I was used to getting my way in pretty much all things, in and out of the bedroom, so for Rose to look me in the eye and tell me to do better?

The words had lit a fire under my ass in a way I didn't have words for.

But not because I thought I had any changing to do, but because I was ready to prove him wrong.

I'd never really thought there was anything wrong with me, nothing that needed serious levels of attention or alteration. It wasn't as if I was bold enough to think I could buy whatever I wanted in life, not how Archie was or, rather, used to be. But I'd done well enough for myself. Born and raised upper middle class, an above-average education, and a trust fund that paid for my degrees. I'd worked hard for my money, but I started with enough to make that work possible.

I'd never imagined myself to be arrogant. Confident, yes.

Arrogant?

I didn't think so.

I knew what I was good at, and I knew what *I* deserved, what I wanted.

Maybe not so much different from Rose after all, if you didn't look at the bank accounts or the cock size, which...

"You look the same way Rob looked after he'd fallen in love with Grayson." Dalton kicked the side of my shoe and threw himself down onto one of the chairs beside mine.

"Well, I'm not."

I raised my glass in toast to him and took a sip, smacking my lips to mock him. The waiter appeared quickly, already knowing our orders by heart after so many consistent visits, and he slipped a glass into Dalton's hand and he mimicked the toast right back at me.

"Are you sure?"

"Quite."

"What has you so distracted then?" He cocked his head and studied me like he'd be able to sniff out the lie. "Is it Owen's friend?"

"Frankie?" I scoffed, rolling my eyes. "I would have taken him to bed, but kissing him was like shoving my tongue into..."

"An electrical socket?" he offered.

"With one-hundred percent less sparks."

Dalton answered that with a knowing sound, and took a sip of his whiskey.

"Frankie is too combative for me anyway. I think I'd much rather love to hate him."

"That'll make Owen sad," Archie said, dropping down onto one side of the couch that flanked the small table in front of Dalton's and my chairs.

"I think he'll survive it."

"You don't have a single nice thing to say about him?" Dalton teased, knowing full well the kind of man I was behind closed doors.

The only good thing I had to say about Frankie, beyond how well he filled out a pair of jeans, was that it was his silly little dare that brought Rose into my bed, and that had to be worth something.

"He's not the worst person I've ever met," I said with a grin.

"I know." Archie looked past me, his own mouth tipping into a smile. "Barclay takes that crown."

"What have I done?"

Barclay came up from behind me with Rob in tow, and they took the remaining seats with the usual grunts and groans that came from middle-aged men and overpriced leather.

"Nothing," Dalton said, raising his glass to the both of them.

"How's Owen settling in?" Rob asked Archie before flagging down the waiter and getting drinks for the three of them.

I'd thankfully paced myself, with less than a quarter of my first round down by the time they had full glasses in their hands. I waited until they caught up, and then returned my attention to the amber-colored liquor.

"He'd like to get out more."

"Are you keeping him tied up at home?" Barclay asked.

"You're getting us confused with that one." Archie flicked a finger in Rob's direction. "But he's adjusting. I think it's a change for him, but he's ready to find a job and a new normal."

"You're letting him work?" Dalton asked.

"I don't think anyone *lets* Owen do anything," I murmured.

Archie gave me an agreeable, if not exhausted, nod. "He's his own man, that's for sure."

"He's yours."

He hummed and took a substantial drink of his whiskey.

"Before the lot of you interrupted…" Dalton cleared his throat. "I was just telling Flynn how he looks like he's in love."

I cursed him under my breath, hating the way it felt when all of their attention turned toward me.

"Are you?" Archie asked.

"Am I what?"

"In love."

"Absolutely not."

Thankful that I'd nursed my drink as long as I had, I poured the rest of it down my throat in one swallow and raised the empty glass in the air to signal for another.

"This doesn't have anything to do with the man from Rapture?" Archie asked.

"Owen's friend?" Dalton clarified.

Archie's grin turned positively feral as he leveled a look at me that had my throat going dry.

I shook my head as Archie said, "No."

"You asshole," Dalton accused. "Who?"

"The twink," Archie said, stare sliding to Dalton like he was absolutely prepared to share all of the gossip.

"What twink?"

Archie looked back to me. "Are you going to tell him or am I?"

"How do you even know?"

"Frankie told Owen and Owen told me. Of course."

"I want you to tell me," Dalton said, angling away from me and giving Archie his full focus. "Flynn is going to lie."

"I'm not a liar."

"Frankie and Flynn made out and it was horrible."

"Agreed," I grumbled.

"So Frankie dared him to kiss someone else. But Flynn has already had his tongue inside of half the patrons at Rapture."

"I think that's offensive," I said.

"Not if it's true," Barclay chimed in.

"Better my tongue than my dick," I countered and he shrugged me off.

"Tongue in half of them, dick in at least a third," Dalton added.

I huffed, scrubbing a hand down my face.

"Frankie picked him a perfect little twink, and Flynn had him up against the wall in no time, all hands and mouths, and all of that." Archie gestured broadly, swirling his hand in the air. "You know how it goes. Anyway, they left together."

"They what?"

Again, all attention was on me, and the heat in my cheeks

would have been warm to the touch if I'd raised my hands and checked.

"Did you take him home?" Rob asked.

"I should have taken him to your house," I snapped. "But no. Just a hotel."

"Which hotel?" Dalton winged up a brow and I glared at him.

"One with a bed."

"And you fucked him?"

"We slept together," I said, not interested in sharing the details with any of them.

There wasn't any harm in kissing and telling, or fucking and sharing, as it were, but I was thinking about the kind of man Rose would deserve and I wagered that the kind of man who talked to his friends about what happened behind closed doors was probably not too high up on the list. Maybe one small thing to change.

"And that's that?"

I dragged my tongue across the front of my teeth. "I don't have plans to see him again."

"But you want to?" Dalton asked.

"He's not on the market," I said. And while it wasn't the truth, it wasn't a lie. Rose didn't think he was on the table for me, but the longer I thought about his smug little declaration at the end of our time together, the more I knew how wrong he was. He deserved a man just like me, and I only had to figure out how to show him as much. But I wasn't going to let on to my friends that I'd been shot down. Not a chance in hell. "We had some fun, that's that."

"Riiiight," Dalton drawled.

"I don't want to talk about him anymore," I said.

"At least tell me his name."

"Rose."

Archie chuckled and clinked his glass against Dalton's. "Cute."

My phone and the text I'd sent to Rose earlier in the day burned a hole in my pocket, and even though I knew he hadn't replied—and probably wouldn't—I wanted to check just the same.

I had some more choice words for him, and it was time for him to hear them.

"This is cute." Dalton reached over and pinched the outside of my arm. "I've known you for almost ten years and I've never seen you like this."

"I'm not like anything."

"You want to see him again."

"I see lots of people again," I said, lips twisting down into a frown. "I've almost seen Val as many times as you and Barclay have."

"But you want to see *him*," Archie teased.

I shook my head, bottom lip pushing out into a pout.

I didn't just *want* to see him.

I needed to.

CHAPTER 10
ROSE

Two in the morning couldn't come soon enough.

My shift had been long and hard, and not in any of the fun ways. My feet were killing me and I could barely keep my eyes open. After I tipped out the kitchen, I clocked out and stumbled into the alley, already half asleep. If I'd been more aware or if it had been any other night, I might have noticed the man leaning against the brick wall near the hood of my car. But it wasn't, and I didn't, and I already had my hand on the door handle when he cleared his throat to call my attention.

I startled in a very tired and undignified way, dropping my keys and my cellphone onto the black asphalt. I heard the screen of my phone shatter, and I glared down at it like it should have done anything differently to have avoided its fate.

"I'll replace it," Flynn said, pushing off the wall and taking a step toward me.

"I'd rather you didn't."

"I caught you off-guard," he said, coming closer until he was near enough to bend over and collect my things from the ground. "It's my fault. You deserve a replacement."

I sighed. "Are we here to talk about what I deserve?"

"No. We're here to talk about what *I* deserve." Flynn handed me back my things, the screen of my phone spider-webbed out from one corner down almost the entire length of the device.

"First we need to talk about how you're here," I muttered, cracking open my car door and tossing my phone and keys onto the driver's seat. Flynn was so close I could smell him again, subtle as a memory.

"I drove." He pointed at the car parked beside mine, a ridiculously shiny sedan that was all black, even the windows.

"You know what I meant."

I wanted to know how he knew where I worked. How he knew *when* I worked. And I wanted to ask what he wanted, even though the tightening in my chest should have been confirmation enough that I already knew. With Cody's reappearance still fresh in my mind, Flynn's arrival was more welcome than I wanted him to know. But I'd given in to him terribly easy last weekend when I'd been on a quest to get over Cody and his betrayal. I found myself now in a comparable situation, but there was a shared history between us already that was impossible to ignore.

Or at least unadvisable.

"I have more money than sense," he offered with a careless shrug, like we'd been talking about the weather forecast and not his stalking.

It was as much of an answer as I'd expected a man like Flynn to give. It was quick, honest, and to the point. Much like him, I realized.

"I'm inclined to agree." I leaned against the closed driver's side door and Flynn stepped around to face me, effectively boxing me in. It should have made me nervous. Everything about him should have been intimidating. From the way he carried himself and the resources at his disposal right down to the way he fucked. There was no doubt Flynn was a threat. Or he should have been. Instead of being scared of him, though, I was hard.

"I've been thinking about you all week," he murmured and heat rushed up my throat. Without thinking, I covered my cheeks with my hands, and the corner of his mouth tipped into a grin before falling back flat. "And I needed to clear some things up for you."

I huffed, rolling my eyes and crossing my arms in front of my chest. "Do you?"

"Yes," he answered, tone solemn. The tip of his tongue traced over his top teeth and his chin tilted toward his chest as he leaned in a little closer, like he was about to whisper. "I don't need to change for you, Rose. I can—and will—give you everything you deserve, and more, just as I am right this very moment."

"Will you now?" The question came out embarrassingly raspy, and I cleared my throat, letting my arms fall to my sides.

There was no point of defense with Flynn. He would tear right through it if it pleased him to do so.

My concession seemed to take him by surprise, but just a flicker in the dark pools of his eyes that anyone else would have missed were they not watching him as intently as I'd been.

As I still was.

"If it's what you want," he said, somewhat softer.

"Is it what you want?"

"I only count for half of it."

I arched a brow, and he took a step closer. "That sounds decidedly not casual."

"I think maybe that's the only change I need to make for you," he whispered.

The words, and his breath, dusted across my cheeks as he said it, and my lashes fluttered before falling closed. Maybe it would be easier to not look at him because something about the way he looked at me made me forget that he was a predator and I was very much his prey. His money, his demeanor, his words, all of them weaved together to make the most dangerous form of camouflage I'd ever seen another person wear.

"Is that an offer?" I asked.

Gently, his nose rubbed across the skin just over my eyebrow, his lips grazing against my temple in the promise of a future kiss.

"The night we met," he whispered the words against my skin, "you called me Sir."

"And you told me I hadn't earned the right."

Flynn cupped his hand around the back of my neck, holding me steady. "Do you want to?"

"Call you Sir?"

He shook his head. "Earn the right."

I pressed the back of my neck into the cradle of his hand, content to let him support me there, at least for a few seconds. Flynn peppered kisses across my forehead, over my closed eyelids, and down my cheekbones. I moaned quietly and shamefully, leaning away from the car to chase after the warmth of his body. I'd never forget what he looked like naked, what he'd *felt* like against my skin. Even with his words ringing alarm bells in my head, my brain focused itself solely on his closeness, his presence. And I wanted more.

I wasn't what some people would consider worldly. I wasn't sheltered either, but I knew there were a lot of things outside of my comprehension and even my interest. I'd seen enough porn to know about BDSM and some of the ways that could look. My cock had gotten hard on more than one occasion at the sight of a man on his knees for another, for the tender touches and even the rough ones. To say I didn't see the appeal of it would have been lying. But wanting it as a fantasy and playing it out in real life felt like two very different things.

Flynn was a dominant man. I'd known that from the first moment I laid eyes on him. From the way he commanded the room to the way he commanded me, I'd been under no delusions that just because he'd gotten onto his back for me meant he'd ever get on his knees. And I didn't think I wanted him there. It would have been awkward and unnatural, undoubtedly for us both, but the thought of me being the one to assume that role turned my blood into ice.

I had fought so hard against so many people to find my personality, my power, and to throw all of that progress away for a pretty man with a perfect asshole and a sinful mouth?

It would be wasteful, but maybe worth it.

"I'm not a submissive," I said.

"I know," he answered quickly.

"Then why would you want me to call you Sir?"

Even as the question left my mouth, my blood had already started to burn hot again, rushing between my legs. My body was answering my own question, and he was close enough to feel the answer pressing against his thigh.

"Because *I* deserve it. Because it was my body that gave you the best orgasms of your life and before you try to shut *that* down, I'm just repeating what you've already told me." His hand slid down my neck, flattening against my spine and racing toward the small of my back, where he pushed his fingers into my skin and urged our bodies closer. "I would want you to call me Sir because it makes me hard and I tend to be very generous when I'm hard."

"I don't want your money," I protested.

"Not with money, Rose."

"Oh."

My forehead fell against his chest, and he wrapped his other arm around me. The hold had almost turned into a hug, although it felt anything but comforting. Flynn's body was coiled, ready to strike as soon as he'd found an opening…or permission.

"Ask me," he whispered.

I swallowed, heart hammering in my throat. "What are you generous with?"

"With my body," he answered, cock jerking against my stomach in solidarity with his response. "With pleasure. With my words, my praise."

"Praise?"

Instead of returning the embrace, I traced my hands up his sides, feeling the hard strength of his muscles and his ribs, the way his entire chest swelled and expanded when he breathed. Beneath my fingertips, his heart beat slow and steady like he wasn't the least bit fazed by me. It made me want to try harder to get a rise out of him. Figuratively, of course, since his cock was already hard and hot against me.

"Consider it a kink," he murmured.

Of all the porn I'd watched, of all the things I understood about BDSM and kink, praise was a new one.

"How does that work?"

Flynn made a very pleased sound in the back of his throat, and with his arms still around me, he pulled us toward his car.

"Get inside," he said. "Get in the back."

The door unlocked as soon as I touched the handle, and I clumsily climbed into the back seat without needing to be told twice. The leather was black, cool to the touch and shiny like the rest of the car. Flynn followed me in and closed the door behind him. It locked again with a deafening latch, and he shifted so his back was against the door, his body angled toward me.

"I've been thinking about you all week." His voice was barely louder than a whisper, but almost deafening in the confines of the car. "I haven't been able to stop thinking about how you felt inside of me. How well you fucked me with that big cock of yours."

I sucked in a breath and groaned, turning my body toward him.

"Take it out," he demanded softly. "Let me see it again. Show me the cock I've been dreaming of."

"Jesus Christ," I cursed almost inaudibly and pulled my dick out of my pants. I was already achingly hard, the slit already slippery with precum.

"I love how you listen," Flynn whispered. "How you do what you're told even if you don't like what that means."

"That makes one of us," I grumbled.

He shushed me, giving me a quick shake of his head to stop my protests. Flynn palmed himself over the fly of his slacks, and I circled my own hand around the base of my shaft to stop it from slapping around.

"You're a good listener because even though you and I don't

know much about each other yet, you know I'm a man of my word and then when I promise you pleasure, I'll deliver it."

My head fell back against the window and more precum leaked out of my dick.

"You can touch yourself however you like, Rose, but I want you to listen to me while you do. Do you understand?"

"Yes," I rasped.

"Yes?"

My balls threatened to explode for how close my orgasm already was.

"Yes, Sir," I whispered, wondering what I'd done to earn it. Was it because I'd listened? Because I conceded? Because I crawled into the back of his car and took my cock out like an obedient slut?

"What did you just think about?" he asked. "Right then when your cock pulsed in your fist?"

I worried about whether I'd be able to get the words out, if I even wanted to. There had to be limits of honesty between us, right? I didn't have to let Flynn know I'd thought about what a slut I was for him, did I? But as quickly as I entertained the idea of swallowing back the truth, my own demands of him came back to me. I didn't want to be with a liar, and I didn't think he did either.

"I was thinking about how you make me do things I never thought I would," I finally answered.

"And I'm not even trying yet." Flynn shot me a near-feral grin. "But it was more than that. Your cheeks went red and your fingers twitched. There was something more. Was it calling me Sir?"

How had he seen all that? Was I just an open book, laid bare with all my truths on display for him to read at his convenience? I hated that. It felt unsafe and wrong, and like I was asking to have my heart broken in the end, when I'd only just managed to get it held back together after Cody had wrecked his way through it.

"Partially."

"I said you could touch yourself," he reminded me, and as if it had been a demand, I stroked my fist up my length and back down again.

Up and down.

I had to loosen my fist, had to move slow, because while I didn't know what was happening between us, I wasn't ready for it to end yet either.

"There you go," Flynn praised. "Just like that, Rose. You listen so fucking well, don't you? You're a good listener. A good boy."

"A good slut." I moaned at him, eyes flying open as the words left my mouth.

The leather seat didn't even make a sound when Flynn moved and launched himself across the car at me. He covered my hand with his and slanted his mouth over mine. Taking control of my pacing, he stroked me harder and rougher than I'd been doing to myself, clearly ready to send me over the edge.

"Is that who you are?" he breathed against my mouth. "Who you want to be? My good little slut? My very best boy?"

It should have been humiliating at worst, demeaning at best, but it worked and my orgasm slammed into me so hard that my vision darkened around the corners. Or maybe that was the lack of oxygen because Flynn had sealed his mouth over mine with such a forceful command, the only breaths I could find were the ones he allowed me between kisses.

Even after my balls had emptied, he kept both of our hands around my dick, slowing his strokes until the tremors and after-shocks had stopped racing up my spine. I was limp and boneless, almost flat on my back with his weight still on top of me. His slacks were wet against my thighs and I didn't know if it was from my orgasm or if he'd come as well.

His kisses slowed as well, tongue moving from urgent explo-ration to tender appreciation, and then against the corner of my mouth, Flynn finally answered the question I'd asked him in the alley.

"That's how praise works, Ambrose."

CHAPTER 11
FLYNN

Thankfully, my approach had worked.

After wiping as much of Rose's cum off his stomach as I could manage without blowing my own load in my pants, he agreed to come home with me.

Even though I'd offered to bring him back for his car later in the day, he'd insisted on driving himself. It was a callback to the night we'd met, but his indifferent expression when we both pulled into my garage had me more off-balance than his look when I'd met him at the hotel. Not that I'd expected him to fawn over my house or anything. I already knew my wealth didn't impress him, but generally people coming over for the first time had *some* kind of readable reaction.

My house was nestled off Coldwater Canyon, a mid-century throwback that I'd spent an obscene amount of money renovating. It was a sprawling single story that hugged the ground, with a front wall made almost entirely of glass. I'd built a small pool in the entry area, housing a monstera plant that I'd kept alive since college, surrounded with enough artistic uplighting to make it look like I knew a thing about architecture and design.

"You live here?" was all Rose asked, throwing a quick glance down at his soiled work clothes.

"Did you want to come in?" I asked.

"That's the point of all this, right?"

His indifference flickered to nervousness, but I watched him try to swallow it back and school his features. He wasn't comfortable, and while I really wanted him inside my house, I didn't want to coerce him.

"You can change your mind," I said softly. "If you're not ready."

He cleared his throat and waggled his head like he was trying to shake the mood off.

"I told you to call me when you were the man I deserved and you did me one better," he said, giving a sincere smile. "The least I can do is stay the night."

"I hate the sound of that."

"I want to come in." Rose closed the space between us and grabbed my hand. "It just reminded me about the difference in the size of our bank accounts."

There wasn't much I could do about the money issue. I came from money and I continued to live with it. I'd never been ashamed of my upbringing and I was thankful for everything it had afforded me. It had given me advantages, I knew, and I'd made sure to use every single one. I'd built myself a good and honest life, and I wouldn't apologize for that.

"If it gets too much, you can leave," I told him. "I don't want that, but I don't want you to hate being here."

"I can just close my eyes if it gets too much, Flynn. Don't worry about me." He gave my hand a squeeze, then a pull toward the door. "I'm just tired from work."

"We'll get you to bed then."

"Feels like it defeats the purpose," he muttered, following me toward the porch.

"I'm very happy to fuck you until you can't keep your eyes open if that's what you prefer."

My front door was made of thin, vertical slats of teak wood, and it unlocked itself on my approach. Pushing the massive panel open, I pulled Rose inside behind me and gave him another minute to adjust.

The inside of the house was just as dramatic as the front, maybe more.

"Does your house have walls?" he asked, taking a step before coming to a stop. He looked down at his shoes, down at mine, down at the pearl-flaked tile between us.

"Not as such."

Rose mumbled something under his breath, then toed off his sneakers and gave them a gentle kick toward the umbrella rack in the corner.

"Do you want a tour?" I asked.

"It all feels pretty self-explanatory."

Rose didn't care about the terrazzo imported from Italy or why my designer had chosen teak wood instead of maple or oak. I doubted he'd be concerned about the salt water pool or the heated floors in the bathroom. As he navigated his way around the open floor plan of my house, I felt the weight of his judgement bearing down on my shoulders, accentuated by every click of my shoes against the tile that rang out over the silence of his own footsteps.

"Where's your bedroom?" he asked, dragging his fingertips across the corner of the kitchen counter.

"Through here."

Apart from the bathrooms, there was only one room with a door in the house, and that was, of course, the bedroom. But the door hinged in the middle, much like the front door, which allowed me to maintain the open floor plan flow if I wanted. Which I often did. We never used my house for entertaining the way we did with Rob's. He was the one with the playroom and the parties and the toys. All things that I'd never really needed for the way I liked to fuck.

"You have a pool," Rose said, taking in the view of the back yard. The outside-facing wall was all glass, again hinged to open up if I wanted air or access to the yard.

"Did you want to swim?"

He shook his head and reached behind him, gathering his shirt and rucking up the soft cotton and pulling it over his head. With his back to me, he let the shirt fall onto the floor, and it looked perfectly at home there in a way I didn't think I'd ever be able to explain. *He* looked at home in my home. Even though he was tired and dirty from work, dirty from me, I watched him and immediately saw all of the organic ways he would fit into my space.

Into my life.

Rose pivoted toward the wall and pointed at the fireplace. "Is that real?"

"Gas."

"Would you turn it on?"

I loved that he wasn't scared to ask for what he wanted, to speak up for what he needed. He'd been so vocal about wanting to top me the first night we spent together, but not shutting down the idea of flipping. Even now, I'd offered and he hadn't told me no, but if he settled into my bed and immediately fell asleep, I think I would have enjoyed that just as much.

Seeing Rose wander and acclimate had me almost as hard as when we'd jerked him off in the back seat of my car, and that was new for me. I'd never wanted someone in my home. I'd never wanted them to feel comfortable or settled around my things. But him?

He was different.

I grabbed the remote off the floating nightstand and pushed the button that would spark it to life. The fire burned huge and quick before settling into a smaller flame. The glass blocked most of the heat, but the fake crackle of the pretend logs echoed off the walls.

"Do you have a hot tub?" he asked.

"Yes."

"Wet bar?"

"Yes," I said again.

Rose turned, flicking open the button of his fly and tugging down the zipper. "A wine fridge?"

"Of course."

He shoved his pants to his ankles and bent to pull off his socks. When he straightened back up, I got a better look at the black lace boy shorts I'd barely caught sight of earlier in the night.

"Condoms?" he asked.

"Yes." I leaned my head toward the nightstand, indicating the location. "Do you always wear women's underwear?"

"They're not women's," he said, taking a step forward and crawling onto my bed. "They're mine."

"Right," I rasped.

"You look overdressed."

I reached for the top button of my shirt and flicked it open. I was still dressed for work, dressed for Cunningham's, dressed to impress—as I always was.

"I feel it."

He knee-walked toward me and swatted my hands out of the way, taking my buttons between his thin fingers and plucking them open one by one. When he reached the bottom, Rose gave a sharp tug and pulled the tails of my shirt free from my pants, then turned his attention to my belt, my fly, my cock.

"Breathe, Flynn," he whispered, following my pants as he pushed them down my legs. My cock still ached from getting him off, and he nuzzled his face against my bulge with a guttural moan that sent shockwaves right to my balls.

I threaded my fingers through his hair, trying to suck in a breath when he open-mouth kissed my cock through the already soaking cotton of my boxer briefs, but I could barely stand.

"If I suck your cock, will you still be able to fuck me later?" he asked.

The laugh that tumbled out of my throat was embarrassingly high-pitched. "Probably not."

"That's a shame." Another sloppy, open-mouth kiss against my shaft. "Guess we'll have to save that for another time."

My mind went fuzzy, a splash of dark around the edges that wrapped around my limbs and threw me off-balance like I was on a carnival ride from hell. I'd always known that I was in over my head with Rose, from his first response to me at Rapture to the headstrong way he'd arranged himself against my body and put his cock into me.

"When you're around, Rose, I don't think I know which way is up."

The confession fell out between us, and I tightened my fingers in his hair. I'd never let a man run me around the way Rose did. I never even gave anyone enough of a chance to flip control, let alone flip *me*. But even on his knees, Rose managed to hold onto the upper hand.

I was in awe of him…of what he'd done to me.

He pushed against my hand and leaned back to look up at me, a lust-drunk grin on his face that looked like he'd finally made himself at home in my space. "That might be the best example of praise kink you've shown me yet, Flynn."

I wanted to tell him to take me apart faster, just finish ruining my life so it hurts now instead of later. Maybe I'd be able to survive it if I didn't put it off.

"It's nothing," I said softly, pulling lube and a condom from the nightstand.

Rose had already stripped me out of my underwear, and I joined him on the bed, lying flat on my back with my feet at the headboard, cock pointing toward the ceiling.

"Let me." Rose took the condom out of my hand and tore the wrapper. He tossed it onto the floor, making more of a mess than we already had with our clothes. He rolled the latex down my length, and I ground my molars together to push off the proximity of my orgasm.

"I love how you touch me," I whispered, hauling him toward the edge of the bed so he was standing with one leg on either side of my head. With my hands around his waist, I pulled him down, smothering my face with his ass and licking a hot stripe from his balls to his hole. "I love how you taste."

"Also good praise," he whimpered, leaning back to brace himself on my chest.

I continued to eat his ass using my tongue and my mouth, my fingers, to get him wet and open for me. Rose tasted like soap and sweat, and I sealed my mouth around him until it was hard for me to breathe, until he rode my face and dug his fingernails into my skin. When it was too much *for me*, I hauled him back, shoving him down my chest. He was so small, so slender, so easy to throw around.

He immediately knew what I wanted, and he arranged himself on top of me, slowly lowering himself down onto my dick. My grip on his hips faltered, and I flexed my hands until I found more purchase around his waist.

"Look at you," I whispered, swallowing and trying to find a breath.

Rose settled down around me and again rested his fingertips against my chest. Looking down, I could see the divots left earlier from his nails, and my eyes lolled back as he started to move, riding me again.

"What about me?"

"You're fucking gorgeous, riding my cock like that. Jesus Christ."

Words were hard, but I'd find them for him.

He hummed, stare flickering from me to the pool beyond the window, to the fire, and back to me again. His cock was dark as the stain on his cheeks and throat, and I curled my fist around it, enjoying the way it felt as he moved it against my palm.

"Riding it like what?" he asked, his mouth looking like it wanted to smirk at me, even though the pleasure kept washing over him in waves. Rose's eyelashes fluttered, his pulse throbbed, and his fingers slid against my skin for how sweaty he was.

I pulled him down at the same time I lifted off the bed, spearing the entire length of my cock into his body. He gasped, back bowing from the intrusion, and it was hard to fight the urge to flip him onto his back, fold him in half, and fuck a Rose-shaped dent into my mattress.

So I didn't.

He landed against the bed with a huff, the air leaving his lungs and ghosting against my throat, which he promptly wrapped his lips around and started to suck a bruise into the skin.

"Like what, Flynn?" he asked again, fingers now digging into my ass, spurring me on.

I grunted, bearing down and bottoming out inside of him.

"Like you deserve it."

"The tables have turned, Sir," he whispered, teeth grazing my collarbone. "Now it's your turn to do the same."

EVEN IN THE LIGHT OF DAY, FLYNN'S HOUSE DIDN'T MAKE ANY SENSE to me. For a man that had so much personality, the place he lived was absolutely devoid of it. From the stark white walls and the uncomfortable furniture, I couldn't tell a single thing about him beyond what I already knew. Even his bedroom was bland and nondescript, save for the fireplace, which was at least a nice touch, if not generic.

I'd woken up alone in his bed, the fireplace still crackling in the wall. The other pillow was cold, leading me to believe Flynn had been awake for a while. I sat up and stretched, kicking the sheets down to the foot of the bed. My clothes were strewn all over the floor, not that I would have wanted to put on cum-stained underwear and dirty work clothes.

Cracking my neck as I looked around the room, I found a pair of gray sleep pants folded neatly on the nightstand. I assumed they were for me since he was nowhere to be found, and as I slipped them on, I took time to appreciate the ridiculously soft material as they slid up my legs.

They were huge on me, which was expected considering how much larger than me he was, and even with the drawstring cinched tight, I had to hold the waistband in my fist to keep them up. Fortunately, or otherwise, there wasn't much spying for me to do on account of how absent his house was of personal touches, so I shuffled off in search of the best lay of my life.

Flynn was easy to find, pacing through his kitchen with a matching pair of pants hanging sinfully low on his hips. The deep v-cut of his stomach had me salivating. He hadn't seen me yet, but he was talking in hushed tones, gesturing with his hands as he leaned over the kitchen island to pour himself a cup of coffee. The white bud in his ear matched the rest of his boring and predictable house.

He looked terribly out of place.

Slinking past him, I hoisted myself on the counter right along-side his bare arm, and without missing a beat, he settled his hand onto my thigh and continued his conversation.

Glancing up at me after he finished his train of thought, he mouthed the question *do you have anywhere to be?*

Your ass, I answered back silently.

The corner of his mouth angled up into a smirk and he shook his head before sliding one of the coffee cups full of brew toward me.

We stayed like that, with his hand on my thigh and the coffee in my hand, until he finished his call and pulled the bud out of his ear and tossed it on the counter.

"My ass, you say?" He asked, coming to stand between my legs.

"I wouldn't say no to the offer if it was on the table."

"It's not *not* on the table, but let me at least get you fed first, get your strength back."

I laughed, jerking my leg away to shake him off. "Do you even have food in here?"

He looked confused. "Why wouldn't I?"

"It doesn't look like you actually live here," I said, gazing past him and into the spacious but sterile living room.

His brows knit together, further evidence of his confusion. "Why do you say that?"

"No pictures," I said. "No art. No color."

"The furniture is art," he protested.

I scoffed at him and took a drink of the coffee he'd made for me. It tasted expensive, which was not surprising in the least. It tasted better than the shit at the restaurant and the instant packets I had at home, I knew that much.

"That's bullshit and you know it."

"The plant?" He asked weakly, straightening up like I'd offended him.

"What plant?"

"The monstera out front."

I didn't even remember seeing a plant, but I'd give him the benefit of the doubt. He was missing the point entirely, which had more to do with his income level than anything else. I didn't want to hold it against him, but after years of working in the service industry, I'd learned that people in the higher tax brackets had a much different way of walking through the world than the rest of us.

"The monstera," I repeated. "Okay."

"Did you want to argue about my lack of art all day or do you have other plans?"

"This is hardly an argument."

The biting comment made me think about Cody and the day before when he'd shown up at my house, and it made me think of catching him in bed with his roommate. Now that had been an argument.

He sighed and scrubbed a hand down his face, turning and leaning against the counter beside me. I brushed my leg against him, hoping he understood I wasn't upset.

"Do you work today?" he asked, glancing at me from the corner of his eye.

"Ah, work," I said, remembering how I'd ended up at his house in the first place. "Not today, no, but are we going to talk about your grade A stalking skills?"

He laughed at that, rolling his eyes. "It's hardly stalking. I'm just resourceful. Speaking of..."

Flynn shoved a small black box toward me, and I quickly realized it was a brand new cell phone. I had no idea how he'd managed to get me a new one in less than twelve hours, but I gathered that he was the kind of man who could get pretty much whatever he wanted, whenever he wanted it.

Me included.

"I told you that you didn't have to do this," I reminded him. "But thank you."

"I know I didn't have to." He shrugged and grinned at me, looking young and playful and a whole different kind of handsome. "But I'm resourceful, remember?"

"Resourceful because of the zeroes in your bank account," I countered. "Buying a phone is one thing, tracking down a one-night stand is another."

"We've spent more than one night together," he said.

"This feels like if you did it, it reads possessive and sexy, but if my broke ass did it, it would be stalking and I'd end up in jail."

"I'd never press charges." He drew an X across his heart.

"Your chivalry is commendable." I rolled my eyes and sighed. "Do you work today?"

Flynn gestured toward the earbud he'd tossed onto the counter after his call. "I already am."

"Do you need me to get out of your hair?"

"I much prefer you in it." He pushed away from the counter and headed toward one of the giant windows. "Do you want to sit outside awhile? It's not too warm yet."

As he approached, one of the giant plates of glass slid open and he stepped onto the concrete pad that led to the sparkling blue pool in the middle of the yard. He hadn't been wrong the night before when he told me he had more money than sense, but I hopped off the counter anyway and followed him out.

Much like the rest of his house, the back yard lacked any personality or defining features. His patio furniture had white cushions so clean I doubted he'd ever used them at all. But he sat down and I sat down beside him.

This was awkward. The daylight, the silence, the residual cum, all of it.

"Can we talk?" I asked, stretching my legs out in front of me.

The yard was made up of concrete pads with green grass between them and I tried to reach my toes to the bright green blades, but they were too finely manicured for me to get close.

"About something in particular?" He stood up and, without warning, dragged my chair closer to the edge of the pad. My toes immediately sank into the grass.

"About this," I said. "About what's happening with us."

"What's happening with us," he repeated.

"Please don't play daft." I sighed and leaned against the back of the chair. Even with the cushions, it was rigid and uncomfortable. Lying on the concrete would have offered more flexibility.

"You're right. I'm sorry."

"I just broke up with my boyfriend the night I met you," I explained. The man had already been inside of me, sharing the truth about where I was at mentally was the least I could do. I wanted us both to go into whatever this was with open minds and complete awareness. "He cheated on me."

"I'm sorry."

"Not your fault," I said quickly, more reflex at this point than anything else.

"You still didn't deserve that."

"How do you know?"

Flynn huffed and shrugged. "Did you deserve it?"

"No."

"That's how I know," he said.

His arrogance was obscenely sexy and I wanted to hate him for it, but that felt unfair. I wasn't under the impression that his attitude was something he had much control over. He was confident and cocky, but in that smooth way that turned you on instead of off. He'd basically won the personality lottery, if not the interior decorating one.

"We need to talk about you," I admitted.

Flynn had occupied the majority of my thoughts for the better part of the past week, whether it was decent or indecent. And I'd spent more time than I'd want to admit to thinking about some of the things he'd hinted around in the moments we'd been together.

"Is it the stalking?" He grinned at me, teeth white and straight and perfect.

"You said that was just being resourceful," I reminded him.

"Six in one."

"I want to talk about the Sir thing," I said, knowing that I had to just get the words out instead of beating around the bush. The Sir thing had taken up most of the thoughts, well that and the hot fucking grip of his asshole. But the Sir thing, and I'd called him that the night before and he hadn't told me no. I didn't think I'd done anything to earn it, that I'd done anything different from before, and he'd been clear the night we met it was a privilege earned, not freely given.

"What about it?" He asked, expression open and blank.

Like his stupid house.

"Tell me about it," I said. "Tell me all about it. Like I'm five."

"If you were five, we wouldn't be talking about it." Flynn smirked, but he knew what I meant. "I honestly am not sure where to begin."

"You're a big boy. Do your best."

The coffee was finally a tolerable temperature and I took a more substantial drink while Flynn visibly gathered his thoughts. While I waited, I looked around, trying to appreciate the space a little more than I had on first glance. It had been unfair to describe the yard or the house as generic. There was character to be found; it just didn't match my understanding of the man.

"Well, Rose, you met me at a kink club so I'm hoping I don't have to explain that part to you?"

Smug asshole.

"I have a first grade understanding of it," I said. "Figuratively, obviously. But a lot that I saw there was way over my head."

"Not mine," he said, "but it didn't appeal."

"You like the praise thing? You're a talker?"

"That's one way to put it."

My stomach growled so loudly, it stopped him in his tracks.

"Are you hungry?"

"I could eat."

The fact of the matter was, I was starving. Normally I grabbed something after work before crashing, but the only thing I'd grabbed last night was my dick.

And then his.

"Let me get some fruit or something." He stood up, knee cracking. "Or do you want eggs? I can make an omelet."

"You don't need to go to the trouble." I stood up to join him and he tried to wave me back into my seat.

"There's more to the Sir thing than just talking dirty in bed."

My breath hitched in my throat, and my knees bent without my approval. My ass was back on the cushion before the weight of his words had even fully processed their way through my brain.

"I'm not submissive," I said, not for the first time.

"Could you be?"

I stood up again, the question entirely unexpected. The answer was no, because I'd fought too many people for too many years to give up control to a man I didn't know anything about.

"I'd prefer to not," I said.

"Come inside with me while I make you something to eat." Flynn held out his hand for me, and I took it, even though I'd stood up to go. It was one thing for us to dance around the semantics of casual and serious, but submission was more of a hard line and one I had no real interest in negotiating.

"I'd prefer to not," I said weakly, shoulders hunched inward.

Flynn studied me silently, head cocked and the inside of his cheek pinched between his teeth like he was reviewing the terms of a business deal or a contract, not a partner. Not me.

"If you want to go, I won't stop you. But you asked about me and I'm trying to give you an answer. The Sir thing is more than telling someone what to do in the bedroom. There's caretaking; there's attention. It's a job."

Cody's vitriol from the week before rang like a gunshot in my ears.

"I don't want to be work for anyone," I whispered.

"You're not work at all, Rose. You're pleasure." He pulled me toward him and I stumbled close, cheek landing against his sun-kissed chest, and I didn't even have a chance to stop the embarrassing sigh that fell out of my mouth. "You're an absolute pleasure."

CHAPTER 13

FLYNN

ROSE WAS A THOUSAND POUNDS OF CHAOS AND CONFLICT IN A hundred-and-ten pound body. Wrapping my one arm around him, he melted against me without another word of protest or disagreement.

"We've been dancing around each other for the past week." I kissed his cloud of hair and inhaled deeply. He smelled like his shampoo and my laundry detergent, and the combination was heady.

"Is that what this is?" His words were muffled against my sternum, and he gently touched one of his hands against my hip.

"Come inside and let me make you breakfast. I'll lay my cards on the table and then you can decide what you want to do."

Gently, I led him back toward the house. Once I got him into the kitchen, I hoisted him up onto the counter and used the side of my finger to lift his chin. His expression met the textbook definition of wary, from his finely-knit brows to the tight line of his lips. But even with that, he looked like a dream.

"No strings with the meal," I promised him. "Just food and honesty, okay? Transparency."

He nodded and I leaned in to brush a soft and chaste kiss against his sleepy mouth. The tiniest moan left his lips and I licked it into mine before he could swallow it back.

"I don't like bell peppers," he said, giving my chest a gentle push.

I gave him a mock salute and went to the fridge, pulling out eggs and cheese and some bacon that I'd cooked earlier in the week to garnish a Bloody Mary for Archie. On the counter, Rose turned and watched me while I cracked and whisked eggs.

"I'm a dominant," I said, aware of how nervous the term and its counterpart made him. "But not like in the movies."

There was a beat of silence while I chopped some of the bacon strips and tossed them into the bowl.

"I don't know what kind of movies you're watching, Flynn." Rose finally chuckled and I flung a dish towel across the island at him. He caught it and swatted it away, the tentative laugh turning more honest the longer it went on. The sound echoed off the walls like a melody, and I closed my eyes to fully savor it in my ears.

"I love a man on his knees for me, don't get me wrong there. But it's not about cuffs and protocol. It's about respect and praise…and sometimes humiliation."

Rose made a sound in the back of his throat, and I poured the omelet mixture into the pan.

"Don't scoff about it." The eggs sizzled in the pan and I pointed at him with the spatula. "I haven't forgotten what you said to me last night and I know you haven't either."

The whole good little slut conversation was going to give me enough wank material for the foreseeable future, even if I never got another chance to hear the words leave Rose's glossy and sweet lips.

"It was a compliment," I continued, hoping I'd be able to find a way to explain the intricacies of how humiliation and praise worked together. It was something I'd wondered about for years because what had always started with yes, and good, and just like that had over time turned into something different.

Something better.

But much like spanking and bondage and kneeling, it wasn't for everyone.

And I wasn't like some people I knew who only wanted to fuck within the limits of a carefully negotiated contract and between the walls of a playroom. No, I wanted to explore and grow and find things that worked and even some that didn't. There was something to be said for trial and error, and the trust that kind of adventure required.

I'd never had it for myself.

But that was by design, I had come to believe. I wasn't one to let people get close, but that were my own fears and insecurities at work. My inability to bare my heart and trust someone enough with those parts of me. Which was ironic because I asked that of my partners by default, even if it was only for a moment, for a night…sometimes a weekend.

"Not that I disagree, but tell me why."

At Rose's question, I flipped the omelet over on itself and gave him my attention while the eggs began to sizzle again in the pan.

"I suppose when you think about the word, you think about a person who enjoys sex more than society thinks they should. Maybe someone who has it more than most?" I posed the last part as a question to make sure we were on the same page. I'd never thought about what it would take to explain myself in the way Rose was asking of me, but it wasn't a bad train of thought. I liked that he was inquisitive, that he wanted to know. It made me believe he was interested, that he wasn't going to eat the eggs and run.

"That's fair," he murmured, sipping at his coffee.

"What's better than being able to bring those feelings, that action, out in your partner? Or if not bring it out, giving them a safe place to share it."

"Is that what you are, Flynn? A safe space?"

"It's what I try to be."

I scooped the omelet onto a plate and slid it across the counter toward him. He inhaled the smell of it, and I got him a fork and knife from the silverware drawer, then refilled both of our coffees.

"Are you eating?" he asked, using the side of his fork to cut the corner of the omelet off.

"I ate before you got up."

I wasn't a big breakfast eater in the first place, but it wasn't a lie. By the time Rose had fallen asleep, it was almost four in the morning and my alarm went off at five. After prying myself out of his arms and forcing myself into the gym, I'd showered and ate a bowl of yogurt while I talked through a contract closing on an apartment building just outside Hollywood with Rob. Rose had woken up during my second meeting of the morning and promptly derailed what was meant to be my third, but they could wait.

I had more pressing matters to attend to.

"And that's how you think it's praise? Finding the good in something that's generally an insult?" Rose's expression tried to look like he had gotten one over on me, but the smug expression was quick to fall away after he forked the first bite of breakfast into his mouth and groaned. He was quick to get a second bite—and a third—before turning his attention back to me looking somewhat more mollified than before.

"When I said it, did it hurt your feelings?" I asked.

"No," he grumbled.

"Then that's how it works."

Rose huffed and finished eating his omelet in silence. I was content to watch him, and when he'd put the last bit into his mouth, he was ready with another stream of questions.

"What about the Sir thing?"

"What about it?"

"You said it has to be earned, but you said you're not like other Doms, so how does someone earn it?"

"Did you want to earn it?" I asked, even though he already had. Just by showing up, by asking the questions, by being willing to play these silly little sex games with me when everything we wanted—and had been given—from life was in opposition with each other.

"I'm not interested in giving up any kind of control," Rose said, lips pursed.

"I'm not asking you to. The less dominant partner is the one who has the control anyway."

There was no point in calling Rose a submissive because he never would be, and the longer I was around him, the less I wanted him to be. He was sharp and feisty and unafraid to ask for the things he wanted. It was confident and sexy as hell, and the fact he did all of that while still taking the smallest amounts of instruction and guidance was unbelievably hot.

"I find that hard to believe."

"You can stop anything we do, Rose." I shrugged, watching the way he nervously tapped the tines of the fork against the plate. "You say stop and it stops."

"Well, good, because if not, that would be rape."

Sucking my lips between my teeth, I bit down and took the empty plate from him.

"I think you know what I meant," I said, if not under my breath a little, wounded from the dig.

"You're right. I do, but I don't trust it." He cleared his throat and dropped his fork. "I can wash up if you want."

I waved him off just like I'd done earlier. He wasn't going to lift a finger in my house unless it was to grab a cock in his hand.

"You can, but you won't," I told him.

He raised a brow like he was challenging me. "Unless you demand it?"

"I don't make demands, and you earn calling me Sir by wanting to call me Sir, Rose. I'm not a hard man to please, but it's a serious thing and I treat it as such."

"Thought you were only into casual."

"Do you get off on calling out all my hypocritical tendencies?"

I walked around the island and again notched myself between his spread legs, enjoying the way he laughed at me and slid his arms around my neck. With him on the counter, he was almost the same height as me, so I leaned in and stole a kiss.

"I'm just trying to make sense of you," he murmured, parting his lips and making way so I could slide my tongue against his.

"My friends say that's impossible." I hauled him to the edge of the counter so he could feel my dick as it got hard for him from the way he kissed me and touched me. "They've been trying for years."

"So, sex is casual, good sex is serious?"

Rose smiled against my mouth and I sank my teeth into his bottom lip until his smug little laugh turned into a moan.

"You have me a little turned around," I admitted, pulling back enough so he could see how serious I was in my confession.

"It's mutual."

"I haven't had a serious partner since I was in college."

Rose wrapped his legs around my waist and pressed our bodies together as much as the spacing on the counter would allow. His hands came together at the base of my neck, fingers tangling in the short strands of hair that had grown too long.

"Are you asking for one?" He dragged the side of his nose against mine, the ghost of a smile visible on his lips.

"I think that's more your speed. I haven't forgotten our first night together, you in those panties talking about all the things you deserve."

It was the truth.

And I didn't think I'd ever forget it for the rest of my life.

"I want a monogamous partner," he confirmed, which was fine with me.

Barclay was the polyamorous one in our group, and Dalton was always more than willing to make his twosome a threesome. It had never been my style to share the way the two of them preferred. No shame to either of them, or anyone else for that matter, but it wasn't for me. I was a little too possessive, a little too jealous.

"What else do you want?"

"I want someone who sees the good in my bad," he whispered, cheeks flushing crimson.

I grabbed his face in my hands, cradling his burning flesh against my palms and I held him steady until he looked into my eyes. "Someone who can maybe talk me through both of those things."

Fuck, he was a gorgeous, gorgeous man. Trusting but wounded, fearful and hopeful all in the same breath. I'd talk him through the end of the world if that was what it came down to. If that was something he allowed.

"I can do that," I said softly, placing a gentle kiss against the corner of his mouth. He arched into me, pressing our chests together as he tightened his fingers against the base of my neck.

"I want to wake up and wear more of your clothes around the house," he said.

Something unexpected surged in my chest at his confession, something raw and feral, and I slanted our mouths together and kissed him until I was dizzy. Until his hands had made their way down my back and around my ass, until my pants were sticky with precum and sweat.

"I'd rather you wake up and wear nothing," I confessed.

Rose wrapped his legs around my waist and raised himself off the counter, his body giving more instruction than his words ever could.

"I think that can be arranged."

CHAPTER 14

ROSE

Uncharacteristically, at no point over the weekend did I get the impression that I'd overstayed my welcome at Flynn's house. The longer I was there, the more I became familiar with him as a person, the more his house made sense. Flynn was steadfast and reliable; he was practical. Every time his phone rang, he answered it, whether it was work or a friend, and he engaged each person in a wholly unpredictable way, at least to my understanding. He was professional and serious with work and jovial and teasing with his friends. He made innuendos and cracked jokes, and it didn't take long for me to realize Flynn was more multifaceted than I'd given him credit for.

I stayed at his house until Saturday afternoon, because I had to go home at that point. I needed clean clothes and I had to work that evening. But from Friday morning to the moment I left, Flynn had done everything in his power to show me the truth behind the words he'd spoken over breakfast. He tended me, made sure I was fed and had enough water. He took me into the shower and washed me with a very commendable attention to detail, then he took me to bed and defiled me with just as much focus and dedication.

My phone battery had died hours before I'd even entertained

the idea of leaving, and when I got home and got it plugged in I had a flurry of messages from a very worried Drake. I knew he was mad that I'd gone incognito, so instead of answering him with a text, I called.

He answered on the first ring.

"You piece of shit," he answered, almost a yell.

"I know, I know. I'm sorry."

I threw myself back onto my bed, charging cord pulling taut as I stretched across the short allotment of space it allowed.

"Where have you been?"

"I worked Friday night and then I went home with that guy from the club."

"What guy?"

"From last week," I reminded him. "The rich one."

"Did you rob him?" Drake laughed.

"Of semen, sure."

"Oh, God!" he shouted in my ear. "Don't *call* it that."

"His ejaculate."

"Not much better."

"Sucked him dry," I said with a laugh and an achingly pleasurable flash of memories. "Wrung his balls out."

"This must be why you're so good at sucking dick," he accused. "Always getting a mouthful of cock so you'll stop talking."

"I'm good at sucking dick because I practiced," I countered, which earned me a very tired kind of sigh from my very best friend. "I'm sorry I didn't call or text, but my phone died when I was at his house and I just got home. If it's any consolation, he intercepted me at work so I'm sure if you reported me missing, the cops would have been able to track him down relatively quickly."

"He what?" Drake asked, and I covered my eyes with my forearm, realizing the error of the casual commentary.

"He met me after work," I tried to course-correct the conversation. "His name is Flynn, by the way."

"Are we on a first name basis so soon after Cody?" he asked.

"Flynn could be the real deal."

If he wanted to be. And after the weekend we spent together, I was relatively confident he did. Even though there was a lot about the things he liked that didn't mesh with the things I wanted, I didn't necessarily think we were incompatible. The one part that had stuck with me, besides the feeling of his tongue spearing my ass open, was the comment he'd made about the less dominant partner being the one with control.

I wanted to say that it felt like a line he spouted to get his way, but after listening to the way he engaged the other people in his life, I didn't think Flynn had a dishonest bone in his body. I also didn't see any harm in putting it to the test if given the opportunity.

"I've heard that before," Drake mumbled.

"Are you worried about me?"

"Of course. You're my best friend."

I rolled onto my side and smiled.

My apartment wasn't anything like Flynn's house and, up until Friday night, I thought I'd had a comfortable bed, a full size mattress I'd saved up to buy four years earlier. At the time, it was top of the line, or at least top of the line for my price range. I knew the pillow soft comfort of Flynn's king size bed was in an entirely different comparison bracket.

I loved my apartment. The colors, the memories, the mismatched items that I'd pieced together over the years. All of it felt like home to me, and even though I'd understood Flynn more in his vast and sterile living space, it had to be miserable and lonely. So many sharp edges, so much white.

"I'll let you know before I go over there next time so you don't worry," I promised.

"If there's a next time?"

"I expect one."

And that wasn't arrogance or pride. I really just had the

impression that, for whatever reason, Flynn liked me. With his looks and his money, he could have his pick of probably any person in the entire city, but he'd set his sights on me. Or his friend had set his sights on me and I got to enjoy the fallout. Either way, I wasn't mad about it and I was happy to see it through as far as it would go.

"Is…" Drake's tone took a serious dip. "Is he a good guy?"

"Do you think I would have spent the night with him twice if he wasn't?"

"I've spent the night with some assholes, Rose. Assholes generally know how to fuck."

"He knows how to fuck," I said. "But as far as I can tell, he's a good guy."

"Do I get to meet him?"

The alarm on my phone started to chirp and I sat up with my back against the wall, stretching my legs out straight and wiggling my toes. "You definitely don't get to meet him."

"Rude."

I tapped the alarm button on the screen of my phone to silence it. "I have to get ready for work, but I really am sorry I didn't let you know where I was. I didn't mean to worry you."

"You better," Drake grumbled. "I'll talk to you later."

I hung up the call and tossed my phone onto the nightstand, then I rolled over onto my stomach and screamed into my pillow.

I didn't want to be excited about Flynn, but how could I not be?

He was older than me. He was established and competent. He was handsome and he was amazing in bed. And not once had he balked at my underwear. I'd honestly expected him to try and steal a pair for as fascinated as he was with them, and the fantasy of Flynn mouthing my cock through some sinfully expensive satin or silk was enough to get me dangerously hard.

"Not now," I told myself as I climbed out of bed.

As much as I hated the idea of washing the weekend away, I desperately needed to get the sweat from sex off of me before going in for another shift. And more than that, I had to get Flynn off my mind so I could focus on work, at least temporarily.

Begrudgingly, I shuffled into the shower, where I did an admirable job of washing my cock and balls. I'd even switched the shower head over to the nozzle attachment so I could clean out in case I had another unexpected visitor at the end of my shift.

I liked that Flynn wasn't scared of getting on his back and taking a cock up his ass, but I very much enjoyed spreading my cheeks for him to pummel me right into the mattress too. I liked the way his mouth felt against my ass and I loved the way his cock felt in the back of my throat. There wasn't a single thing about him that hadn't brought me some form of pleasure, even the silent week we'd spent apart when I'd been under the delusion that Flynn had to be anyone besides himself to be deserving of me.

His pride and confidence had been on full display when he'd shown up at my work, proving me wrong over and over again. If I sat with the thought too long, I almost felt ashamed for the assumptions I'd made about him and the kind of person he was. Flynn wasn't some typical, rich, Brentwood prick. He had money, but it wasn't part of his personality, at least not in the way I'd expected it to be.

At every encounter, every turn, he proved my pre-conceptions about him wrong. And so it felt patently unfair of me to not give him a fighting chance. What I did know for certain, though, was that he wasn't the one who had battles to fight to make things work.

It was me.

I was the one with the preconceived ideas and the hard lines about who I was and the things I wanted. Flynn wanted me back, but he also wanted a man—wanted *me* to get on my knees and do as I was told.

Even if it was casual.

The idea of it had me rolling my eyes so hard it gave me a headache, and while I got dressed for work, I tried to turn the ideas of him over in my head. I didn't think I had more questions for him, but I was ready to take him for another road test.

Thankfully, I didn't think it would be terribly long until I saw him again, but I also knew the time couldn't go fast enough.

I was already halfway to head over heels, and that didn't sound like a good idea for anyone involved, least of all...

Me.

CHAPTER 15

FLYNN

"Do you think my couch is boring?"

Standing in my kitchen with a glass of wine in hand, I posed the question to Dalton, who sat at the island. He'd only had a sip of his drink, so when he looked over his shoulder toward the couch in question, I knew I'd get an honest answer out of him. Or at least out of his face. The man was a horrible liar—it was one of the things I liked the best about him.

"It's…" His brows drew together, expression making it evident he was running through a mental thesaurus as fast as he could without looking suspicious.

"Boring," I said.

"Utilitarian," he countered.

I scoffed and chased the sound down with a drink of wine.

"Is this about Rose?"

"Is what about Rose?"

Dalton pursed his lips, unimpressed. "You've lived here for years and you've never once asked my opinion on your furniture."

"The fact that you immediately assume the question has to do with a man is proof enough that you've harbored less than savory opinions about my couch for as long as I've had it."

Dalton raised his hands in surrender and laughed at me. "Guilty as charged, but it's not such a glaring problem that I felt it necessary to call you out on it. But now that we're on the topic, did you want to talk about the dining room table too?"

"Oh, my God!" I snatched my wine glass from the counter and stalked past him into the dining room, glaring at the teak table designed to match the wall panels. I stared at the extremely expensive piece of custom furniture, another frown deepening as I tried to see my house through Rose's eyes. "Oh, my God."

The second iteration of the phrase had a decidedly more resigned feeling than the first, and as soon as I felt Dalton at my back, I turned and weaved around him, heading for the back yard. He followed after, laughing the whole time, then joined me at the loungers with a sigh.

"It's not the end of the world, Flynn. It's just furniture and you can afford to replace it."

I glared back at the pieces inside my house before turning my attention to the lush—albeit also utilitarian—landscaping against the far wall of the yard. The space was still mostly concrete with soft grass between the pads and a well-manicured wall of ivy and some other kind of greenery I'd never bothered to learn the name of. It gave the house some color without being bold or brash, and I tried to think back to the version of myself who'd bought the house thinking that either of those was something to be avoided.

"How long have you known that you're attracted to men?" I asked, deliberately changing the subject.

Dalton barked out a surprised laugh. "That answer is probably going to take more wine than you have in this whole house, but in summary, just since college."

"Was it Barclay?"

Our friend group was very close—had been for many years—and while I'd met them all due to my association with Archie, Dalton and Barclay had known each other just as long on their own. While none of us had ever shied away from sharing toys or partners when the situations called for it, Barclay had always had some kind of way about him. He was a natural flirt, older than most of us, and more good-looking than most men had any right to be. He'd been in a holding pattern with another man, Val, for what felt like years, but neither of them had made any sort of commitment to the other beyond the promise of a good time.

"Believe it or not," Dalton started, gaze going soft as he stared off into the distance. "When he and Dennis were together, they were quite the monogamous pair."

Dennis, of course, being Barclay's former long-term partner, a man who'd stumbled into bed with a professor at the college, promptly breaking Barclay's heart and changing the entire trajectory of his life.

"I remember. But I meant before."

Dalton shook his head. "When he's committed, he's all in. But no, even before he met Dennis, he and I…"

The way he trailed off convinced me there was a story, but I also trusted he was right in that I didn't have enough wine to get it out of him.

"Enough about Barclay," I said.

Clearing his throat, Dalton took another swallow of his wine and asked, "How long have you known?"

"Forever, I think, but it's been a struggle. People don't seem to really like bisexual men so I don't talk about it much."

Growing up, I was raised and conditioned to find women attractive, but even if I looked past the social constructs of society, I enjoyed the female form so I knew it was more than that. But the first time Billy Roberts had accidentally grabbed my cock along with the flag in a game of sixth-grade flag football, I'd known there was more to it than I'd suspected.

It had been easier to keep my attraction to men a secret, choosing instead to date cheerleaders by day and then fuck football players on the weekends. High school was probably when I stumbled onto my natural affinity for using my mouth to get me into and out of trouble, because I'd yet to meet a man in the closet who didn't like being told what a good boy he was for taking a dick up the ass like he'd been born for it.

As an adult, I'd dated men and women, I'd slept with both,

sometimes even at the same time, but I'd never wanted to have a relationship that lasted longer than a few days. It was partially a result of seeing Barclay getting his heart shattered in college that turned me off the idea, and partly because I didn't want to have to choose one person for the rest of my life. People had always treated my bisexuality like a choice I made, a deliberate attempt to sit on a fence instead of picking sides, but that was never what it had been for me.

I understood the concepts of polyamory and open relationships, and knew I could lean into something like that to appease my fear of commitment, but I was also too jealous for that kind of thing. But I also knew I couldn't ask someone else to let me play around and not give them the same courtesy. So, it had always felt easier to keep everything casual in every way.

And then there was Rose.

Rose, who was so gorgeous and playful and wonderful, and I'd immediately been willing to throw myself at his feet to get a chance with him. I realized after meeting him how absolutely transparent my attempts at casual dating had been, because one look from him, one kiss, and I was on my knees and begging for more. Like a man lost in the desert or something equally trite and metaphoric.

"Oh, you talk plenty, Flynn," Dalton teased, and I huffed out a laugh, closing my eyes and resting my head against the back of the chair.

"But yes, to your other question. It's about Rose."

"Is his name really Rose? Like the flower?"

I thought about how pink and sweet his ass had tasted when he let me shove my tongue inside of it.

"It's a nickname." I shifted my weight and crossed my legs at the ankle. "His name is Ambrose."

"That's obscene."

I laughed again. "I know. Hence, Rose."

"And I take it you've seen him more than once?" he asked. "More than a casual weekend."

"I've been seeing him here and there for a few weeks," I answered. "He did a pretty good job at putting me off for the first week."

"Getting you off?"

Another laugh. "He told me the first night we met that he deserved better than me."

That earned another sharp rebuke from Dalton, who waved his empty wine glass at me. I snatched it out of his hand and stood, walking back into the house to get the bottle of wine we'd left open on the counter. I topped him off and brought the bottle outside with me, pouring another drink's worth into my own glass and arranging myself back down in the chair.

"He's probably not wrong."

"Well, I was inclined to disagree with both of you, and I told him as much."

"You must have been real convincing." Dalton waggled his eyebrows at me and took a sip off the top of his wine.

"I would have been, but everything feels a little different with him."

"Oh, shit." Dalton heaved a petulant breath and twisted his mouth into something that looked like a stark lack of amusement. "Are you next to fall?"

"What?" I chuckled and shook my head. "Absolutely not."

I wasn't an idealistic man. I was an optimistic realist on my very best days and a brooding pessimist on my worst. Just because I'd come around on the appeal of seeing someone in a more serious way didn't mean I was anywhere near delusional enough to think that there was a forever in anything for me and Rose.

"You say that like it's a hard and fast fact."

"I know myself well enough to know it is," I said. "Whatever Rob and Archie have found with Gray and Owen isn't for me."

As I uttered the words, a sharp pang stabbed through my ribs, penetrating my heart. It was the first time I realized that there was jealousy lurking somewhere in the depths of my chest around them all finding some real kind of love and happiness for themselves. Seeing Rob, of all people, so content in his push and pull with Grayson had hit me the hardest, I suspected. Even though I was closest with Archie, I saw more of myself in Rob than anyone else in our friend group, and that longing was raw and rough.

"Your face says otherwise," Dalton said softly.

I squeezed my eyes closed and blinked them wide open, hoping to clear the expression and the feeling at the same time.

"Rose wasn't wrong that he deserves better than me," I admitted. "But I'm not the worst he could do."

"How *did* you get around that, by the way? I'm dying to know."

"I was honest with him." I drank some wine and let the rich floral taste roll around my mouth before I swallowed. "I told him I didn't need to change, that I could give him everything he wanted."

"If what he wants is orgasms and bland home furnishings."

I had half a mind to throw the contents of my glass right onto Dalton's very overpriced white t-shirt. But I put it to better use, taking another drink instead.

"I was honest," I explained. "About what I wanted and what I could give, and that seemed to be enough."

"For now."

"Thanks for your vote of confidence."

Dalton breathed out a laugh and shrugged his shoulders on a long inhale. "You've never been the kind of man to take no for an answer. I didn't expect you to start now."

"None of us like being told no," I said.

"Guilty as charged." Dalton set his wine on the table next to the bottle and rubbed his hands down the front of his jeans. "Just be careful."

"What?" I angled my face toward him, caught off-guard by the change of tone and the worry in his voice.

"Just be careful," he said again. "We don't like to be told no and all of us have a habit of doing everything we can to turn a no into a yes."

"That's called being a skilled negotiator," I countered.

He gave me a stern look that made me feel like there was a lot more to the story than he was letting on.

"You know what I mean," he said.

But I didn't.

I really didn't know at all.

CHAPTER 16
ROSE

My Thursday night shift was absolutely dreadful. It was slow and the customers I had weren't tipping, and by the time the dinner "rush" passed, I was ready to call it quits. The week had been relatively anti-climactic after I settled down Drake's frantic Saturday afternoon phone call, and I'd chatted here and there with Flynn, but we hadn't made any solid plans to see each other. I'd spent my down time with Drake and eating packaged ramen.

It was normal.

It was all the things I did with my time before I met Flynn, but somehow they felt boring and dull *after* him. Not like his house had much to offer besides a pool—which I hadn't been able to stop thinking about since I'd seen it. I worried I was more fascinated by him, and I had way too much downtime since I'd seen him last to think about the implications of that.

Thinking about Flynn made my chest feel light, but it was impossible to not remember the tragic line from *Ever After* going on about birds and fishes and where they would live. I couldn't have met a man any more different than myself when I'd met Flynn. He had to know I wasn't as well off as him, I didn't think many people were, but I also didn't think he understood just how broad of a gap there was between our tax brackets.

There were some things in life that were conquerable, but the longer I stewed over Flynn and his cheekbones and his shitty furniture and his expensive car and his stupid house, the more I understood what I needed to do.

I had to break things off with him.

It didn't matter that he was sure that I deserved him. He was right about that. I *did* deserve a man like Flynn, and I deserved the kind of life his money could offer, but this wasn't a dream world. This was the real world where boyfriends told you they loved you and then fucked their roommates behind your back. This was the real world where the novelty of a man with less money and nicer underwear wore off sooner rather than later.

I pulled my phone out of my pocket and opened my messages, sending one to Flynn.

Me: Can we talk?

He didn't reply right away.

Flynn: Out with friends for a bit.
Me: Is that a no?
Flynn: It's more of a I'm out with friends so not right now, but if it's an emergency, I can step away and give you a call.
Me: Why didn't you just say that in the first place?
Flynn: Why are you being so combative?
Me: I'm not.

Another long pause.

Me: I can see the sigh you're sighing.

As soon as I sent the message, my phone started to vibrate in my hand, Flynn's name flashing across my screen. I debated letting it go to voicemail because I didn't want to interrupt his night out, but I was the one who'd reached out.

"Hello?" I leaned against the wall beside the time clock and closed my eyes.

"What's wrong?"

Flynn sounded worried, almost distressed, and that brought some semblance of a smile to my face. I squashed it quickly because my plan was to break up with him. His concern shouldn't please me and it definitely shouldn't send the butterflies in my ribcage all around the place like a damn tornado had touched down.

"Nothing's wrong," I rasped, clearing my throat and scrubbing a hand down my face. I hadn't shaved in a couple of days and the rough stubble on my cheeks abraded my palm.

"Do you know what I do for work?"

I squeezed my eyes closed. "No."

"I make deals for a living. Extremely high dollar deals that can make or break corporations."

"Are you bragging?" I interrupted, even though there was a part of me that loved to hear the pride in his voice. Flynn always radiated some sort of magnetic confidence around himself, but when he switched from playboy mode to work mode, it was an admirable shift in demeanor.

"It's not glamorous work," he said. "What I'm telling you is that I can read people, oftentimes better than they can read themselves. I was practically trained in reading between the lines, so for you to send that message and then tell me nothing is wrong lands a lot like an insult."

"To your ego?"

He snorted. "What's wrong, Rose?"

"I just…" I trailed off, the words falling short. Even if I could find them, they wouldn't be enough.

"Where are you?" he asked.

"Work."

"For how much longer?"

"I…" Blinking slowly, I forced my eyes open so I could check the clock. "Another couple of hours."

"I'll be there in twenty minutes," he said.

"You don't have—"

"I'll be there in twenty," he repeated, disconnecting the call before I could fight him on it again.

With a trembling sigh that rattled my bones, I slid my phone back into my pocket and counted down the agonizingly slow minutes until Flynn burst through the front door in a frenzy of expensive clothes and delicious-smelling cologne. He was dressed like he always was, half of a suit, jacket discarded somewhere else. Shiny black shoes, black slacks that hugged the muscular spread of his thighs, and a dark green button-up, sleeves rolled up over his forearms and the top two buttons undone.

A raucous noise followed in after him, and I counted four other men who looked like if you put their bank accounts together, they held as much money between them as the entire state of Colorado. One of them laughed particularly loud, and Flynn grimaced, reaching behind him to smack the man upside his head. He turned back around, eyes searching the restaurant for a second before he found me. When our stares locked, he tugged at the open collar of his shirt and closed the space between us like he owned the place.

For all I knew, he could have.

When he reached me, Flynn came to a quick stop, taking my face into his hands and angling me toward the bright chandelier lighting over our heads.

"What's wrong?" he asked. It was only then I really heard the panic in his voice, overlaid with the worry that shone through his eyes. "Are you hurt?"

I huffed out a breath that felt like it wanted to be a laugh, but didn't have the energy. I shook my head, curling my fingers around his wrists.

"I'm fine," I said. "I'm fine."

I wasn't fine.

I was embarrassed and heat flooded my cheeks, but his hold made it impossible to get away from him. It was impossible to shake the feeling that my inability to understand—let alone articulate—my feelings had brought him away from wherever he'd been and right to my work, with all of his friends in tow no less.

Flynn let out a breath, but didn't let go of me, intuitive eyes still scanning over my face, reading every single one of my secrets.

After what felt like an eternity, he let go of my cheeks and took a step back, letting his hands fall down at his sides. "You were going to break up with me, weren't you?"

I opened my mouth to protest, but quickly snapped it closed when I remembered that was exactly what I'd been intending to do.

"Why?" he asked.

The stupid fish and bird comparison shoved itself to the front of my mind again. I pursed my lips to stop myself from saying it. "It just…"

"Rose."

I immediately recognized the sound of my manager's soft voice behind me.

With a grimace, I turned away from Flynn and gave her an apologetic look. "Hey, Ashley."

"You just got seated a party of five by the window," she said.

I managed a nod and angled my eyes back toward Flynn. "I'll go get them right now."

"Thanks, Rose."

I sighed and looked up at Flynn. "We can talk later," I told him. "I have to work."

"We can move to another table," he said.

"I still have to *work*, Flynn." When I stressed the fact this was my job, placing my hand against my chest in emphasis. "This is my job."

He licked his lips, biting the corner of his lower lip between his teeth before sidestepping out of the way so I could get past him.

I took a step and he reached out, grabbing my arm and drawing me back to a stop. He was so close and he smelled so good, and I felt the tension rolling off of him in waves. He'd been *sincerely* worried about me when he gathered up all of his friends and hauled them away from wherever they'd been to the shitty little restaurant I worked at. I figured if I touched his chest, his heart would be racing, so I did.

And it was.

The frenetic pace of his heart caused mine to skip and sputter, and I yanked my hand back like the touch of him had burned me.

"Right." He let go of my arm, looking like it hurt him to touch me too.

"I'll be right over."

"Don't let them rile you up," he said, expression ever apologetic.

I inhaled a breath, steeling myself against whatever Flynn thought I needed to prepare myself for.

"This is my job," I reminded him, as if I hadn't just said it. "This won't be the first table of rich assholes I've had to deal with and it won't be the last."

But instead of following him toward the corner where his friends had set up shop, I slipped into the back and locked myself in the bathroom. I knew time was short, so I splashed some cold water on my face and fiddled with the collar of my shirt until it felt like I could breathe without struggling.

"You can do this," I told my reflection. "They're no one to you."

I repeated the mantra to myself, hoping that even though the urgency of Flynn's arrival had thrown me off-guard, that I'd be able to regain a hold on my usual level of casual banter that paid my rent and kept me employed.

But as soon as I stepped back onto the restaurant floor, I could feel all of their eyes on me, Flynn's included. I made sure I was quick to flash them a bright smile that portrayed all of the confidence I wanted them to think I was feeling. And it wasn't that rich and handsome men—which they all were—always threw me off-balance the way they had. It was that Flynn and I had been...

Dating?

I don't know.

Whatever we'd been doing, and I'd been on the verge of

breaking up with him and he'd just shown up at my job with all of his friends. It was my first time meeting them, first time *seeing* them, and I had no idea what he'd told them about me or what their impressions of me were. They couldn't have been good, considering the five of them looked like they'd crawled out of a centerfold spread in *GQ* or something and absolutely slummed their way down to the still very overpriced restaurant where I worked.

Even if I hadn't been two breaths away from calling things off with Flynn, this was not how I'd want to meet his friends for the first time. I wouldn't want to be in work clothes with my hair a little too greasy to be presentable and my face a little scruffier than I normally liked it. But I hadn't intended on seeing Flynn. I hadn't thought to dress up or use some dry shampoo in my hair.

And with all of those very self-conscious thoughts bouncing around my brain, I reached the table and prayed that my voice didn't crack.

"Hey, guys. My name is Rose and I'll be taking care of you tonight. Can I get you started with some drinks?"

CHAPTER 17

FLYNN

As soon as Rose left to get water for the table, four sets of amused and inquisitive eyes landed on me.

"Don't," I warned.

"He's young," Rob whispered.

Dalton rolled his eyes. "Like you're one to talk."

"That man"—Rob pointed at the direction Rose had walked off in—"is younger than Grayson."

"How old is he?" Archie asked, leaning back in the booth and crossing his arms over his chest.

"I honestly don't know," I said.

"It doesn't matter," Barclay muttered, glancing toward the kitchen, his voice low.

"Thank you."

He shrugged.

"Why did you drag us here, though?" he asked, turning his heavy stare toward me.

"I didn't drag any of you anywhere," I reminded the bunch of them.

We'd been out for drinks, as was our Thursday tradition. Archie had been a little nervous about leaving Owen alone so soon after his move to California, with Frankie back on the East Coast and everything. But Grayson had been quick to offer himself and his best friend Wesley up as chaperones for the night. It was clear to me Archie hated the idea, but much like the lot of us, Grayson could be persistent when he knew what he wanted.

"You can't just leave a meeting of the Trophy Doms Social Club early," Archie interjected.

Hearing the nickname that Rob's boyfriend Grayson had teasingly given our friend group had the hairs on the back of my neck spiking on high alert. It was too close to the judgement I'd received from Rose about the state of my house for comfort, and I hated to even entertain the idea I wasn't anything without my bank account.

"Will you please stop calling us that? Grayson isn't even here to smack you over it."

"Grayson knows better than to smack any of us, I think," Archie countered.

"He just smacks Rob around." Dalton laughed.

"He knows better," Rob said, but the flush on his cheeks indicated that there might have been some recent changes to the dynamic of their relationship that none of us were privy to.

"You still haven't answered the question," Barclay said.

"There wasn't one." From across the room, I could see Rose headed back toward us, tray of water glasses in hand. "Do not say something asinine in front of him."

"Or what?" Archie threw his head back and laughed just as Rose reached the table.

My heart hammered against my sternum as Rose's thigh grazed the outside of my arm. He leaned past me to set water onto the table, then tucked the tray under the crook of his arm and stepped back.

"Have you five had a chance to look over the menu?" he asked.

"We haven't even thought about the menu," Dalton almost purred.

I smacked him and narrowed my eyes in warning.

"There's cocktails on the back," Rose offered, reaching in front of me and flipping my menu onto the other side. "I'll give you some more time."

"I'll have a whiskey," Rob said. "On the rocks."

"Same," Archie said, letting his menu fall to the table.

"What about you?" Rose asked me.

"Water."

Barclay laughed at my answer and threw his menu on top of mine. "The rest of us will have whatever whiskey you're getting for the first two."

"Four whiskeys and a water," Rose summarized.

"Not well," Barclay added.

Rose feigned insult, pressing his hand against his chest. "I'd never."

That retort earned half of a smile from Archie, and a moment of peace after he headed to the bar before they started in on me again.

"Things with Rose are not cut and dried," I said.

"They rarely are," Archie mused.

Of the group of them, Dalton was the only one I'd even remotely entertained the idea of sharing with, and with the four of them ganging up on me, I debated if I wanted to tell any of them anything ever again.

"And you can say you didn't drag us here, but in the decade or so I've known you, I've never seen you get up and go after a man. So of course we were going to tag along," Barclay said.

"Had to see what the fuss was about," Archie agreed.

"Well." I gestured toward the bar on the other side of the restaurant. "Now you see."

"He looks positively decadent," Dalton said. "Now I see why he hated your house."

Archie chuckled and Rob leaned in a little closer. "He hated your house?"

"He hated my furniture."

"I hate your furniture too," Rob agreed, nodding like the dislike of my furniture was common knowledge between them.

"You didn't hate it enough to not fuck on it."

"I'll fuck anywhere."

"You used to," Dalton said. "Before Grayson collared you."

Rob flipped him the bird, and Archie smirked.

"Why do you care if he likes your things?" Rob asked me, one inquisitive brow raised right into his hairline.

Before I had to admit the truth, Rose was back with drinks for the four assholes I called my best friends. He threw a quick, indecipherable look down at me, dropping a straw for my water on top of the stacked menus.

"You five don't strike me as the eating type," he said, looking back at my friends.

I swallowed, feeling the heat and the judgement radiating off of him. I knew I was a lot on my own—he'd told me as much and he hadn't been the first. Rose was going through *something*, though, something that it felt important for him and I to discuss, but as long as he was at work and as long as my friends were at this corner table in his section, I didn't think I'd get the chance.

That just wouldn't do.

I pushed my chair back and stood, towering over him as I always did. He shivered and turned his attention to me.

"Where's your restroom?" I asked.

"In the back," he said softly. "By the kitchen."

Archie let out a catcall kind of whistle, and I shot him a warning look and a middle finger for good measure. Rob ruffled Archie's hair, and the two of them lapsed into a conversation, quickly taking Dalton and Barclay's attention as well.

Rose took a step away from the table and I followed after him.

"Can we please talk?" I asked.

He didn't stop walking, heading toward the kitchen. "What did you want to talk about?"

"Whatever was bothering you when I called," I said.

His supervisor, boss, whoever she was, the woman who had chastised him for letting my friends dehydrate upon arrival, gave him a terse look. I had half a mind to reach into my pocket, pull out my wallet, and gag her with a hundred dollar bill or five.

Though, I knew Rose wouldn't appreciate the gesture...or the potential job loss.

"I didn't ask you to come down here," he said.

"I know. I came because..." I trailed off, words catching in my throat.

I came because he'd sounded upset and I didn't want him to sound that way anymore. I didn't want him to feel that way. Because if I was going to be serious about someone, about him, I was going to mean it. It wasn't like I had any experience to pull from, but I was a smart man. I could figure it out, but had I gotten this one wrong?

"I'll finish serving you and your friends tonight," he said, squaring his shoulders and staring up at me through the golden fan of his lashes. "But one of you better order some food because the tip on four glasses of whiskey isn't even worth my time, and this shift has already sucked enough."

"Is that why you're upset?"

"I'm upset because I'm broke. Upset because I need this job."

"I heard that!" Ashley called from around the corner. She didn't sound angry, but Rose grabbed my arm and shoved me toward the back door.

I turned the knob before my face slammed into the metal, and both of us stumbled down the steps and onto the gravel. Rose huffed, cheeks red, then he turned to face me with his hands braced against his hips.

"I'm upset because I need this job and you don't need a job at all," he said.

I scoffed, in absolute disbelief that Rose assumed I didn't need to work. Just because I did different kind of work than he did, just because I wasn't chained to a desk forty hours a week, didn't mean I didn't work. I had done that for years. I'd slaved through years of schooling and hours of evening and weekend overtime to get to the money and the status I had now.

"I very much need a job, Rose."

"Do you ever go to it?" he snapped.

I pulled my phone out of my pocket and tapped the home button. My screen illuminated and I shoved it into his chest.

"I'm always at work," I said, gesturing for him to scroll through my alerts. "Even when I had you pinned against a wall at Rapture, even when you were in a thousand dollar a night hotel suite with your cock up my ass, I was working."

His shoulders sagged and he handed my phone back to me.

"We have different jobs," I said. "Different lives. That's not a cause for concern."

"How much did your couch cost?" he asked.

I shrugged. I didn't know and when I bought it, I hadn't cared.

"Mine was seventy-five dollars at a thrift store," he whispered.

I exhaled, stuffing my phone back into my pocket, even as another email vibrated its way into my inbox.

"I came from money, Rose, and I won't apologize for that because I didn't have control over it." I took a step back and fidgeted with the buttons on my shirt, undoing the second one so I could catch a breath. "And I won't apologize for having money now because I've worked hard to get where I am and I'm not sorry about it."

"I think we should break up," he murmured.

I slashed my hand through the air between us, cutting the thought off before it could get to me. "No."

"What?"

"Absolutely not."

He made a frustrated sound in the back of his throat. "That's not how this works."

"It's exactly how this works." I took a step toward him and he took a step back.

"Maybe in your world, but not mine."

I took another step toward him, lowering my voice. "I don't know if you noticed this or not, but from the first time I kissed you, you've been a part of my world, Ambrose."

He shivered, a whimper falling out of his mouth. "Say that again," he rasped.

I licked my lips and stretched my arm, placing my hand against the brick wall and boxing him in. Another shiver worked its way up his spine and when he blinked up at me, it was with a dark and heavy look.

"You're part of my world," I said.

He shook his head, eyes closing. "The other part. My name."

"Ambrose?" I allowed myself a deep breath of him, noticing the way he didn't smell like my sheets anymore, didn't smell like my shampoo, but instead his own.

"This won't work out between us."

His protest came out sounding like a whimper, like he wanted to mean it even though he didn't. Like the words were on autopilot and his body was crashing on the course.

"How do you know that?"

"Just a feeling."

I gently pressed my finger against the underside of his chin and tipped his face up until he managed to look me in the face again.

I'd been with a lot of attractive people in my life, men and women alike, but Rose was one of the prettiest men I'd ever seen. The vibrant sky of his eyes was absolutely unmatched and I knew I'd never meet anyone after him that could even dream of comparing to him in any way.

And maybe that was why I'd been gone for him from the very first kiss. There was something inside of him that had connected to something inside of me. The pull was undeniable, and there was *something* groundbreaking between us. The desire to chase after it was why I'd been so immediately willing to break away from the tried-and-true rules that had governed my life for as long as they had. The need to touch him and find out more about him had been enough to have me thinking—even temporarily—that I needed to change for him. And if I had needed to, I would have. But the things Rose needed, the things he *wanted* were all things I was able to provide him. That I was willing to share.

"I think you're wrong," I whispered against the tuft of white-blonde hair that seemed to float on the top of his head.

"That's your prerogative."

"Give me a chance to prove it."

"How?" he asked.

"Don't worry about that." I kissed his temple, the top of his ear. "Just give me time to show you what it's like to be with a man like me."

"I don't want to be with a man *like* you," he murmured, but even as he said the words, his fingers scrabbled against the top edge of my belt pulling our bodies flush.

"With me then," I corrected. "I'll show you what it's like to be with me."

"How long?"

I didn't have a good answer for that because I hadn't thought that far in advance. Negotiations were done in the bedroom or the boardroom, not alleys behind restaurants while I pleaded my case to a jury of one.

"A month," I suggested.

I could work with a month. Four weeks, maybe five weekends if I counted the days right. It would be enough time to get to know him, which I was desperate for, and maybe if I was lucky, make him fall in love with me so hard that he didn't even bother to tell me the time on our little deal had run out.

"What if you don't like being with *me*?" he asked, angling his head to the side and giving me more direct access to his ear, which I licked, and his neck, which I peppered with kisses.

This had to work.

As much as I wanted him to want *me*, I also needed to understand what it was about him that had me absolutely and almost immediately head over heels for him.

"Then you were right all along." I nipped his earlobe between my teeth, praying that he wouldn't be and choosing to pose a much better question before letting him get back to work. "But what if you're wrong, Rose? What if you're wrong?"

CHAPTER 18
ROSE

If I had a dollar for every time I thought about how different Flynn was from other men, I'd be as rich as he was. Unfortunately, I didn't, though the fact that each of his friends had tipped me a crisp hundred dollar bill on their seventeen-dollar glasses of whiskey sure helped the situation a lot. Their generosity—or their arrogance—had helped ease the strain of a dead Thursday night in ways I was too embarrassed to say.

Five hundred dollars right into my pocket, plus the $125.00 I earned on the rest of my slow-as-sin shift. That was almost my rent made in one day. As I folded up the bills and slipped them into my pocket, I tried to not think about how it was spare change for them. How none of them would even notice the money missing from their wallets, but how I'd be able to breathe easy with it in mine.

What if you're wrong, Rose?

After our interlude in the alley where my breakup was refused like it had been negotiable, Flynn went back inside and rallied his friends to finish their drinks. He got them out of the door with a grumbled round of protests, and a text message promised that he'd see me later. I didn't know when later was, but as soon as I clocked out, my phone buzzed with an incoming message.

The rush of heat in my chest should have been confirmation enough for me that I was in over my head with Flynn, but I pulled my phone out anyway, a stupid huge grin on my face that quickly fell when I found Cody's name instead of his.

Cody: Are you ready to talk?

My mouth went dry and I smacked my tongue against the roof of it a couple times, trying to draw up some saliva so I didn't choke.

Ignoring Cody's message, and the dread that filled my shoes like cement, I swiped through to Flynn's message thread and sent him a text.

Me: Is it later yet?

He was quick to reply.

Flynn: I was just about to text you.

I knew it.

Flynn: Do you want to come over?
Me: You're asking
Flynn: Considering you tried to break up with me earlier tonight, I didn't know if I was in a position to tell you anything.
Me: You *told* me I couldn't break up with you.
Me: You've been telling me all about praise and yes, sir and all of that and I don't think you've really shown me everything that entails.

He was slower to reply, and I waited until my nerves convinced me I'd said the wrong thing. I shoved my phone into my pocket and grabbed my bag from the locker in the back of the restaurant, said goodnight to Ashley, and slipped out into the alley where I'd parked. Fumbling around my things, I slid into the driver's seat and locked the door behind me, staring down at my phone and waiting for an answer.

When it didn't come, I sent one myself

Me: Did I say something wrong?

His answer came fast as lightning, followed by another.

Flynn: NO.
Flynn: I'm just trying to be mindful of what I put between us.

I wasn't sure what that meant, but I closed my eyes and waited for him to explain. It took two more messages from Cody and a heavy nervousness that washed away any sort of excitement or hope I'd felt about Flynn until he answered.

Flynn: Do you work tomorrow?
Me: Not until 5
Flynn: Come over.
Me: And what? You never answered my question.
Flynn: Come over, Rose.

He sent me his address and I didn't even bother trying to pretend I wasn't going to do what I was told. I copied it into my maps and headed toward the part of town I'd never be able to afford. The whole drive, Cody's messages echoed around my head, and I called Drake, hoping for a distraction.

When he answered the phone, it was loud, like he was at a bar or club, but he yelled at me to hold on and then after a beat, the background noise quieted down.

"Can you hear me?" Drake asked.

"Yeah."

"Are you okay?"

"Yeah," I said again. "Why wouldn't I be?"

"Because you've been weird ever since you met that rich guy and I wanted to make sure he didn't fifty shades you."

I laughed at the statement. Flynn definitely wanted to do some fifty shades shit with me, but not in the *Criminal Minds* kind of way that Drake was thinking about.

"He's fine. I'm going to send you his address, by the way, because I'm going over there tonight."

"Stranger danger. Proud of you."

"He's hardly a stranger at this point," I said.

"What's his favorite color? His favorite movie?" Drake asked. "Do you even know his last name?"

"Judging by his house, it's gray." I chuckled at my own little inside joke. "I don't know the rest, but I do know what his face looks like when he comes if you want that description for the memory book."

"I'd rather hear about that one in person."

It briefly got louder in the background of the call before quieting down again.

"Where are you?" I asked.

"I'm at The Cathouse," he said. "Went out onto the patio to make sure you didn't need to be saved like the damsel in distress you are."

"No, I'm fine. I just…I'm a bit in my head. Cody texted me tonight."

Drake cursed under his breath. "I fucking knew it."

"What do you mean?"

The bright lights of the city began to fade into the subtle street-lamps of the residential area where Flynn lived. The houses weren't close together, and there was plenty of room on the streets and up the long and winding driveways…a complete contrast from my packed apartment block. The difference in our incomes was clearly more of an issue for me than it was for him, and I needed to commit some energy to getting over it if I wanted things with Flynn to work out in the long run.

But…

Did I want them to work out?

Why did I even care?

Sure, the dude was hands down the best fuck I'd ever had, but what else about him was there to keep me interested and inspired? His attraction to *me* surely didn't hurt, but there had to be something more substantial than that, right? And at the end of the day, he was asking me to give up a lot of things that had been very important to me for a long time. My desire for control in the bedroom, for one. But he'd given things up too, hadn't he? Even if being seriously casual had been a joke at first, Flynn surely was the one putting himself out for me in ways I'd never even imagined to ask.

The very least I could do was manage some concessions of my own. At the end of the day, I enjoyed Flynn's company. Rather, I enjoyed his company when I wasn't stressing about how opposite we were, and that needed to be something I made peace with. If a rich dude wanted to fuck me in expensive hotel suites and all over every boring surface in his very bland house, who was I to say no?

But Drake was right.

I didn't know much about him beyond the physical, and maybe it was worth asking some of those questions. Or seeing him in a setting where we couldn't end up—or at least socially shouldn't—with our clothes off.

"Cody was here earlier," Drake said, my ex's name drawing me right out of the pleasant softness of my daydream and back into the present conversation.

"Did you talk to him?"

"Fuck no!" Drake almost shouted at me. "I hate what he did to you. But he tried to talk to me and I brushed him off."

"What did he say?" It was a sick curiosity that compelled me to ask, even though a huge part of me didn't care about the answer.

Let him miss me.

Let him sit with his mistakes.

"He asked how you were." Drake hummed, a conniving sound that I was all too familiar with.

"What did you do?"

"I told him you were seeing someone new. Someone better than him."

"Someone without a last name or a favorite color or favorite movie."

"He obviously has all of those things," he said. "You just don't know them."

"Yet," I supplied, turning onto Flynn's street.

"Yet," Drake agreed. "But it made Cody a little agitated, I think, a little jealous. It's probably better you're not home tonight."

"Do you think he's going by the apartment?"

I pulled into Flynn's driveway and parked near the door. His car wasn't outside, but he had a three-car garage tucked against the side of the house. And he didn't strike me as the type to risk rust and water damage by parking outside anyway.

"I don't want you to have to get a restraining order or anything like that," Drake said. "I just want you to know he was asking about you."

"He asked if I was ready to talk." I cut the ignition and dropped my head against the headrest. Flynn's porch was illuminated, the monstera he was so fond of standing proud under a wash of warm white light.

"What did you tell him?"

"I didn't answer him at all. He sent two more after that, but I didn't read them."

"Good. Let him know you're over him by ignoring him. He doesn't deserve your attention."

The front door opened, drawing my stare. The lights inside of the house threw Flynn into a dark silhouette against the stark whiteness of the walls and the sharp lines of the teak wood door.

Drake was right. Cody didn't deserve my attention, but Flynn did.

He'd committed himself more to me in the past handful of weeks than Cody had in the months we were together. And here I was, waffling back and forth like there was any sane or reasonable excuse why I shouldn't be with Flynn. I'd come so close to talking myself out of being with him, that if he'd been any other man besides the one he was, I might have lost the chance for good.

"You're right," I said, straightening up and unlatching my seatbelt. "I just got to Flynn's house so I'll talk to you later."

"When later?"

"Sometime tomorrow. I'll text you his address."

"Good. Thank you."

"Thank you for watching out for me." I shouldered open the driver's side door and swiveled, dropping my feet onto the ground.

"That's what friends are for," he said.

The background noise turned loud again and I knew Drake was making his way back into the club. I told him goodbye and disconnected the call, then copied and pasted Flynn's address into a text message and sent it off.

The nerves from earlier that had finally started to wane during my conversation with Drake were back in full force as I walked from my car to the porch. When Flynn's face came into focus, I found it nearly impossible to swallow. It was mind-blowing that I'd ever had the audacity to look at this man and tell him he didn't deserve me. I was the one who didn't deserve *him*.

I'd fought him at every turn, and he'd fought back, not willing to give up without one hell of a fight. And I hadn't appreciated that until I'd almost lost him.

"I'm sorry." I stepped onto his porch, sliding my phone into my pocket.

He cocked his head to the side, expression curious. "For what?"

I closed the space between us and wrapped my arms around his waist so I could rest my cheek against his chest.

He'd changed clothes from earlier and instead of wearing the suit I so often saw him in, he had on the same pair of gray sleep pants from the last time I'd spent the night. No shirt, so my skin pressed against his, immediately sending heat waves from my head down to my toes.

"I haven't been fair to you," I murmured.

Flynn stroked his hands through my hair and down the back of my head, down my neck and over my shoulders.

"Come inside, Rose. Let's talk."

CHAPTER 19
FLYNN

Rose shuffled into the house like he was about to get grounded.

He kicked his shoes off just inside the door, and I glanced down at him in time to watch him slide his socked feet across the tile like he was ice. He stopped quick enough, clearing his throat and changing to a normal step. I led him toward the couch, which I knew he hated, and sat down. Patting the cushion next to me, I waited for him to follow suit before asking, "What do you mean you haven't been fair?"

Rose scrubbed a hand down his face then sprawled out across the couch. He tucked his back into the crook of my arm, one hand resting on my thigh and the other flung over the back. With his legs splayed, one knee bent and foot on the floor, the other hanging off the far edge. He tipped his head back and I stared down at him, immediately willing myself to not get lost in his eyes.

"I haven't been fair to you from the start. I've been telling you what I want, what I *deserve*."

The sneer in his voice led me to believe he was recalling the conversation we had before he'd left me at the hotel, but I could also tell he wasn't done so I waited to respond.

"And then just deciding on my own that we're too different to work, even after you tolerated the rest of it. I tried to break up with you and—"

"And I told you no."

"Not only did you tell me no, but you still invited me over here? You came to my work and you answered my texts, and now I'm here?" Rose closed his eyes and let out a breath so huge I wondered if he was going to melt into the couch.

"We both had preconceived ideas the first night we spent together. I think that's fair to say about anyone."

"But I kept carrying them." He covered his face with his hands, and I swatted them out of the way, grabbing both of his slender wrists between my fingers and pinning them to his lap. His nostrils flared and his lips parted.

"Are you still?"

He shook his head.

"Neither am I." I tightened my hold around his wrists. "Would you feel better if we started over?"

"Started over how?"

I needed to let go of him, but I didn't want to.

"My name is Flynn Galloway, and I very much would like to kiss you right now."

"What's your favorite movie?" he asked, wiggling his wrists out of my grip.

"What?"

"Favorite movie," he repeated, like it was a logical answer to my kissing statement.

I couldn't remember the last time I'd watched it, but I gave him my answer just the same, "Midnight in Paris."

"I'm Ambrose Baker, but you can call me Rose." He got his hands loose and moved quickly, flinging one slim leg over my lap and straddling me before taking my face into his hands. Our noses brushed together and I watched his eyes flutter closed, the long fan of his lashes hiding the gorgeous blue sky of his irises.

"Rose."

I barely managed his name before his mouth was on mine. He

kissed me similar to the way he did on the first night, but with all of the want and none of the hesitation. Grinding his hips down hard against my lap, I raised up, pressing one hand against the middle of his back and the other his waist. With my fingers splayed, I dug my nails into his skin, opening my lips wider and allowing him to steer the kiss. Rose let his hands slide away from my face, working their way between our bodies. His fingers were treacherously close to my erection when my brain cleared enough for me to realize that once again, I'd let him take control.

"Slow down." I grabbed his wrists again, moving his arms and pinning them down at the small of his back. The shift caused his back to arch, and he angled his chin up so he was looking down at me.

"I don't want to go slow," he whined, swirling his hips. "You make me unfairly hard."

"We just met," I reminded him, hoping to call back the spirit of starting over that we'd led in with.

Rose made a disgruntled sound, shoulders going sluggish.

"I need you to know that I'm not looking for anything casual," I whispered.

He dropped his forehead against mine and let out a quiet whimper. If I was getting a second chance at starting over, I was going to rewrite our history into what he'd deserved all along. What both of us deserved.

"But I am a dominant man, and there's something I refuse to compromise on."

Rose went soft against me, save for the long and hard erection between his legs. His breath puffed against my cheek in a warm, slow rhythm that could have put me to sleep for how comfortable it was.

"What's that?"

"I'm in charge."

Rose snorted, the sound lodged as deep in the back of his throat as I wanted to shove my cock.

"And what does that mean exactly?" He purred the question,

nuzzling his face against mine, rubbing his chest against my front, doing everything to gyrate and grind on me without using his hands to touch.

Fuck, he made it impossible to think.

"What does that mean?" I grunted, pushing up off the couch and taking Rose with me, only to pivot and drop him down onto his back. I arranged myself between his legs, his hands now pinned against the arm of the couch behind his head. His eyes went wide, nostrils flaring as he felt the hard ridge of my cock push against his leg. "It means that you do what you're told and I make sure you feel. Really. Fucking. Good. While you're doing it."

I punctuated my words with gentle nips against the underside of his jaw, and he answered with a moan so wanton I was confident the message had been received.

"If I want your gorgeous, thick cock up my ass, I'll tell you how to put it inside of me," I whispered, kissing my way up to his ear.

Rose wrapped his legs around my waist and threw his head back.

"I'll tell you when and how. I'll tell you how fast and how hard you can move."

"Flynn."

"And if you're on the bottom, Rose, then I'll make those decisions for myself. I'll decide when you get to come and how long you're going to come for."

"Feels impossible," he rasped, half a laugh.

"Just wait and see."

He moaned at that, turning his head to press a kiss against the corner of my mouth. His tongue darted out, trying to lick past my lips and get inside, but I redirected, licking a stripe beneath his ear.

"I..." He groaned when I bit his earlobe, then swallowed so loudly I heard it. "I've never done anything like this before."

"That's fine, baby." The endearment earned another groan from him. One that went straight to my balls. "I don't have any issue talking you through it. In fact...I very much prefer it."

"D...do I..." Even though they were single syllables, his words wavered. "Do I call you Sir?"

That was the question of the hour, wasn't it?

I'd presented myself to him in a different way the first time we'd met, acting like his submission was something that we both had to work for when I knew the truth.

When I knew it was something that should be freely given.

And taken.

But I'd postured like an arrogant prick at first, pretending that it was something special to be at my feet, when in reality the gift was clearly Rose on his knees. Not the other way around.

I shifted my weight around so I could keep him pinned, but raise up enough to get a good look at him. "Do you want to?"

Rose blinked, holding my stare as he licked his lips. The answer was obviously not what he'd expected based off how things had gone the first time. But I was serious when I said I wanted to start over. When I told him I wanted thirty days to show him what it could be like for us.

"Sometimes, maybe," he whispered. "Do you want me to?"

He blinked up at me, his face washed with arousal, but also so much transparency and eagerness it sucked the breath right out of my lungs.

"Yes," I told him.

A broad smile spread across his mouth before settling into a smirk that reminded me of the man I'd met. The headstrong little twink with lacy underwear and a penchant for talking himself right into the pants of anyone he wanted to get naked.

I pulled away, rolling back onto my knees. I'd let go of his hands, but he kept them in place above his head, a posture that made my cock surge with desire. I kept moving away until our bodies weren't tangled and he had free range of movement.

"Get up then," I instructed.

Rose crawled off the couch, his knees shaking and his erection tenting the fly of his black work pants. He held his hands up and shrugged, almost in a *you get what you get* kind of gesture, but the sentiment couldn't have been further from the truth.

"Look at you." I leaned back on the couch and spread my legs, pointing between my knees. He shuffled in front of me, and then I tugged at the waistband of my pants, letting my cock spring free. "Look what you do to me."

His stare flickered down to my dick, and then his hands went for his own belt.

"No."

He went still.

"Tonight, you just listen and do what you're told. Can you do that for me, Rose?"

He chewed his lower lip between his teeth, the shiny flesh going pink around the white outline from the bite, and nodded.

"Let me hear you, baby. I like to talk and I like to be talked back to."

"Yes, Sir," he whispered, and it took all my strength of mind and fortitude to not spill all over my hand on the spot.

"Start with your shirt," I whispered. "One button at a time."

Rose undid his shirt, button after button after button, bringing the porcelain expanse of his chest and stomach into view.

"Off," I said.

With a fluid shrug, the shirt slid off his shoulders and onto the floor, exposing his perfect pink nipples and sharp angles of his collarbone. Rose was so small, so slim, and so unbelievably sexy.

"*Now* the pants."

He opened his belt and fly, shoving his pants to his ankles. He wasn't wearing fancy underwear, and I couldn't get control of myself fast enough to stop the frown from flickering across my face. I'd never dated, never been with, a man who wore women's underwear before I was with Rose, and the novelty was far from wearing off. In fact, I didn't think it was novel at all. I figured it was my new favorite kink.

"I wasn't expecting to see you," he said, stepping out of his pants and kicking them to the side. At the same time, he bent over to peel off his socks and add them to the pile. "Sir."

"I don't for one second believe you only wear lace for other people."

"No, but laundry."

I chuckled and beckoned him closer. He shuffled until his knees were inches away from the couch, coming to a stop when I held up my hand.

"Can I buy you some things to wear?"

As I made the ask, my dick throbbed in my hand, threatening once again to burst all over us both.

"Clothes or…?"

"Does it matter?"

A red flush rushed up his cheeks, causing him to look absolutely cherubic. It made me want to come on his face. I didn't know why. Just that the need to make a mess of him was a very real and tangible thing that had taken up residence in my chest.

He answered with a small shake of his head. "No, Sir."

"Well then?"

"Yes," he whispered. "Yes, Sir. I think I'd like that very much."

I rubbed at my sternum, the need turning into an ache and growing into something far more dangerous than either of those feelings on their own.

"Good. Now get on your knees and open your mouth, Rose." I kept talking as he moved to the ground, bracing himself against my thighs as I pointed my cock toward his plump mouth. "Just because we're starting over doesn't mean I've forgotten how good it feels to fuck the hot sleeve of your throat, baby. Now open up and swallow me down like the good boy I know you are."

I wasn't a large man in the dick department, but Rose was small everywhere *but* there, and with him on his knees and my cock beside his face, I looked positively massive. Heat rushed up my spine at the thought of stretching his jaw with my dick, and I grabbed myself hard around the base to pinch off the blood flow.

Rose's cheeks were flushed, and his tongue darted out, lapping up the precum that had already started to bead against the tip of my dick. He licked the flared underside of my crown from left to right and back again, and I had to reach down and tug my balls away from my body. Starting over or not, this thing between us felt new and my body reacted in kind. The familiar thrill of a first time hovered in the air around us, sparking invisibly in the air.

"Stop playing," I whispered. "I told you to suck, not lick."

He opened his mouth like he was going to protest, but I'd been clear with my expectations and if either of us wanted this to last, which I was certain we did, he had to listen. I threaded the fingers of my left hand through the soft curls of his hair and guided his mouth farther down my length. I didn't shove him or jerk him around, but my grip on his head was firm and strong, telegraphing my expectations.

Rose was quick to comply, sealing his lips around my shaft and sinking down until his nose was buried against my stomach. His non-existent gag reflex was going to be the death of me.

"Stay like that," I coaxed, relishing the sharp puff of breath out of his nostrils as he breathed around my erection. "God, your mouth is so good. Have I told you that you suck me better than anyone else ever has?"

I pulled his head up, my cock slipping out of his mouth with a wet pop.

"How many people have sucked your cock before?" he asked, mouth twisted into a smirk.

Dragging my tongue across the front of my teeth, I guided him back down to his place nestled around the base of my shaft.

"Enough to know what a fucking treasure you are." I gasped when he flattened his tongue against the underside of my shaft and flexed his throat muscles to swallow.

Rose's stare flickered up, making it clear to me he knew exactly what he was doing, what he was capable of. Letting go of his hair, I stretched my arms out across the back of the couch and gave a slight lift of my hips. He hummed around me, near a choke but not quite. Rose would be a perfect cock warmer with a throat like that, with his mouth and his tongue all hot and wet around me. I imagined myself working from home with him between my legs, taking calls while he lapped and suckled on my dick, drawing cum out of my balls whether I wanted to come or not.

It was all within reach, and I was ready to reach out and take it.

"Do you want my cum, Rose?"

I stared down at him, clenching my jaw to fight back my orgasm. He looked like he'd been born to get on his knees and shove my dick into his mouth. The way his plump and glossy lips stretched around my girth, the way his cheeks darkened to almost the same shade of red as my shaft, he looked like a debauched Renaissance painting that had been commissioned just for me.

In response, he hummed, eyes rolling back a little in his head. Spit leaked out of the corner of his mouth and he tried his best to slurp it up before it landed on the couch.

"Can you keep it all in your mouth like it is right now?" I asked.

He slurped at me again.

"Of course you can," I said, swallowing back a groan. "Keep me in your mouth just like that and give me your hand."

Rose extended one of his hands toward me and I licked his fingers, sucking them into my mouth one my one. I had to bend forward to reach him, sandwiching him between my legs and driving my cock deeper into his throat. It was hot and it was heaven. It was everything.

He was everything.

I leaned back when he did finally sputter around my dick, and I spit in his hand. "Touch yourself."

His hand was between his legs so fast, I almost missed the movement. When he curled his fingers around his own thick length, he groaned, the pleasure he brought himself vibrating down my shaft and straight into my belly. The sound of my spit trapped between his palm and his cock shattered the silence of the room, and his mouth inched up and down as he stroked himself toward his own end.

"Good boy, Rose. You're such a good listener. You look so perfect on your knees choking on my cock. This is so good, feels so good. Isn't this good?"

He groaned again, back bowing and arching as he continued to jerk himself off. Spit leaked freely from his mouth now and tears had joined the saliva in the curve of his mouth and the dip of his chin. On his knees for me, he was practically in bondage, and if it had been any other night, any other circumstances, I would have taken a picture so I'd never forgot how unbearably hot he was.

But I committed it to memory instead, closing my eyes and bucking up into his mouth until the head of my dick pressed against the back of his throat.

"Suck the cum out of me, baby," I rasped, curling my fingers around the back of the couch so I didn't fly out into space when he hollowed his cheeks around me. "Get yourself off first and then swallow my load right into that perfect fucking throat of yours. I want to come so deep in your throat, I can't even taste it when I'm finished."

It was one of the easier demands I'd ever made, and Rose came all over his hand in less than a minute, his mouth drawing my own release almost immediately after. I tangled my fingers into the hair at the back of his head when my orgasm approached, and I fucked his throat so hard, I was certain I'd shot deeper into him than anyone ever had, leaving no taste of my cum in his mouth or on his tongue.

After my bones re-solidified, I kissed him again, just to make sure.

I was right.

CHAPTER 20
ROSE

Sometime very early Friday morning, I found myself back in Flynn's bed. His long fingers drew lazy shapes up my side and across my ribs, sparking gooseflesh down my arms while I watched the fire crackle across the room.

After our talk, I'd sucked him off in the way that he already knew he liked, then I let him fuck me with my legs flung up over his shoulders, my body folded nearly in half for how hard he pounded me into the mattress. The whole time, he never stopped touching me, never stopped kissing me, licking me. He never stopped praising me. I was quickly growing addicted to not just him, but the way the descriptive and complimentary words fell out of his mouth and into my ears.

Maybe I had a praise kink too.

Or, at least, a *being* praised kink.

"Do you work today?" he asked, pressing a kiss against my bare shoulder.

"Not until late."

"Can I take you shopping today?"

With a soft huff, I closed my eyes and rolled over to face him. We were both naked, the sweat from the last round of sex finally drying, but the spit and cum undoubtedly still sticky around the corners of my mouth and in his pubes.

"No," I murmured, pulling his hand up to my lips and kissing it.

Flynn's body almost went tense, like he tried to get upset at my denial, even if his muscles wouldn't cooperate.

"You agreed," he reminded me.

"There was no timeline on it."

I wasn't telling him no to be contrary. In fact, quite the opposite. I told him no because in less than twenty-four hours, he'd already convinced me that everything he had to offer was everything I needed. The assertive and sincere way he approached me, explained what he wanted from me, what he was asking...it was hot. I'd been with dominant men in the past, but never a man like him. And it was one thing for me to agree to his thirty day trial run, but allowing myself to get used to him? That was a bridge too far. Because the pleasure I knew this man was going to give me in the next month would be incomparable to anything I'd known before. I also knew the novelty of *me* would wear off long before the calendar page flipped over.

Being with Flynn was going to be work because I would have to find my pleasure where I could, which would be easy since he offered it so freely. But I would have to do it in a way that kept me protected enough for when the eventual end of things came around. Thirty days was a blip on my radar. Hell, I didn't even remember anything that happened in the month of February, and that wasn't even that long ago.

Being with Flynn would bruise, but no amount of praise from his mouth would heal the scars left by him.

"You agreed to thirty days," he said, as if I was the one who needed reminding about the terms of our coupling. "You agreed to be all in so you could see what it's like to be with me."

"And you'll see what it's like to be with me."

Flynn rolled on top of me, notching his broader frame between my legs and dragging his tongue across the swell of my Adam's apple.

"I like what I've seen so far," he whispered against my skin, nipping his way up toward my jaw. "If thirty days is all I get, I want to take full advantage of the time."

Even as I scoffed, I threaded my fingers through his hair, arching against him as his cock hardened against my thigh. Mine was already hard, or still hard, depending on how you wanted to look at it. Flynn just had that effect on me apparently.

Another first.

"Are you going to buy me thirty pairs of underwear?" I asked, teasing and wrapping my legs around his waist so he couldn't move away. "One for each day we have?"

"Thirty at least," he confirmed, lips hot against my ear. "Ninety meals, a thousand orgasms."

"That feels adventurous."

"I've never been scared of a challenge," he said, raising up onto his arms to look down at me. "I'm here, aren't I?"

I swallowed, hating the idea of being *a challenge*, but also knowing I was. Knowing I could be. But I didn't want to be a challenge or a game. I didn't want to be something worth conquering. I wanted the truth behind the words he spilled over me when we were in bed together. I wanted to be beautiful and good and *worthy*.

"You're not buying me ninety meals," I said.

The rest didn't feel important.

"So you're saying I *can* buy you thirty pairs of underwear, though?"

"If you want to waste your mon—"

He kissed me, silencing the rest of my protest, which I was happy for. I let my mouth fall open and his tongue slid against mine like silk. Flynn kissed me deeper, using his whole body to rub and grind against me, pouring promises and praise onto my tongue. I lapped it up like the eager slut he'd turned me into, giving myself over and reaching between our stomachs and taking both of our dicks into my hand.

Flynn groaned, content as I was to finish against my fingers instead of inside of me or across his stomach. I stroked us both through another orgasm, happy to take the weight of him on top of me after he came. I loved that he was big and he was dominant, and I loved that he wasn't afraid of taking my cock up his ass when it suited either of us. I loved a lot of things about…

No.

"Your hands are almost as good as your mouth," he whispered against my ear, breath coming in harsh and tired pants.

I hummed at the approval, giving both of our half-hard cocks another squeeze. "What time is it?"

"Does it matter?"

Flynn slowly untangled my legs from around him, leaving me cold and messy. I watched him climb out of bed and walk to the bathroom, the tanned globes of his ass firm and lifted. The muscles in his back were solid and visible, his thighs much the same. He went into the en suite, wetting a washcloth and coming back to sit on the edge of the bed.

Watching Flynn gave me a sense of contentment that coiled in my belly and felt a lot like fear. It was a dangerous emotion, something that I needed to try my best to keep in check, even though Flynn made it nearly impossible to keep my guard up around him.

He took my hand and cleaned me up, wiping our cum from the webbing of my hand, one finger at a time. His gaze sat intent on the task, his eyes tracing over my skin like lasers as he searched out dirty spots that needed cleaning. Flynn softly wiped my stomach, the fold of my thigh, and farther back still over my well-used hole. When he wrapped the cloth around my shaft and gave a gentle pull up my length, I moaned, arching off the bed and happily rolling toward him for more.

"Let me get you now," I offered, holding out a freshly cleaned hand for the cloth.

He made a tutting sound and shook his head, keeping the cloth out of reach. "I can get it," he said.

I yawned, stretching out against his sheets like a starfish. "What if I want to?"

"Then you can do it next time." He stood up and gave a

rougher tug down his own cock than he'd given me, corner of his mouth twisting into a grimace as he moved, no doubt from the sensitivity. "Or the time after that. Or the time after that."

He gestured in the air with the rag and padded back into the bathroom where he gave himself the same cleaning he'd offered me, though with noticeably less care and kindness. I took the opportunity to slide out of the wet spot and get comfortable on the sheets. The fire still crackled across the room and I yawned again, waiting for him to come to bed, hating how easy it would be to get used to him and everything he had to offer.

The intrusive thoughts about sabotaging my relationship with Flynn before it even had a chance to get started were the last thing I remembered before falling asleep. I wasn't even aware of him coming to bed, but when I woke up to sharp-angled rays of light slashing their way across my face, I realized I had. Flynn was still absent from the bed, but quiet sounds from the kitchen confirmed he was still in the house.

I hadn't planned on spending the night and I didn't have any clean clothes. I sure as shit didn't want to put on my dirty old laundry-day underwear again.

Let him take you shopping, an annoying voice in my head whispered. *If you let him buy you nice things, you could keep them here and this wouldn't be an issue.*

The logic was sound, but that didn't mean I liked it.

Wrapping the sheet around my waist, I crawled out of bed and kicked my legs free. The sheet was massive, but there was only so much bunching and gathering I could do and still keep myself covered. I shuffled out into the main part of the house and found Flynn hunched over the island, glaring at his laptop screen, phone beside his hand.

"Are you working?" I asked.

He sat up, back going rigid before he turned toward me. There was a change in him, something so clear I would have been able to see it in the dark. His furrowed brows softened, and the chocolate of his eyes turned golden when he saw me. His hands fell into his lap and his head cocked to the side, mouth twisting from a frown into an appreciative line.

My cheeks burned from his appraisal, so deep it hurt, and I shifted the gathered sheets into one hand to cover half my face with the other.

Flynn snapped the lid of his laptop closed and shook his head. "It's not important."

"I didn't mean to intrude."

He shook his head again. "You're not."

"Why are you looking at me like that?"

Flynn's gaze raked over me, from my toes to the tangled mess of hair on top of my head. I should have stopped in the bathroom before coming out. God knew what kind of disaster I looked like with my curls all tangled and my eyes probably puffy from how late we were up the night before. I had to look like awful, but the way he watched me gave me the distinct impression he saw a different version of me than I did.

"How am I looking at you?" he asked.

I swallowed, turning my attention toward the floor instead of his face. But even as I tried to count the grain in the wood planks beneath my feet, I could feel him watching me, studying me, cataloging me.

Devouring me.

"Like that," I said, waving my hand toward him dismissively.

"Like you're gorgeous?" he asked, causing the ache in my cheeks to deepen. "Like you're the most beautiful man I've ever seen?"

"Flynn."

I didn't know why I said his name, because as much as I wanted him to stop, I never wanted him to stop.

When was the last time anyone besides Flynn had called me beautiful?

Called me gorgeous?

I was always pretty, or cute, or something as equally diminutive. Because I was small and slight, and apparently those bigger words were only reserved for bigger people. But hearing them directed at me with such a staggering kind of sincerity… I wanted to believe them.

Wanted to believe him.

"Am I looking at you like you suck my cock better than anyone I've ever met?" He stood, an erection visible behind the soft cotton sleep pants he wore. "Because you do."

"It's just the gag reflex," I mumbled, suddenly uncomfortable with the praise.

"It's not." He adjusted his erection, moving his hips to the side as he pulled his palm over his length. "It's your lips and your mouth. Your tongue. It's the way you look at me with those ethereal blue eyes of yours, tears streaking out the corners as I slide into the back of your throat like it was made for me."

It was my turn then to adjust my own erection, quickly growing behind the knotted sheets in my fist.

"It's the way when you lay with your head off the bed, I can trace the length of my shaft as it stretches your throat and you touch yourself at the same time because you like it so much…" His voice caught on the last word and he trailed off. "You like how I worship you with my hands and my words. My body."

"If you don't stop talking like that, we're never getting out of the house," I said, even though there was nowhere for us to go, no plans for us to keep. Just Flynn and his money desperate to buy me sexy panties that he could take off of me, ready to give me a thousand orgasms and a hundred meals, or whatever he'd said before. It was just these promises between us that shouldn't have meant anything, but instead meant everything.

"Am I looking at you like when you're not here and I jerk off, I think about you fucking me?" he asked, closing the space between us and covering my hand with his own. I loosened my grip and he held the sheet between his fingers before it could fall.

He was, actually.

He was looking at me *exactly* like that.

"Do you?" I managed to ask, even as it was hard to keep my

eyes open, hard to stand in front of him and not put him on his back and do just that.

"I don't believe I've stopped thinking about you since the first second I laid eyes on you," he said softly, biting the tip of his tongue between his canines. "I'm worried I'm never going to think about another man ever again."

Another feeling blossomed in my chest, just as dangerous as happiness, but even more catastrophic. I let go of the sheets and pulled my hand out of his, rubbing a slow circle on my sternum to alleviate the tenderness there.

"Would that really be so bad?" I asked with a weak laugh, already knowing the answer was yes.

"THE TWO OF YOU ARE A NIGHTMARE," I MUTTERED, STARE FLICKING back and forth between Grayson and Archie, who hadn't shut the fuck up since I arrived at Archie's house twenty minutes prior for an impromptu Sunday brunch.

"Just wait your turn." Archie waved me off without even a glance, his attention still solely focused on Grayson, who looked more bored than I'd ever seen him, and that was saying something because historically Rob kept him on his toes.

"Well, let's ask Flynn what he thinks," Grayson said, which brought both of their stares level with mine.

I grabbed Archie's lemonade and took a swallow, which earned me a smack in the arm. But it was his house and he hadn't even bothered to offer me a drink when I got there. Desperate times and all that.

"What do I think about what?"

Archie sighed. "Grayson doesn't want to move in with Rob."

"I don't blame him. You wouldn't want to live there either," I said. "The lack of window dressing in his house is disturbing."

"All of you rich assholes are obsessed with glass," Grayson snapped.

Much like mine, Rob's house was an ode to modern architecture with lots of white walls and giant plate glass windows. I was fairly certain the downstairs library at his house was the only room that had curtains, the rest of the space nearly constantly drowning in natural light. It was a look, that was certain, but I'd at least built up the back yard a bit around my own place so the sunrise didn't feel like waking up on the surface of the sun itself.

"I am sure he would let you hang curtains," Archie said.

"There's no place for them!" Grayson threw his hands up. "The glass goes all the way up."

"Redesign it," I suggested.

"Rob would never."

"Owen doesn't like my house," Archie said, a small frown pulling at the corners of his mouth as he looked around. His place was relatively modest compared to the rest of us, but it still dripped with quiet luxury. And since his boyfriend moved in, there were dozens more personal touches than before, all of which I'd never have expected from Archie, but he allowed because he loved Owen so much.

"He likes you."

"He loves you," Grayson said.

"And you love Rob," I reminded him.

Grayson sighed, tipping his head back and staring up at the ceiling. "It's a lot."

"What does your little friend Wesley think?" I asked.

Even though Grayson had immediately taken a liking to Archie, his best friend was a twenty-something named Wesley Sutton. He'd come around on a handful of occasions—working for Rob, living with Grayson, and being about ten years away from being able to handle his liquor.

He was a good kid.

Grayson, on the other hand, was an absolute menace.

"Wesley practically lives with his boyfriend now, so I know me moving in with Rob would give him the out he's been looking for to cut the tie."

"So you refusing to move in with Rob is keeping Wesley from

moving in with his boyfriend?" I arched a brow. "That feels selfish."

He rolled his eyes and Archie laughed, finally realizing that I'd finished his lemonade in the absence of my own. He took all of the empty and near-empty glasses into the kitchen to get refills, leaving Grayson and me at the table together.

"It *is* selfish," he agreed, looking a decade older than he was. "But it's complicated."

If anyone knew about complicated these days, it was me. I gave him a sympathetic nod and told him as such.

"I like where this is going," he said, leaning close. "Let's change the subject before your stubborn best friend gets back."

"He cares for Rob," I said. "And you."

Grayson's face softened, but went hard again as Archie came back from the kitchen with fresh drinks and a charcuterie board.

"Tell me about your complicated," Grayson said.

I'd agreed to come over because I wanted to talk about it… no, I *needed* to talk about it. Rose had me all turned around, and I could barely keep track of what I was meant to do and who I needed to be. First, I'd made him see that I didn't have to change at all to deserve a chance with him, which had been easy. But as things progressed, I realized he needed a little more care than I'd thought. He was nervous around me, skittish, and so I'd proposed a thirty-day plan to prove my worth to him.

The idea by itself was absurd because I'd never had to prove myself to anyone. That wasn't a life or a struggle I'd ever known, and maybe that made me cocky or arrogant, but so be it. Much like Rose, I knew my worth. I'd committed to this test run to ease *his* nerves, but the game wasn't sustainable. I couldn't go as far in with him as I needed to if I knew the risk of him leaving was on the horizon.

As much as it pained me to admit it, I had a heart and that would break it. It would be easier than breathing to fall in love with Rose, who bloomed under my hand, from my praise and my words. He was a manifestation of every dream I'd never realized I had, and I didn't want that to end in a handful of weeks. I worried if I asked for more, if I changed the terms, that I would lose him altogether, though.

"Rose is complicated?" Archie grabbed a small pickle and shoved the entire thing into his mouth.

"Extremely."

"Why?" Grayson asked.

"Because I want more than he's willing to give," I said.

Grayson let out a bark of laughter and reached forward to assemble a finger sandwich from the charcuterie tray between us. "Trust me, that's not as insurmountable as you think it is."

"It feels that way."

It had only been two days, but every second I spent away from him had me feeling like I was sliding down a mountain while he continued to climb toward the summit. He had caved in and let me take him shopping Friday afternoon, but when he saw the price tags, he balked at thirty pairs. I wouldn't have even noticed the change in my bank account, but Rose was verging on angry over the cost, so we settled on seven and the promise of a fashion show before the weekend was over.

I thought about how badly Rob must have wanted Grayson to move in with him, the same with Archie and Owen, because that proximity was heady, it was potent. But it worked both ways, and while having Rose around more might make sure I won in the end, I might also end up losing parts of myself that I hadn't planned.

"He didn't want anything to do with me at first," I told Grayson. Archie already knew the gist of the story. "But I proved that he did."

"How?" Grayson interrupted.

"I told him."

Archie scoffed.

"Of course you did," Grayson muttered. "The whole bunch of you, I swear. Go on."

"I told him to give me a chance and he did. He saw that I was right. But he wasn't all in, you know?"

"Oh," Archie mused. "I know."

"So then I said give me thirty days. Thirty days to show you that this is worth your while."

"Fool."

"I know," I agreed. "I don't want thirty days. I can't do thirty days." I scrubbed a hand down my face, shaking my head. "I can't be the man I want to be for him if I *know* there's an expiration on it."

"And you can't take it back?" Archie asked.

"I would rather thirty days than nothing."

"Liar." Grayson slashed his hand through the air, leaning back in his chair and crossing his arms in front of his chest. "You want all or nothing."

"Can you blame me?"

"All of you are the same," he said.

"You're no exception to the rule, Grayson," Archie countered, brow raised. "You can give us your cute little Trophy Doms nickname, but you're not exempt from the moniker yourself."

"Being dominant and rich aren't the only membership requirements. Do you really think that's all the five of you have in common?"

I threw a sideways glance at Archie, and he shrugged, as lost by the comment as I was.

"I've been told no more times than either of you will ever," Grayson said under his breath. His features flashed with sorrow, but he was quick to shake it off. "None of that matters. We're talking about you and your resistant little flower."

I rubbed circles on my temples and sighed.

"So you want him to be as in as you are," Grayson surmised.

"I want him to *want* to be in."

"I'm starting to think you're the one who's making this complicated."

"If he would stop being resistant to"—I gestured at myself—"me, then this wouldn't be an issue."

"Resistant how?" Archie asked.

"With…the money."

Archie laughed, and so did Grayson.

"Trophy Dom," he cackled.

"Speaking as someone who also has a partner who is resistant to money…" Archie cleared his throat and turned his back on Grayson. "There's not much you can do besides wait it out. He has to see that you're more than your money."

"Patience isn't a strong suit," I said.

"Another mark of a Trophy Dom," Grayson chided.

"How can I help him see it?" I asked, ignoring Grayson's barb.

"I'll talk to him."

Archie and I both snapped our necks turning toward Grayson.

"You'll what?" we both asked.

"I'll talk to him," he said again, looking smug.

"That's the opposite of a solution."

"You can send Owen if you'd rather," Grayson suggested.

"Or I can send no one. My end goal is that Rose wants to be with me. Not that he runs screaming for the hills."

I finished the rest of my drink and pushed the chair back from the table, needing space. I found some in the living room, but Grayson was quick to follow, coming to sit beside me on the ottoman. With his legs bent at the knee, his khakis hiked up enough to expose his bare ankles, and his white sneakers were so clean it looked as if they'd never even set foot on asphalt. I couldn't imagine a world where Grayson would be able to plead my case more effectively than I could.

"I can talk to him myself," I said, sounding disgruntled.

"Of course you can," he agreed, smacking my arm with his elbow. "But you have friends who care about you. Who want to see you happy."

"Are we friends now?"

He pressed a hand to the center of his chest, feigning insult. "All I'm saying is, sometimes a fresh perspective helps."

"Is that what made you come around?" I asked him, thinking back to the tumultuous beginnings of his relationship with Rob.

"Your other friend and I both had some work to do," he said. "But to your point, yes. I did have someone talk me through it."

I exhaled, thinking of all the ways I wanted to talk Rose through it. My face must have showed the thought process because Grayson made a disgusted noise in the back of his throat and kicked me.

"Head in the gutter," he said, "Another Trophy Dom trait."

"Again, you're more like us than you think."

"That's offensive." Grayson stretched his legs out, crossing them at the ankles.

Out of the thousand ideas I'd had over the last two days about how to backtrack my commitment without Rose worrying that I wasn't reliable, none of them felt workable. It would be easier, I wagered, if I was a man like Rob or Dalton. Far more dominant in the expectations of their partners than I'd ever been. Not that Dalton had ever had a partner. But Rob…

I glanced at Grayson and took him in, really took him in for maybe the very first time. He was younger than me, younger than all of us, but he carried himself with all of the confidence and surety we'd spent decades gathering on our own. He was a stubborn man who knew what he wanted, and he wasn't scared of doing the work to get it, even if that work took him out of his comfort zone.

I'd done the same with Rose, with my initial concessions all the way to my thirty-day agreement. That wasn't the kind of person I'd ever been. I didn't compromise. I was generous in the bedroom and in the places that it counted, but when it came to my own wants and needs, I was as selfish as they came.

Or so I'd thought.

"What would you say to him?" I finally asked, shoulders sagging under the weight of the question.

"Like I'd ever tell you." He scoffed and stood, fidgeting with the cuffs of his shirt.

This was out of character for me, but Rose had me out of my head. I couldn't think straight when he was around and it was even worse when he was gone. It didn't feel egregious to ask for help. The last thing I wanted to do was scare Rose away, though, and Grayson was as formidable a personality as me.

"I like him, Grayson." I propped my elbows on my knees and looked up at him, hoping he could see the truth of it in my face. But maybe also hoping he saw the lie because I didn't *just* like Rose.

"Just tell me where to find him, Galloway. I'll take care of the rest."

Shoving my Sunday night tips into my pocket, it was impossible to not think about how easy my life would be if Flynn had his way. I'd made a couple hundred dollars, which was better than nothing, but still far less than he'd spent on me when he'd taken me shopping Friday afternoon.

As it was, the lace and satin on the panties he bought for me over the weekend were the most decadent pieces of clothing I'd ever owned, and the way the ones I currently wore cupped my balls was deserving of sonnets and songs. The material had long since warmed from my own body heat, and the soft touch of them on my most sensitive parts had me strung as tight as a high wire, even without Flynn nearby.

He'd wanted me to stay the whole weekend, and of course I wanted that too. But I'd told him no. I spent as much of the day Friday with him as my heart could manage, then I'd gone back to my very small one bedroom apartment where I shared a pizza with Drake and fielded more angry texts and calls from Cody. Flynn knew I worked over the weekend and even though he was clearly anxious to see me again—and the underwear he'd bought me—we didn't have set plans.

I figured I would give him a call in a couple of days and maybe make plans for later in the week. I didn't want to appear too eager, even though I was. Things with Flynn had the potential to be *so good,* if only I could let them, but it was near impossible to get over myself. For as much as I wanted him, there were still so many things about him that triggered my alarms. I hated it. I fought myself on it. But it wasn't going to be an easy road.

And, anyway, what was the point.

Thirty days and then nothing.

God, this was stupid.

I pushed the door open, debating the sanity of every life choice I'd ever made, tripping over my feet when I found a shiny black Audi parked right next to my car. Much like Flynn had done in the past, a man leaned against it, legs crossed at the ankle and arms folded in front of his chest. I'd never seen him before, but I would have bet my pocket full of cash he knew Flynn. He looked up when the door opened, the alley light washing his face in a pale amber glow that made him look closer to my age than Flynn's. I wondered who he was. How old he was. What he wanted.

He gave me a onceover, then straightened up, uncrossing his arms and stretching one out to me like he wanted a handshake.

"Do I know you?" I asked, coming to a stop after the door swung closed behind me.

He cocked his head to the side, chin tipped up while he stared at me down the bridge of his nose. He was taller than me, but still short. He'd just learned how to better compensate for it. I mirrored the posture, wondering how it would make me feel.

"You're about to." He gave his hand another shake in my direction until I took it and returned the gesture. "I'm Grayson. I'm friends with Flynn."

"I figured."

Grayson let go of my hand and shoved his into his pocket. "You're Rose?"

I nodded.

"Short for something or did your parents just like to garden?"

I huffed, blinking slowly. "Short for Ambrose."

"That's a hell of a name for..." He looked me up and down as he trailed off, leaving the quiet part unspoken.

"Go on," I encouraged. "Hell of name for someone like me?"

"Someone like you?" He repeated it back to me like the intent of my initial statement wasn't clear. "What do you think I meant?"

"Nothing."

"What do you think I meant?" he asked again, voice taking on a stern edge that compelled me to answer him.

I gestured at myself, then at him, and shrugged. "I'm not anything special."

Grayson laughed and pushed off the car, coming toward me with long and sure strides. He looked like he was ready to smack me upside my head, so I squared my shoulders and again tried to look at him the way he'd looked at me, down the nose with the chin held high.

He stopped in front of me and grinned, blue eyes sparkling. "It would take a man with a name like Ambrose to bring Flynn Galloway to his fucking knees."

The words registered, but they didn't make any sense. I cleared my throat and took a step back, but my heel bumped into the stair and I fell right on my ass. Embarrassed and tired, I didn't even bother getting up. Grayson, for his part, looked absolutely unbothered. He kicked my feet out of the way and sat down beside me, both of us starting at our cars across the alleyway.

"What's your damage, kid?" he asked.

"I'm not a kid."

"What's your damage, *Ambrose*?"

I could hear the eye roll in his voice.

"I don't know what you're talking about," I mumbled, rolling a rock underneath the peeling sole of my black sneaker.

"Can I level with you?" he asked.

"Please do."

"Flynn is a friend of mine. I don't know him as well as my boyfriend does, but I know him well enough to know that the way he was acting a month ago is not the way he's acting now, and the only difference in the timeline is you."

"Acting how?" It was hard to get the words out because watching and listening to Grayson was like seeing myself dream cast in a movie. He was the kind of person I'd always wanted to be. Bold and confident, even though he wasn't stacked like a body builder. It wouldn't hurt to have a little money, but he didn't seem like the kind to flaunt it the way Flynn sometimes did, even if unintentional.

The lace between my legs brushed against my soft cock as a reminder of that.

"Not himself." Grayson tapped his temple, then his chest. "All tangled up over the curly-haired little angel who won't give him the time of day."

"I give him plenty of time," I said.

"When?"

I swiveled toward him, eyebrows raised. "Excuse me?"

"When do you give him time?"

I knew there was nuance to the question. Grayson wasn't calling into question the number of hours I spent with Flynn, but the timing of those hours. A flash of shame heated my cheeks and I turned away.

"Weekends," I answered. "At night. But that's all he wants from me. That's all—"

"Thirty days, right?"

I covered my face with both hands, pressing my fingertips into my closed eyelids and then swiping down my face. "That's what he said."

"He wants more."

Grayson said it so quickly, I wasn't sure I'd heard him right. But I tamped down the spark of hope that fizzled in my chest because I didn't know this man from Adam and who knew what his intentions with the conversation were.

"More…?"

"More than nighttime. More than thirty days. More than half-commitments."

"Then why is that what he asked for?" I knew why. It was a compromise that would get him me, and he had been willing to take pieces and bits if he couldn't get the whole thing.

I stretched my legs out and let my ankles drag through the alley gravel. Grayson's sneakers were so crisp and white, I wasn't sure he'd ever worn them before coming to see me. I was so out of my league with him, with Flynn, with all of them.

"Are you for real right now? Are you always like this?" Grayson stood and dusted off the backside of his khakis, turning to face me with his arms once again crossed in front of his chest. His attitude had changed from when I'd stepped into the alley. Where he'd started as agreeable and friendly, everything had shifted toward protection and defense.

I nodded, looking down at my lap as the fight went out of me.

"Why?" he asked. "I mean, is this how you treat Flynn? Because I can't imagine why he'd keep coming back for more of *this*."

"Hey." I stood and brushed my pants off, stepping toward him with my hands balled into fists at my sides. "Fuck you."

"Fuck you," he spat back at me. "I came by because Flynn was all torn up over how bad he wants you and I wanted to help him out, but I really just don't see it."

I worked my jaw back and forth, but didn't say anything in response to Grayson. Mostly because I didn't know what to say. I was being unfair and defensive, I knew it. But it wasn't something I could simply reprogram or turn off. Giving Flynn a chance would have been a hell of a lot easier if I could.

"Is it him?" Grayson asked, pacing himself in a small circle like he wasn't quite ready to give up on me yet. "Is it the money?"

"The money's part of it," I admitted.

"Listen, Ambrose—" he started in again, but I cut him off.

"Rose."

"Listen, Ambrose," he repeated, ignoring me. "Everyone has money. Some of us just have more than others."

"He has more than most," I said.

"And so do I." Grayson shrugged. "But my boyfriend has more than me. Hell, he has whiskey in his kitchen that costs more than what I spend on clothes in a whole year. That's his prerogative, not mine."

"I don't want his money."

"And I don't want Rob's money, but I want Rob, and they're kind of a package deal."

Grayson looked at me like I was a child and he'd just explained a very simple concept that I should have grasped years before. I flexed my hands, stretching out my fingers and then cracking each knuckle to alleviate some of the tension that had built in my bones.

"There are plenty of reasons to not be with a person," he went on. "If they're mean in a not-sexy way, or if they don't tip the wait staff, or like…I don't know. Plenty of reasons. But if you run a perfectly good man off because he was raised well and had some shit handed to him on a silver platter, then you're really narrowing your playing field. I mean, you want more than this for yourself, right?"

Grayson's attention moved past me toward the restaurant, then down my clothes, and finally to my car.

I sighed, kicking a pile of rocks down the alley.

"I don't want to get used to it," I said quietly. "And then lose it."

"That's the risk with any relationship. And honestly you don't strike me as the type to let him spoil you beyond measure."

"He's already done too much."

"Says who?" Grayson asked.

"Says me."

"Are you in a partnership or a democracy?"

Headlights flashed down the alley and a car came rolling down the gravel, coming to stop less than two feet from where Grayson and I stood. The driver cut the ignition and when the lights turned off, I immediately recognized the make and model, and shortly thereafter, the man in the driver's seat.

"Shit," I cursed under my breath, steeling myself for whatever vitriol Cody had for me this time around.

"Do you know him?"

"Unfortunately," I groaned. "My cheating ex."

Cody shouldered the driver's side door open and came around to the front of his car, eyes narrowed into judgmental slits. He'd clearly already appraised the situation and made up his mind about who Grayson was and who he was to me. He looked angry, borderline furious and barely restrained.

"Why aren't you answering my calls, Rose?" Cody took a step toward me, and Grayson moved, putting himself between us.

"Who are you?" Grayson asked, his tone half-sneer and half-laugh.

"Who am I?" Cody scoffed. "I'm his boyfriend."

"Bet you're not," Grayson said at the same time that I also refuted the claim.

"Oh?"

"You might have been in the past, but he's moved on from men who don't appreciate a good thing when they see it." Grayson's mouth was pulled into a tight and unimpressed line.

"I appreciate you just fine, don't I, Rose?"

"Appreciated him right into someone else's bed, I hear."

For every angry breath Cody took, Grayson seemed to get stronger. The casual way he batted back every insult Cody tried to hurl was only making him angrier and making me more worried. I didn't know Cody to be a violent man, but Grayson was practically a stranger, and I didn't want to have to explain to Flynn how he'd gotten injured on my account.

I curled my hand over Grayson's shoulder, trying to pull him back, but he refused to stand down.

"I'm not afraid of a man with more volume than sense, Ambrose," he said, turning his attention back to Cody with the most bored expression I'd ever seen anyone wear. "You can go now."

"I'll go when I'm ready."

"Alright, well…we'll go then." Grayson turned his back on Cody and studied me silently before saying, "I think I get it now."

"Get what?" I asked weakly.

"The damage."

He turned back to Cody who had started to huff and puff. I appreciated Grayson trying to fight this battle for me, but I didn't need him to do it. I didn't want that from him—or from anyone.

"I don't know how many times I have to tell you that we're through, Cody," I said, finally getting Grayson out of the way. "I don't want to be with you anymore."

"You know I did you a favor, Rose." Cody made a tutting sound with his tongue against the roof of his mouth. "What real man is going to want a little femme like you?"

"Oh, I can think of at least one," Grayson said under his breath.

"Who? You?" Cody scoffed.

Grayson shook his head. "I couldn't afford him. He deserves someone much nicer than me and far better than you."

"Fuck you," Cody sneered.

Grayson scrunched his nose and chuckled. "I'll pass."

"Cody, please go. I don't want to keep doing this with you."

"We're not done," Cody said.

"You very much are. So go on and get back into your car that we both know smells like a pile of Black Ice air fresheners and stale iced coffee, and do whatever it is people like you do on Sunday nights." Grayson gestured toward Cody's car, and I looked away until Cody got back inside and peeled rubber down the alley. When the noise of his engine died down, I collapsed back onto the stairs, hands trembling.

"You didn't need to involve yourself like that."

Grayson ignored what I said, instead asking, "Was he always like that? Or only after?"

It was hard to admit that I'd disregarded the signs, that I'd settled for a man like that, but my adrenaline from the encounter was already crashing and I didn't have it in me to lie. "I think always."

"Flynn would never," he said, like I needed any convincing that Flynn was a better man than Cody. There'd never been any doubt in my mind as to the caliber of Flynn's character.

"I know."

"Do you think you don't deserve to be treated well?" He glanced down the alley in the direction Cody had driven. "Do you think that piece of shit is the best you can do?"

"It's just…it's…he only says it really when…when we…"

Grayson widened his eyes, swirling his hand in a circle like he wanted me to get the words out. "For Christ's sake, Ambrose. We all know he has a praise kink; it's not a secret."

"He only says it in bed!" I shouted before I could take the words back. "Or I only hear it in bed. It's all around the sex part and not the other part."

"Didn't you just tell me that the sex part is all you've given him?" Grayson went to his car and pulled open the driver's door. "If so, that feels unfair. Flynn is a good man, a great one even. From what I hear, he's tried on more than one occasion to meet in your middle instead of his, and I think we both know his is where the both of you really want to be." He lowered himself into the seat and pressed the power button. The engine roared to life and he closed the door behind him, but unrolled the window.

I got the impression the only thing Grayson liked more than his boyfriend was the sound of his own voice.

"So while you're waiting for your little twink knees to quit knocking together, maybe you can think about what that could mean for both of you, then you can get over yourself, and go make an honest man out of him. Alright?"

I slowly nodded, because I wanted that more than anything. Even if I hadn't felt before like I deserved it, I wanted it. I wanted Flynn and I wanted him for more than thirty days, so that was what I was going to have.

I WAS GETTING READY FOR BED WHEN SOMEONE KNOCKED AT MY FRONT door. I knew it wasn't any of my friends because they would have barged right on it with no preamble. I hadn't ordered food and I didn't have plans with Rose, so finding him on my porch just shy of ten on a Sunday night caught me a little by surprise.

"Is everything okay?" I asked in lieu of a greeting.

It was out of character for him to just show up, and I worried he was going to try and break up with me again.

"Did you know Grayson was coming to my work?" he asked.

"I did."

"Did you ask him to?"

Dragging my tongue across the front of my teeth, I shook my head. I stepped out of the way and gestured for him to come inside, which he did. That had to be a good sign, right? Rose toed off his dirty work sneakers and kicked them into place in the corner, dumping his phone, wallet, and keys on top of them.

"Did he say something stupid?" I asked

Rose exhaled the beginnings of a laugh. "He does talk a lot, doesn't he?"

"He has his moments, but he means well."

Rose nodded and closed my front door behind him, then reached for my hand. His palm was cool and clammy, his fingers thin against my own. He led me into the living room and sat us both down on the couch, turning our bodies so our knees bumped together.

He looked worried, a stray curl loose across his forehead. I reached up to push it back into the tangle on top of his head, and Rose closed his eyes with a quiet—if not resigned—sigh.

"I haven't been fair to you," he whispered.

"I think we had this conversation the last time you tried to break up with me."

I fucking knew it.

"We need to have it again," he said, taking both of my hands. "Because I still haven't been fair to you."

"You're giving me a chance," I reminded him. "Which is all I asked for."

"It's not, though."

I never would have admitted it out loud, but I was scared to open my mouth lest I start begging and pleading him to change course.

"What are you saying?" I finally asked.

"I don't want to do thirty days with you." Rose caught my stare and held it, his eyes looking anything but sad. I hadn't imagined him to be so heartless, so jovial at the prospect of breaking my heart. "And I don't think that's what you want from me either."

"I'll take it," I rasped, fingers tightening around his.

"Do you remember the night we met?"

I didn't imagine there would come a day when I ever didn't remember the night I met Rose. From my failed attempts with Frankie to the dare that had absolutely changed the course of my life. I'd always remember the way Rose's body felt against mine, his tongue in my mouth and his legs around my waist. And later still, taking him back to that hotel and letting him rut into me the way he had. There were a thousand memories wrapped up in those few hours and I'd never forget them for the rest of my life.

But I didn't want to say all that if he was only going to walk away from me, so instead I told him, "Yes."

He nodded, straightening his shoulders and turning up his chin. It was a pose I'd seen on Grayson more than once and I fought back the urge to laugh at the comparison between the two. What I would give to have been a fly on the wall for whatever Grayson had said to him that made him realize he didn't want to be with me anymore.

I couldn't be mad at Grayson, though. Even if my first instinct was to drive over to Rob's and throw Grayson out of a window. If anything, he'd expedited the inevitable. Better to break my heart now and not later.

"I told you I wouldn't settle for less than I deserve," Rose went on.

I remembered that conversation very well.

"And I think that's what you're doing now."

"How do you figure?"

"Thirty days?" He winged up a brow, and I turned my attention down toward our joined hands. "I had the courage to speak up for what I really wanted. Now it's time for you to do the same."

"What do *you* want?" I asked instead.

Rose shook his head. "That's not what I said."

"I want you," I whispered, raising his hands to my mouth and dusting kisses across his fingertips and his knuckles. "I want all of you in all the ways, all the time."

"More than thirty days?"

I nodded.

"Ask for what you want then," he said gently, untangling our fingers so he could start working open the buttons on his shirt. I covered his hands with mine, stilling the motion.

"I want you," I said again, hating the tremble in my voice. "I want to be your partner, your boyfriend, whatever you want to call it."

"You want to be my Dom."

I swallowed, the weight of the realization hitting me like a cement truck. I pleaded with myself to find the fortitude to look him in the eye when I said the next part, and even as the words came out a little shakier than I would have liked, I succeeded.

"I want to be your everything."

"That's admittedly terrifying." Again, Rose worked his hands out from my hold, but instead of returning to his buttons, he moved toward my face. He cradled my cheek with one hand and pressed the other against my chest, right over my heart. His stare was so bright, so intense, I had to close my eyes for fear I would say something else outlandish or daring.

"I know," I agreed.

"But…" He trailed his thumb across my cheekbone. "I think I can be brave."

My eyes flew open, not sure I'd heard him correctly. The smile on his face was small and crooked, but the truth was clear in his eyes, the rest of his expression.

"What are you saying?" I needed to ask. I needed to be sure.

"I want to be your everything too," he said, lashes fluttering. "I think I deserve that, don't I?"

"You deserve that and more."

"Longer than thirty days," he whispered.

"As long as you'll have me," I promised.

I curled my hands around his waist and pulled him onto my lap. He let out a soft laugh, but he gave me the chance to move him around until our stomachs were pressed together and he sat a head above me. He looked like a goddamn angel up there, the light behind his hair casting a glow around his head and through the loose curls of his hair.

"What did Grayson say to you?" I murmured, petting my hands up and down his sides to make sure he was real. To make sure *this* was real.

Rose huffed and shook his head a little. "I don't think Grayson likes me."

"Impossible."

It didn't matter if Grayson liked him or not, because I was very close to loving him and I was finally going to get my chance to fall

all of the way into that. I owed him a bottle of whiskey nice enough to say thanks, but not so kind that he'd believe I didn't care about whatever he'd done to make Rose think he had a sour opinion of him.

"What does it look like? Being your everything, I mean?" he asked, turning his attention to my chest, which was bare. His fingers flexed and danced across my pecs and up my clavicle, over my shoulders and down my arms. His touch was electric, sparking ideas and feelings that I'd only ever dreamed of before him. And it wasn't like he was the first person to ever touch me, far from it. But he was the first special one, of that I was certain.

"It looks like twenty more pairs of underwear for starters," I said, and he tweaked my nipples with a bratty laugh. Instead of pulling away, I groaned and arched into him, pressing my quickly growing cock against him.

"Just twenty?"

I huffed a laugh. Oh, how the mighty had fallen.

"It looks like you meeting my friends."

"I already have." He ground against me, looking more like a devil than an angel.

I grabbed his waist, dragging him to a stop because I had no interest in coming in my pajamas when his perfectly tight and hot body was right in front of me.

"Officially."

"What else?"

"I don't know beyond that," I admitted. "I've never done this before."

Rose jerked his body to the side, the momentum pushing me down at an angle so my head landed against the arm of the couch and my back flat against the cushions. With one of my legs on the couch and the other braced on the floor, Rose adjusted himself over top of me, giving me another grind of his hips for good measure.

"More of the praise part, I hope."

I closed my eyes and nodded, tongue darting out to wet my

lips. I had a hundred words of praise and promise on the tip of my tongue, but spilling them all over him after being prompted to do so felt far too contrived.

"Plenty more," I assured him. "You'll be begging me to shut up before the week is through."

"I doubt that."

I blinked him back into focus, tugging his arms so he fell against my chest. He pressed his forehead against mine and I opened my eyes, taking in the parts of his face I could see with the narrow field of vision.

"Are you sure this is what you want?" I asked.

In response, he rubbed his erection against me.

I bit back a groan, giving a small shake of my head. "I know you want that. I want that too, but I mean…the rest of it."

"Flynn." He pushed himself up a little, giving me space to see the earnest sincerity in his eyes. "I've never met someone like you and I don't think I ever will again."

"Not sure that's a compliment," I murmured.

He smacked my chest, which broke some of the tension for a second, only for things to turn somber and serious within the next breath. Rose was terrified. I could see it in the finest wrinkles around the corner of his mouth when he tried not to frown, the tightness in his shoulders when he tried to keep himself composed above me.

"I know that if I want to be with you, I need to give up some of my control," he said.

I wanted to argue the point, but he wasn't wrong. There were ways I liked things, especially in the bedroom, and while I could have great sex without those rules…it was infinitely better with them. I wanted that for me, for him…for us.

"It's not a bad thing," I told him. "It's…it's trust. It's responsibility."

"It's terrifying," he said.

"I don't ever want you to be scared of me."

"Not of you." He shook his head, quick to correct me, which

did something to the knot that had begun to form in my stomach. I couldn't bear for another good conversation with Rose to go bad. Not when I was so close to truly getting a chance to be with him in all of the ways I wanted. "It's just me. My life. The way I've had to be up until now. I can't just turn it off."

"Not a switch."

"Barely a dimmer."

I chuckled and pulled him back down, silencing his worries with the softest kiss I'd ever given another person in my life. Above me, Rose went soft and pliant, melting against my chest and making way for my tongue to dip past his lips. I kissed Rose until I was ready to take his clothes off, forcing myself to pull away long enough to remind him, "You've given me a chance before. Give me another one and I'll show you how freeing giving up control to someone can truly be."

ONE OF THE THINGS I LOVED THE MOST ABOUT FLYNN BEING SO MUCH bigger than me was the way he could control me with his body, his hands, his mouth.

"Get out of these," he murmured against me, setting to work with steady hands between my legs. Together, we got me out of the rest of my clothes and I was on his lap again, but naked. He wasn't wearing much either, just loose and soft pajama pants, but in light of the things we'd just talked about, the things he'd asked of me, I felt unbelievably naked.

Flynn traced his hands up my sides, whispering against my mouth as he moved. He counted his way up my ribs and around my shoulders, holding me strong and hard against him while he dipped his tongue into my mouth. He kissed me like it was a confirmation of everything he'd just said to me. Like he was offering himself—signed, sealed and delivered—as long as I could meet him halfway.

"I want you," I begged against his mouth, grinding against his lap.

In that moment, I wasn't just physically naked, I was emotionally bare as well. Grasping at something I knew would make me feel better, something that would overshadow that fear with another more pleasurable feeling, I ground down against the burning hot erection between Flynn's legs.

"Not tonight." He bit my bottom lip between his teeth and pulled, drawing me closer to him.

"Why not?" I made another circle with my hips, hoping to convince him.

Flynn groaned and trailed his hands back down to my hips and holding me still. Fuck, he was strong. He was so big, so handsome, so powerful. How had I ever stood a chance? Whatever he had for me, I wanted, and whatever he wanted from me, he could have. I couldn't think straight around him, and I didn't want to. It was almost enough to erase everything that scared me, everything I'd fought so hard against for years before him.

"You're drunk on the adrenaline," he murmured. "The fear, the exposure. I'd feel like I was taking advantage."

I fisted his hair in my hands and tried to angle his head for another kiss, but he was so solid beneath me. So unyielding.

"I promise you're not."

He smiled and pressed his lips against mine, barely a ghost of the kiss I so badly wanted from him.

"This is giving up control," he whispered. "This is trusting me to know what's best for us both."

"Your cock doesn't feel like it thinks this is best."

He laughed and kissed me again, a little bit deeper, but still nowhere near what I wanted. Flynn's hands shifted and cradled my ass, reminding me again how much bigger and broader than me he was. I closed my eyes and mentally focused on the way his hands spread against me, the points of contact where every finger pressed into my skin. He stood, the pressure points deepening, and I dropped my head against his shoulder.

"My cock isn't in charge," he said into my ear, walking us both into the bedroom.

He carefully laid me down on top of the blankets and lowered himself over me. I wrapped my legs around him and held him against my chest, and he seemed content with that level of entanglement. But his hips stayed still as he kissed me, brushing my hair back from my face and peppering his lips around my chin, my jaw, my cheeks, even over my eyelids.

Flynn kissed me until my legs unwound from his waist and I was boneless beneath him, drunk for real on the way his mouth made every cell in my body come to life screaming his name. He kissed me with his tongue, his hands, his body, using everything he had to drive me mad until I stopped begging him to fuck me. Until I realized he'd been right all along and the soft touches and deep and soulful kisses were exactly what the both of us had needed most.

I didn't remember an end to our make-out session, but I must have fallen asleep because the next thing I remembered, sun streamed through the windows, casting shadows across the foot of the bed. Flynn was asleep beside me, not on top of me, curled onto his side with one hand settled gently against the swell of my waist. One of my legs was stuck between his, our bodies close and warm and touching everywhere we could manage except for our mouths.

Smiling—and trusting—I closed my eyes and went back to sleep.

It had been four days since that encounter, since those truths were laid on the table, and nothing had been the same since.

And that wasn't a bad thing.

I sat across from him over dinner, sharing sushi that didn't cost an arm and a leg. The restaurant choice had been a concession for us both, but the tension of the debate was quickly forgotten as soon as we'd slid into the same side of the booth and opened the menu. Flynn's hand rested steadily on the top of my left thigh, inching up with every roll that landed on our table. The touch was intimate, but not sexual, and it was easy as breathing to lean into him comfortably as the night went on.

"I want you to meet my friends again," he said after taking a sip of his hot sake.

"They're intimidating," I admitted.

I'd often thought back to the night the five of them showed up while I was on shift. There wasn't anything decidedly aggressive about them. It was only a combination of their looks, their stature and, of course, their wealth. But it was impossible to think about them without thinking about Grayson…and the conversation we'd had in the alley on Sunday night.

"You're intimidating," Flynn whispered, nudging his nose against the spot above my ear.

The words felt like they were meant to be praise, but they raised my guard just the same. Grayson's voice made its way back into the front of my mind.

What's your damage, kid?

"How do you figure?" I asked, angling my head toward Flynn without pushing him away.

"Tell me first why you don't believe it."

I sighed and leaned against him. "I don't want to do this exercise."

"Please?"

The waiter came by and collected our empty plates without a word, which I supposed was the kind of service a place like this offered. I'd always been told it was rude to not engage the customer when you came by the table, but apparently I was out of my element in more ways than one. Flynn's question might as well have thrown me into a whirlpool for how uncomfortable it made me, but I wanted to answer him honestly and fairly. I'd spent enough time jerking both of us around because of my own worries and fears about being with a man like him. After we'd agreed to give things an honest go, the least I could do was offer him sincerity and truth.

"You know how you kissed me at Rapture that night we met?" I asked.

He was still leaned in close to me, nose buried in my hair in a way that had me feeling far more special than I had any right.

"I think about it often," he answered.

"No one has ever kissed me like that before."

"All the more reason to do lots of it now." His hand crept higher and he used his body to press me into the corner of the booth.

Admittedly, I didn't hate the idea.

Kissing Flynn was almost as good as sleeping with him, two things I enjoyed above many others. But there was something about the way he kissed that set the rest of it apart.

"I'm trying to answer you," I gasped, his fingers grazing a little too close for comfort considering just *how* public we were.

"Right." He withdrew his hand, but not his body. "Sorry."

"I...I'm younger than you."

Flynn hummed in my ear, clearly disagreeing with me.

"I don't have as much—"

"You have me," he interrupted, and I closed my eyes. "Aren't I worth something?"

"Worth a lot of things." I cleared my throat. "Did Grayson tell you about Cody?"

The subtle flex of Flynn's hand against my thigh was as much of a yes as any verbal confession would have been.

"Vaguely."

"I really liked him. At the time, I thought I could have loved him. But..."

"Grayson said he cheated."

I nodded. "With his roommate. I caught them."

"I'm sorry."

I set my hand on top of his, threading our fingers together even as his palm pressed down against my leg.

"I'd just found out right before that night I met you, and I...he had me all upside down about things. I wasn't myself."

Flynn waited for me to go on, almost still as a statue beside me.

"I think...I think the way things went with him has me

convinced that I don't deserve to have good things or that I won't be able to keep them because I couldn't keep him."

"Why would you want to keep someone who cheats on you?" Flynn asked, not sounding cruel in the slightest, which only made my cheeks burn with more embarrassment.

"I didn't, but…I'm trying to explain why I am how I am."

"I don't have a problem with how you are," Flynn offered. "I happen to actually enjoy who you are very much."

"I know and I love you for that—"

The words were out of my mouth before I could stop them, and if Flynn heard the ill-timed confession, he didn't acknowledge it in any discernible way. I gave my shoulders a wiggle and tried to brush off the admission and get back to the point, even though I wasn't sure what the point *was*.

"I think the moral of the story," I said, "is why should I expect you to stay faithful to me when Cody didn't manage it."

Flynn pulled away from me slightly, giving his neck a crack before he shifted his body even *more* toward me. He took my hands in his and moved me as well until our knees brushed together and my back pressed against the restaurant wall. I had nowhere to look but into his eyes, nothing to smell but the subtle waft of his cologne and the ginger on the table to my right, nothing to feel but the heat rolling off his body in waves so intense I actually wondered if I was going to combust.

"That's why I was the way I was before. With the demands, and the back and forth, and being so fucking stubborn about you," I whispered.

Flynn's dark eyes did a slow study of my face, from the tight lines I knew had popped up around the edges of my frown and mole by my ear that I'd spent two years debating getting removed. He scanned me and catalogued me, hands still hot and big around mine, body and presence more commanding than anyone I'd ever met.

It was silly, I thought, in that moment to have ever been back and forth about a man like Flynn because he was just that. He was a man, where Cody had been a boy, and sitting under the weight of Flynn's stare for even a single second should have been enough confirmation to me that I was in safe—and talented—hands.

"That feels like an apology and you don't owe me one," he said quietly. "You're here now, and that's what matters. But to your earlier question, Rose. You can expect me to be faithful to you because that's the kind of man I am, and I have no issue doing the work to prove that to you. I don't know anything about Cody besides what Grayson had to say, which wasn't very complimentary, but I know myself better than most men do."

"I know." In fact, I'd never doubted that fact about Flynn in the least.

"I've worked hard for all the things I have," he went on. "The house, the car, the bank account…the ability to buy you as much underwear as you like."

With that, he gave me a soft and seductive grin that reminded me exactly how close to my cock—and said underwear—his hand really was.

"And the one thing I want you to know about men like me, Rose, is we protect the things that are ours. And you're mine, aren't you, baby?"

I choked out a noise that I hoped sounded affirmative.

"That's what I thought," he murmured, still holding my stare with the intensity and heat of a thousand burning suns. "And if protecting you sometimes looks like getting whiplash because you're scared or nervous, than I get whiplash. If protecting you looks like getting on my back and spreading my legs so you can rut into me until your bones turn to jelly, then you climb on top and fuck me into oblivion."

"We're in public," I whispered, more for myself than anyone else because my cock had hardened so fast at his words, I worried about how we'd get out of the restaurant without getting the cops called for an indecency charge.

"I'm not scared of work. I'm not scared of a challenge. And I've never backed down from a fight. You can push and pull all you need to, Rose, but I've known since the first time your lips touched mine that I was all in for you."

"Shut up," I begged, wrapping my hand around the back of neck and pulling his mouth against mine.

Flynn hummed happily as our lips crashed together, and I hoped his mouth was able to swallow down the whiny and desperate moans that I made as my body lit up under his touch. I wanted to kiss him more, kiss him harder, deeper, but the quiet clank of chopsticks against porcelain in the background reminded me we were in public.

We were *in public.*

"I want you so much," I whispered. "But you scare me."

He pressed his forehead against mine, lips slightly parted and eyes closed. His dark lashes fanned out against his cheekbones. My hand was still curled around the back of his neck, fingertips playing in the clipped ends of his hair while we both worked on calming ourselves down.

"I'm scared too," he said softly. "You've made me question every single thing I've ever wanted for my life and I'm not always sure what to do with you."

"But you don't push me away. You don't back off."

"That's not the kind of man I've ever been and I don't see myself starting now."

I gulped down a swallow. "Am I just a game? A challenge for you?"

"For Cody maybe."

I winced at his name on Flynn's tongue, hating that Cody still took up any space in my head or my life. I'd wanted him to go away. Told him we were over so many times I'd lost count, but like a cockroach, he kept coming back. Even if I blocked his number, he knew where I worked, he knew where Drake liked to party. There were ways for him to find me, to annoy me, to taint the happiness Flynn was offering me on a golden fucking platter.

"I can wait out your doubts, Rose. I'm not afraid of them."

"I am," I rasped.

"Come out with me after dinner." He stroked his thumb across my bottom lip, pulling down until the cool air of the breath inhaled over my tongue. "Come meet my friends again, get to know *me* better, and give me a chance to treat you the way you want. The way you deserve."

"How do I deserve?"

Somehow we'd made it back to the start, the earlier question hanging in the air between us, but this time turned toward Flynn, where I much preferred it.

Flynn huffed out a breath, mouth angling up into the barest tease of a grin before falling back into place. He leaned in closer to me once more, his lips soft against mine as he answered.

"You deserve to be fucked in dark corners in public places because I can't control myself around you. Because I can't wait to get you home."

His voice was so soft, I almost felt the answer from his mouth louder than I actually heard it with my ears.

"You deserve your back against the wall, a cock up your ass, and a hand over your mouth so no one hears you whimper when you come. And it's because I want you so badly, Rose, I can hardly breathe when I think about it sometimes. I want to worship you; you deserve to be fucking worshiped. Revered."

I made a very awkward noise in response to that, half moan and half strangled-off cry for how close his words had brought me toward a very unplanned orgasm in the middle of a sushi restaurant. Though, the thought of fucking Flynn in public, like he'd just said…

A shiver tore through my body, radiating from the base of my spine up and down and out and all over. I sucked in a breath, ready to respond.

But Flynn wasn't done talking.

"Then you deserve to come home to a nice bed with soft, clean sheets, and you deserve to have a man on his back with his legs spread wide so you can bury yourself so deep inside of him the only thing he can see is you."

"Is…is that what it's like for you?" I managed to ask, the words crackly and quiet between us. "When you're with me?"

He didn't have to answer because the truth was right there between us. It was in the way he tolerated me, the way he waited for me, the way he touched me. When we were together, Flynn was like a satellite, orbiting me. I hadn't noticed it before, but his words, the confession. It clicked everything into place and I understood for the first time just how much he'd put on the table for me. Flynn hadn't balked at my nerves or my back and forth. He'd waited and he'd tried, he'd backed off and regrouped, never walking away even when I'd all but asked him to.

"Every single time, Rose," Flynn said, the words sounding as much like praise as the rest of it. "Every single time."

CHAPTER 25
FLYNN

Kissing Rose was the best part of my day. When I kissed him, everything felt steady and real.

Solid.

Like whatever we were finally starting to build was going to last.

And beyond that, he was willing to meet my friends. Like *really* meet them, and that filled me with a giddiness so childlike, I was almost embarrassed about it. But it was Rose who brought those feelings out in me, those wants, those needs. I wanted him to hear how I was feeling. To truly understand the way he'd come in and upturned my life.

For the better.

And when he'd straddled my lap and let me tell him as much, I swear my heart grew in my chest near to the point of bursting. I would tell him every hour of every day if it meant he would keep rewarding me with those soft and pleased kinds of looks he so rarely gave out.

Rose had stayed over the last night, taking me apart with nothing more than his teeth and the gentle friction of his newest pair of lace panties.

I woke up late and worked from home, making him French toast and coffee after he stumbled out of bed. He had to work lunch, so he'd lingered as long as he could before heading back to his house with a promise to return later that night to meet my friends.

And while I waited for him, my phone buzzed so fast and steady against my palm, I could have used it as a goddamn vibrator.

Archie: I don't know if we should even let you come tonight.
Archie: SCAB
Me: What are you talking about?
Dalton: He's upset you skipped out on us last night.
Me: I was occupied.
Archie: With Rose?
Dalton: Of course with Rose.
Rob: Grayson likes him, be nice.
Me: That's not the praise you think it is. Have you met Grayson's friends??
Rob: Wesley is sweet. Just naive.
Dalton: Naive is an understatement from what I hear.
Rob: He's sweet. And he loves Grayson, and so do I.
Archie: Owen is also rather fond of Grayson.
Archie: And Wesley
Me: YOU are fond of Wesley.
Archie: Stop trying to distract me.
Barclay: The bunch of you are insufferable.
Dalton: This is solely your fault. You brought me around this group of people. You can't try to back out of the relationship now.
Barclay: I absolutely can.
Me: I'm coming tonight. I'm bringing Rose with me.
Rob: Good. See you later, then. Grayson will be pleased.
Dalton: You need Flynn's man to please your own? I thought that was more up Barclay's lane.
Rob: You know what I meant.
Dalton: I know times are a-changing. At least, I've heard.

Me: I'll see you later. Be nice or I'll foreclose on all your favorite properties.

Barclay: I'd like to see you try.

I dropped my phone back into my pocket at the same time Rose rapped his knuckles against my front door. There was no point in trying to play it cool because, around him, I was anything but, so I practically ran through the house to let him in. On my porch, he looked tired and a little worn down, but when I opened the door and his eyes locked on mine, his smile softened and his shoulders relaxed.

"Hey," he said quietly, almost nervous.

"Hey, beautiful." I stepped out of the way to let him in.

Rose had a black backpack slung over his shoulder and he toed off his shoes, kicking them into a pile in the corner like every time he came over.

He buried his face in my chest, and I wrapped my arms around him, just happy to have him back in my space.

"I don't look beautiful right now," he mumbled.

"Hush." I stroked my hands through his hair and walked us both into the house, Rose still pressed tight against my chest. "Can I get you in the shower? I got you something for tonight."

He groaned, digging his chin into my chest and shooing a sharp look up at me, but when I arched a brow, his face once again softened.

"Thank you," he whispered. "For whatever it is."

"Let's get you rinsed off."

Rose threaded our hands together and followed me into the en suite. He started to pop open the buttons of his shirt, but I stopped him with a quiet click of my tongue. HIs hands fell to his sides with a sigh, and I started the shower before turning back to him and picking up where he'd left off.

"I like being around you, Rose," I whispered, working my way down to his waist. "I like being inside of you, and I like it very much when you're inside of me."

I tugged the tails of his shirt up and out of his pants, then slid the sleeves down his arms and past his wrists. The shirt fell to the floor, and the flush on his cheeks rushed down toward his throat and his chest. I plucked at his belt, then the button and fly of his black chinos.

"I like the quiet moments when we're just together too," I said, somehow sensing the question about whether I was only with him for sex hanging on the tip of his tongue.

He swallowed audibly as his pants fell to his ankles, revealing a pair of relatively simple but still silky, black panties. I licked my lips, almost losing my train of thought as I traced my finger over the ridged outline of his half-soft cock.

God, he was perfect. There were only two things that could make him better so far as I was concerned. One of which being the blessing of my friends. Their approval was far from a deal breaker for me because, as I'd told Rose more than once, I was already all in with Rose. The other, of course, being some degree of submission from him.

I'd been careful to tread far more carefully around that road than the rest, and the way he'd opened up to me the day before had proven that to be the right decision. I wouldn't go so far as to call Rose skittish, at least not anymore. But he doubted my affection, sometimes doubted my sincerity. His ex had hurt him, that much was clear. Thankfully, I had no issue cleaning up the mess and picking up the pieces.

Every time Rose shut up and let me pour praise over him, he brightened and healed, and I was happy to see it. Even happier to be part of the cause of it. But I hadn't asked him to kneel, hadn't asked him to call me Sir. We'd danced around it, talked about the implications of the power exchange, but to me, it felt like there was still a bridge to cross there.

Rose hummed, walking his fingers up my chest until they reached my mouth where I kissed the pads of his fingers. He traced my lower lip and I darted out my tongue to lick it, which earned me a sharp and surprised intake of breath.

"There's something else," he said. "Something you're not saying in there. I can hear it between the words. In the quiet."

"I think a lot about the first night we met. The first time we kissed."

Regretfully, I pulled his panties down to his knees. Rose braced himself against my shoulder and stepped out of the silk, leaving him naked and exposed. His skin was nearly as white as the marble countertop behind him, washed out and pale. I balled up his underwear, raising them to my nose and taking a deep inhale.

"That's gross," he murmured, shaking his head and staring down at his feet. "They're sweaty. I've been working all day."

"You think I don't love that?"

I had half a mind to shove the balled-up material into my mouth so I could taste it, but that wasn't what I had planned for the night and if I was late getting us to Rapture, I didn't doubt for one second that my friends and their respective dates would herd themselves over to my house and let themselves in without knocking.

"I love the way you taste," I told him, putting the underwear into my pocket instead. "The way you feel and the way you smell. The way you sound when you call me Sir, even if you don't mean it in the ways that I want you to mean it."

He hummed at that, an indecipherable sound.

I helped him into the shower, leaving the door open so I could keep my hands on him. He tried to protest as the spray rained down onto the dark hunter green of my shirt, but I didn't care. I washed Rose thoroughly; then I shampooed his hair and rinsed him properly off. Once he was clean and had quit trying to argue with me, I wrapped him in a towel and let him dry himself in peace.

I'd gone shopping for him earlier in the evening, hoping he wouldn't protest over any of the things I'd wanted him to have. They were just as much for me as for him, I was ready to remind him, and I wasn't in the business of depriving myself of anything I wanted.

Rose found me in the bedroom, sitting on the edge of the bed beside the bag that held his gift. He eyed me thoughtfully from the doorway, backlit and glowing like an angel. Even though we were leaving soon, I had the fireplace on because I knew he liked it. I watched him drop the towel in the bathroom and pad across the room, the orange sparks from the fire casting him in a much more sinful glow than the white of the bathroom had allowed.

Without a word, I watched him shift his weight and straighten his spine, right his shoulders. He tipped his chin and tilted his head, like he was an impervious king staring down at his subjects, and it should have had me desperate to flip the roles, but I found that I liked the watchfulness, the dominance.

The pull between Rose and me would keep me honest.

"Would you kneel for *me*?" he asked, voice barely louder than a whisper over the crackle of the fireplace.

I'd do far more than kneel for him, I realized, a rush of adrenaline curling around my spine and almost sending me straight to his feet.

"If that was what you wanted."

My shirt was still wet from the shower, the water cooling and sending shivers down my arms. Rose took a step forward, then another and another and he was between my spread legs, fingers deftly working their way down the button front until I was naked from the waist up.

"What do *you* want?" he asked, tracing his fingers over my shoulders. He was so close I could touch him, so I wrapped my hands around his waist and kissed his stomach, slow and wet.

"I want to make you feel good."

"What else?"

I chuckled, nipping at the thin skin around his ribs until he wiggled away from me, his hands still on my shoulders, up into my hair. Rose tugged my head so I was forced to look up at him, and I let him because it made him happy to control me like that.

"I want..." I trailed off, not sure about admitting the idea that had just forced it's way to the front of my mind. I let the silence turn into a deliberative hum in the back of my throat, then I dragged my tongue across the front of my teeth.

"Tell me," he coaxed.

"I want to take you bare," I whispered. "I want to fill you full of cum and then put you back into your gorgeous panties and let it leak around and ruin the lace. I want you to bury yourself so deep inside of me that I can't tell where you end and I begin…"

His fingers tightened in my hair, his cock growing harder between us.

"I want you to ruin me for other men." As if he hadn't already. "And then I want to make you breakfast, make you lunch, make you dinner. I want to clean you and dry you and *keep* you. I want to take care of you in all the ways you deserve, even if you don't ever find the words to ask me to do it. I worry sometimes that I want to consume you."

Rose opened his mouth and snapped it closed, seemingly caught off-guard by the confession. I was hard by that point too, thinking about the truth of the words and all the ways I wanted to own and defile the man between my legs. We were already going to be late to Rapture, might as well go big.

"I want *you* to get onto your knees," I said, and he did. Without blinking, without thinking. His hips moved out of my hands and I finished loosening my pants, taking my cock out and holding it tight around the base. "I want you to like being here. Like this."

Rose's lashes fluttered, and I tapped my cock against his cheek, dragging it over his mouth and across his face. He parted his lips and stuck out his tongue, pupils dark and massive as black holes against the crystal blue of his irises.

"I do," he rasped, the words choking off as I pressed my cock against his waiting tongue.

"Suck on it," I told him, definitely not a question and almost a demand. I slid toward the back of his throat, pleasure roaring through me like an unstoppable tidal wave. He sealed his lips around me and swallowed me into the back of his throat in that way he always did.

Rose blinked up at me, tears already pooling in the corners of his eyes from the stretch. Using my fingers, I pushed his curls back from his face, relishing the way he preened under my attention, under my touch. I pulled all the way out, enjoying the way saliva tracked from my cock to his lips, slicking down his chin.

"I love sucking you off," he said, voice low and so reminiscent of the power he'd put on display the first night we spent together. "Love taking you apart with my mouth and ruining you for everyone else."

"There's no one but you, baby."

His eyes rolled back in their sockets a little and he angled his head to the side, using the tip of his tongue to lick the spit off his mouth.

"I want to call you Sir," he whispered. "In the ways that you want from me."

"Rose."

"Can I do that tonight? That's what would make me feel good. I can tell because my hands get tingly when I think about it."

I hadn't expected that, and I didn't know what to say. It felt indecent to sit there with my cock in his hand and Rose on his knees, him confessing to me an interest in something I'd been willing to table for later.

"And you said you wanted to make me feel good, right?" He widened his eyes, mouth opening and closing before he added on, "Sir."

I almost came on the spot.

"Anything for you, baby." It was a vow, and then Rose took my cock back into his mouth, back into his throat. "You're so good at sucking my cock. So good at being on your knees for me."

Rose groaned in agreement, the vibrations catapulting me headfirst toward the brink of my orgasm and head over heels into love with him.

CHAPTER 26
ROSE

With my head in the clouds from the things Flynn said to me during our little tryst, I could barely focus my eyes on the panties he'd bought for me. But as we climbed the front steps to Rapture, the soft lace and silk hugged my cock and balls like they'd been made to do it.

"Just know," Flynn whispered before we stepped through the front doors of the club, "no matter what happens tonight, we go home and I take those off of you with my teeth."

"You better."

I liked that he referred to his home that way, like it was a place for both of us to go. Like he expected me to come home with him when our outing was done. With any other man that would have infuriated me, but with Flynn…it made me feel very safe and very protected.

"My friends are normally upstairs," he said, the music almost immediately drowning out the sound of his voice. "Did you want to get a drink first?"

I looked up at Flynn and batted my lashes, hooking one of my fingers behind the placket of his shirt and pulling him down closer to me. "That's up to you, Sir."

He growled in response, and I couldn't fight the laugh that bubbled up out of me. I was absolutely and admittedly drunk with power, but I was far from under the illusion that Flynn was ever anything besides in control. He would have gotten onto his knees for me if I asked, but he knew that wasn't what I really wanted. I just wanted to see if he would. Maybe it was a bit of a test, but that felt reasonable.

"It does something to me when you call me that." He said the words right into my ear, one hand braced against the bar behind me and the other gentle against my waist.

"Do you want me to stop?"

"Do you want me to fuck you in a dark corner before we even make it home?"

I grinned. "I'll have a Sprite, Sir."

Flynn exhaled loudly and righted himself, taking our joined hands and using mine to adjust the bulge between his legs. Heat pooled low in my stomach at the feel of him. The knowledge that I was the one to put him on edge, to shove him over, and bring him back all at the same time? It was amazing.

Again.

Drunk with power.

But I didn't want to take advantage. I didn't want to lose my grip.

I wanted to get comfortable enough to allow Flynn the opportunity to give me all of the things *he* said I deserved.

Over my head, he ordered drinks and I scanned the crowd, curious if there were any familiar faces. I half expected to see Drake's bright pink hair, but it had been a few days since I'd connected with him and I didn't know what his plans were. I needed to be better about staying in touch, especially after the way he'd fielded Cody for me, but I was wrapped up with work, and Flynn, and fucking Flynn, and sucking Flynn, and—

"Here's your drink."

Flynn handed me a small glass filled with bubbling soda and a slice of lime. He had a whiskey in one hand, as usual, and my hand in the other. I was happy to follow behind, letting him navigate us around the corners of the dance floor. I didn't have to watch where I was going or worry about who was in my way. He moved us through the crowd like it had been practiced ahead of time, and a quiet voice in the back of my head wondered if that was what he meant when he talked about all the Sir things.

I knew it wasn't only for sex, but…

At the base of the stairs to the loft, he stopped and turned to face me, his expression almost worried and very serious.

"What's wrong?" I asked.

His attention flickered toward the loft before falling back to me. "My friends and I…we don't really have boundaries," he said.

"Are you telling me that you fuck them? Because I was under the impression that—"

"Jesus, no." Flynn raised up the hand with his drink, brows knitting together and his whole face turning sour. "I just told you I wanted to come inside of you. I didn't take that lightly."

A couple stumbled into us with a laugh, pushing past us and heading up the stairs. Flynn grabbed my hand with a grunt and hauled us out of the way and toward the wall, very close to where we had our first kiss.

"Not to misdirect, but if I didn't tell you earlier, I liked that whole train of thought you were on," I said. "We should get tested."

"And we will, but that wasn't the point."

"Boundaries," He repeated his statement from earlier. "We share beds sometimes. Share partners others."

"Often?" I tilted my head to the side, more curious than anything else.

"When the situation allows," he said. "Not since you. Not… there's no infidelity."

"Are you poly?"

It felt like something I should have asked ages ago, and the way Flynn shifted his weight nervously from foot to foot didn't do much to alleviate my worries.

"I'm whatever feels right at the time," he answered. "I told you I didn't do relationships before you and that's the truth. Have I been with more people than one at the same time? Also the truth. But I'm not a cheater."

I swallowed, looking down at my soda. "I didn't think you were."

"My friends and I…we've always been open with each other, with words and with actions."

"And partners," I reminded him.

"No touching without permission," he said quickly. "No engaging."

Something flashed across his face and everything clicked into place. The worry, the hesitance, the misunderstanding.

"You're telling me the lot of you like to watch."

Flynn took a huge swallow of his drink, like the whiskey would wash away his nerves. "We don't have to. They don't have to."

"I need you to stop." I pressed my hand against his chest, and he stood straighter, almost like I'd tapped a reset button. His hands hung down at his sides, fingers splayed over the top of his glass, the other hand tapping against the outside of his thigh. His expression had gone almost neutral, bringing into focus the sharp angles of his nose and his cheekbones, the softness of his lips.

"We can go," he offered.

"I said I need you to stop," I repeated.

Flynn went still.

I closed my eyes and dropped my head against the back wall, hating myself for all the seeds of doubt and worry I'd sown in this man's mind. I was young, but I should have been old enough to know better, should have had some shred of self-awareness so I could understand how my actions impacted others. On the tail end of Cody destroying my life with his carelessness, I should have been more careful myself. I should have stopped and thought.

I shouldn't have ever kissed Flynn the way I had.

I should have never let him compromise the things he wanted just to earn himself a shred of my time. Though the dedication did wonders for my ego and the praise was almost good enough to convince me it was true.

"I want you to answer me yes or no," I said, fingers still firm against his chest. "No explanations and no judgement. Just your truth. Can you do that?"

His jaw worked back and forth. I could tell he hated the limitations, hated being told what to do.

"Yes," he said gruffly.

"Do you want to watch whatever fuckery your friends get up to tonight?"

"Yes."

"Do you want me to watch it too?" I arched a brow.

"Yes." Another twitch in his jaw was enough to let me know that if he had more words, the answer would have been, *Yes, if you want to.*

"Do you want them to watch me?"

He held his hands up in the shape of a T.

I rolled my eyes. "What?"

"Doing what?" he asked.

"Let's assume that after this little game of questions is over, it's purely yes, Sir and no, Sir and thank you, Sir from me for the rest of the night."

My cock jerked at the thought of that, but I didn't let on.

"Is that what you want?" he asked.

Jesus, the way my man loved to please. I was going to get a complex about it. Earlier he'd been talking about how I ruined him, but I was the ruined one because how could I ever accept anything less than *this* from anyone ever again?

"Your time out is over," I said, ignoring him. "Do you want them to watch *me*?"

"Yes."

Another spasm down the length of my cock, but that one was impossible to hide. Flynn watched the way I shuffled my weight around, his eyes narrowed and focused like the predator he was.

I let my hand fall to his waist, fingers dancing across the top of his belt. "Would you like showing off what's yours?"

Flynn's nostrils flared, and I was certain we both thought about the new underwear he'd just dressed me up in before we left.

"Yes."

"Do you trust me to stop you if I'm uncomfortable?"

He inhaled a sharp breath, gaze dragging over my face as if he'd find the answer there. The silence stretched and he kept watching me, and I kept looking back at him with the same quiet expression I'd started with.

"Yes."

"Questions are over."

I'd barely gotten the words out before Flynn moved in. With a quick movement, he set his glass on a table and walked me back against the wall. His hands were free and he grabbed the under-side of my thighs, hoisting me up until our mouths were level, then he angled his head and crashed our lips together.

The ferocity of the kiss caught me off-guard, and my Sprite fell out of my hand, shattering at his feet. If it got him wet, Flynn didn't give any indication, instead wrapping my legs around his waist and spearing his tongue into the depths of my mouth. I slid my now free hands around his neck, tangling my fingers into his hair as he deepened the kiss.

Flynn's cock was hard and hot, pushed against my ass like if he had the power to fuck me through all of our layers of clothing, he would have managed it. He pressed my back against the wall to hold me steady, then his hands trailed up my legs and my sides, down my arms and somehow around to my head. He kissed me and held me until everything had gone blurry and hazy, and I couldn't remember why I'd ever not been sure of this man in the first place.

Because this kiss was so much like the first, but I knew Flynn better than I had that night. I'd become familiar with his hands and his body, his mouth, his moans. Flynn kissed me like he was in love with me, like he had been from the start. And that should have been an absurd idea, but I couldn't find a single shred of disbelief in me. Every action he'd taken lined up with the theory, and by the time he broke away for a breath, he'd proven the hypothesis.

I wished I hadn't been so quick to end the game because I knew Flynn would never lie to me, and the question was on the tip of my tongue…somewhere in the back of his throat.

"There's rooms upstairs made for this kind of thing," a voice said, very close to both our ears.

"Fuck off," Flynn muttered, barely moving away enough to get the words out.

Even at his denial, he slowed the kiss and I managed to pry my eyes open, finding a rather amused-looking Grayson standing half behind him with a young man I'd never met with him.

"You're an animal." Grayson smacked the back of Flynn's head, and Flynn rested his forehead against mine, breath hot against my already kiss-swollen lips. "Let Rose down."

I would have been happy to let Flynn fuck me into the wall, but there was more to whatever was between us than sex, so I gave my hips a wiggle and let my legs unwrap from his waist. Slowly, he lowered me to the floor and stood back at his full height, which dwarfed the three of us.

I patted my lips with the tips of my fingers, and Flynn scrubbed a frustrated hand down his face. I grabbed it and brought it to my mouth, kissing his fingers before letting his hand fall away.

My heart skipped, letting me know Flynn wasn't the only one in love, and I promised myself I would tell him.

Sooner rather than later.

Just not right then, because Grayson made a show of looking down at the massive erections between our legs and scoffing. He waved Flynn off and grabbed me by the crook of my arm, tugging me out from the pocket made by the wall and Flynn's imposing figure. I threw a glance over my shoulder, relieved to find Flynn looking relaxed, his mouth angled up into a quiet kind of laugh as Grayson hauled me away.

"Figure out how to get that under control, Rose," Grayson said, pulling me and the third man back toward the stairs. "Because this is Owen. Owen, this is Rose, and I think the two of you are going to be great friends."

CHAPTER 27

FLYNN

KNOWING ROSE WAS IN SAFE—IF NOT IMPULSIVE—HANDS, I TOOK A minute to recover my breath and my composure after Grayson and Owen hauled him up the stairs. Rose, for his part, seemed comfortable enough with Grayson from their first meeting that I didn't feel the need to interfere. My suspicions were confirmed when I did make it up the stairs and found the three of them leaning against a wall in the corner. Grayson had a drink and an animated expression on his face while he talked and gestured wildly with his hands.

"He's settling in well," Dalton said from the couch, prompting me to tear my attention away from Rose and let it land on my friends.

Dalton sat on the couch with Archie beside him, who eyed Owen like a hawk. Rob sat alone at a chair across from them, back to Grayson.

"Where's Barclay?" I asked, taking the empty seat next to Rob.

"Home arguing with Val," Dalton muttered, shaking his head.

Archie took a sip of his whiskey and rolled his eyes. "For someone who isn't in love…"

"Whatever is going on with him and Val is complicated," Dalton said.

"Do you know more than the rest of us?" I asked.

"Of course I do." He grinned at me.

"He's our friend," Rob said.

"And he's fine," Dalton promised. "He's been reeling a little since Dennis's engagement and Val has been handling the brunt of it. That's all."

"That's not fair for Val," I said.

"Lots of things aren't fair for Val," Rob added.

"Val is an adult," Dalton reminded us. "He can make his own choices."

"It's no fun to talk about them when they're not here." Archie's attention again flickered over Rob's shoulder toward Rose, Owen, and Grayson in the corner. Owen was the one talking now, far more subdued than Grayson could ever be. I turned my gaze back to Archie and watched a soft smile flutter across his face while he observed them.

"Let's talk about yours," he said, the soft expression turning quickly into a sharp and devilish grin.

"Yes," Dalton agreed. "Lets."

"What do you want me to say? You've met him before."

"Meeting someone at work isn't the same as meeting them in the wild," Archie said. "And I'm personally offended that Grayson has spent more time with him than the rest of us."

"Owen has too, at this rate," I said.

Dalton rolled his eyes. "Owen talking to him is the best thing that could happen to either of you."

"How do you figure?"

"I don't want to make assumptions here, friend, but I would wager that the two of them have more in common than the two of you."

"I doubt Flynn has been secretly in love with Rose his whole life." Archie laughed.

As much as it pleased me to see my friend able to make light of the ten years he spent estranged from the man he was clearly meant to spend the rest of his life with, there was some subtle kind of truth in his words.

Maybe I hadn't known it was Rose specifically, but had I been waiting for a man like him my whole life? Absolutely. I hadn't expected him to be younger than me, and I hadn't planned on being in my thirties by the time I found him, but he was here now and I knew. I understood why my brain hadn't wanted me to bother with anyone else who'd dared to come before him. It felt almost like I'd been saving a part of myself for him, and that was special.

If not mentally unhinged.

But I was in love with Rose Baker, and I wanted to be looking in his eyes the moment he realized he was in love with me too.

I'd almost told him as much earlier, but thought better.

"I like him," I said.

"You love him," Rob corrected, and even in the dark of the loft, the flush that colored my face was enough of a tell to earn a whoop out of Archie. A sound so loud it drew the attention of the three men huddled in the corner, brows knit together in some kind of serious concentration and discussion.

"He doesn't know."

"He does," Rob said. "He just hasn't told you he knows."

My breath lodged in my throat, but Rose was headed back to me at that point, flanked by Grayson and Owen on either side of them. Grayson kicked the edge of Rob's shoe until Rob let his arm fall off the armrest of the chair, and Grayson lowered himself to perch on the edge. Rob's hand returned protectively to his knee at the same time Archie hauled Owen right down onto his lap, and Rose came around to stand beside me, unsure of where to go or what to do next.

"Everything good?" I asked, reaching for his hand.

His jaw was set, but not tense, like he'd made some sort of decision over there in the corner and, for better or worse, he was going to stick with it.

"Did you want to sit?"

The corner of his mouth twisted into something that was almost a smile, but mostly a grimace.

"Can I…" Rose trailed off, but used his body to finish the sentence. His knees landed on the floor beside my feet and he folded his hands together across the top of my knee, blinking up at me with wide and unsure eyes.

I knew Archie said something, or maybe it was Dalton, but I didn't hear the words over the whooshing in my ears as my focus widened and then narrowed down to one singular point in front of me.

"You don't have to do this," I said.

It wasn't that I didn't want it, but…

I supposed there was no but, really.

"I want to see how it feels." Rose cleared his throat and tipped his chin down. "Sir."

"You're going to make him come in his pants," Grayson said.

"How embarrassing," Archie chimed in.

I gave the both of them the finger, my stare still locked on Rose and the angelic expression that had manifested on his face as soon as he landed on his knees.

"Do you like it?" he asked softly. "Do you like me here?"

"I like you everywhere," I promised him, the very real truth.

"But here especially?"

I managed a nod, still in awe of the sight before me.

"What did you and Owen and Grayson talk about?" I asked. "You don't have to tell me if you don't want to."

"Are you worried?" He tilted his head to the side, chin angled up again like he did when he was trying to be brave.

Like a king on his fucking knees for me.

"Curious."

"Owen had a lot to say," he whispered, changing the direction of his head tilt, clearly still processing whatever they'd discussed. "And I don't want to tell you the whole of it, but I swear it was good."

"Obviously, if it brought you to your knees."

I petted my hand across the top of his head, threading my fingers through his hair and appreciating the softness of his blond curls. The hum he let loose vibrated up through my bones and I fought the urge to tighten my hand and pull.

"I like being on my knees for you," he said. "At least I like it when your cock is in my mouth. I didn't think there'd be any harm in trying it without."

A knot of worry that I didn't even realize had tied itself together in the center of my chest unfurled at his words, and I grabbed Rose under his armpits and hauled him up onto my lap. He was slim and small, and he landed easily against the tops of my thighs. He squished his legs on either side of me to get a proper straddle, and I held him steady with my hands around his waist.

There'd evidently been a part of me that was worried this was all for me, not for him. That we'd both made concessions for each other at the beginning of our relationship and this was another one of them. But as he arranged himself against me, the swell between his legs burned hot and apparent, a reminder to me that Rose wouldn't do a single thing that didn't please him. And I knew, I trusted in the very depths of my gut, that if there ever came a day when *I* no longer pleased him, he wouldn't do me anymore either.

"I think I'm in love with you," I whispered.

Rose's mouth split into a grin and he rolled his eyes at me, a small shake of his head to go along with it.

"I know you're in love with me," he said.

Not the response I'd been hoping for, but…

He leaned down, his glossy lips sticky and warm against the shell of my ear. "I think I'm very close to falling in love with you too, Mr. Galloway."

I groaned at that, fingers bearing down around the soft curves of his waist.

"Say that again."

"I'm close to falling in love with you." He bit my earlobe and I bucked up out of the chair, grinding him down hard onto my lap.

"The other part."

Rose chuckled low. "Mr. Galloway?"

"That's a thousand times better than Sir."

No one had ever, at least not outside of a business context, but something about the way my last name sounded coming out of Rose's mouth like that, thick with sex and promise?

It would be my undoing.

"You like that, Mr. Galloway?"

He was a little shit, and he knew exactly what he was doing. So, I was thankful he didn't stop me when I slid my hand around to the front of his shorts to busy myself with the fly.

"Right here?" he asked.

"Unless you want something more private."

My fingertips dragged across the lace of the newest pair of panties I'd bought for him and I worried Archie's earlier commentary about me coming in my pants was treacherously close to coming true.

"Can I have both?"

"Jesus Christ." With my free hand, I grabbed the back of his neck and kept his face buried against the side of my throat, both our mouths beside the others ears.

I shoved my hand behind the waistband of his underwear and fisted his dick, long and hard, thick and already wet with precum smeared all across the tip. Rose moaned into my ear, hips giving a little buck.

"My friends are all watching you," I whispered, stroking him down to the root. "They're watching you writhe around my lap with your cock out. They're watching what's mine. Do you remember that time we were together, Rose? When I told you your body was mine?"

He managed a whimper.

Our bodies were so tightly squeezed together, it was hard for my hand to move, but judging by the way his cock twitched in my hand while I spoke, he was already dangerously close to coming.

"I want you to know how lucky you are," I went on. "Sometimes Archie doesn't let Owen come for days."

"I would die," he rasped.

"Owen loves it. He begs for it."

"I'd die," he said again, digging his forehead into the side of my face.

"I'd never make you wait, baby," I promised him. "You're too perfect when you come. I want to see it every day."

"Every day," he murmured. "Every day, every, oh, God…"

"You're gorgeous when you want it. Humping my lap and fucking my fist like you've never had an orgasm in your life."

He huffed out a desperate sound, teeth flashing against the shell of my ear.

"Look how much I'll give you when you get on your knees for me. I'll give you everything, Rose. I swear it. Everything."

"Just you."

"Everything," I repeated.

"You."

I tightened my hold, pressing the side of my thumb against the slit of his cock. The heat between his legs burned like a furnace, and Rose moaned, throwing his head back in line with the long curve of his spine.

"Everything," I said one more time.

His muscles seized and he fell forward, hot jets of cum spurting out against my fingers.

"Everything," he choked out between breathy sobs and gasps. "I want all of it. All of you. Flynn. Mr. Galloway. Oh, *God…*"

Another fountain of cum leaked out of his cock, and I jacked him off through the entirety of his orgasm until he went soft and boneless in the safety of my lap.

"It's yours," I said, tucking him back into his soiled panties and doing up his shorts. I shifted him around with his back against my chest and he curled up in my lap like a tired cat. On the other side of the room, Grayson and Dalton had a man I'd never seen before trussed up in ropes, hanging from the ceiling with his cock so ready to burst, it was purple.

"It's yours," I said again to Rose. "*I* am yours."

"His money isn't going away," Owen had told me once we got into the loft and he and Grayson pressed me into a quiet corner. "You can either love him with it or not at all."

The conversation had rattled through my brain the entire night, and when they'd said their piece and we'd split off to go find our men, going to my knees at Flynn's feet had felt as natural as breathing. It hadn't felt like a concession in any way, and I wondered—I hoped—I was finally seeing the light at the end of the tunnel with him. That I'd gotten over *myself* enough to feel okay with the things he liked.

Or better than okay.

I felt good about them.

Really good.

And it was that feeling that had carried me right into Flynn's arms and a dark corner of the loft, with my brand new cum-stained panties shoved into my mouth to muffle my shouts and his cock so deep inside of me I couldn't tell where our bodies became separate.

He came with his teeth buried in the side of my neck, sweaty forehead against my ear and a thousand promises on his tongue.

And I believed every single one.

Flynn was gentle when he put me down, and the panties went into his pocket. His second collection of the night.

"Is that why you want to buy me so many?" I asked, doing up my shorts and hoping my balls didn't hang out the leg. "So you can steal them all back?"

"I want to buy you so many because I like the way you smile when you put them on."

"And when you take them off," I said.

He kissed the top of my head. "The best smile of the two, that's for sure."

"What about when you get me off?"

"That's less of a smile and more of a…" He made a slack-jawed expression which I sincerely hoped looked *nothing* like my actual orgasm face, but I ignored the hilarity of his expression, tucked myself against his side, and threaded our fingers together.

"Mr. Galloway, you need to take some acting lessons if that's what you think I look like."

"How do you know?" he asked. "Have you ever seen yourself?"

"I don't make a habit of watching."

Flynn dragged me to a stop and brought his lips against my ear, immediately sending a shiver up my spine. "We'll have to change that very soon then, won't we?"

"Will we?"

He made an affirmative hum in the back of his throat and resumed walking toward the stairs.

The night had been awesome. Watching Grayson and Dalton rig someone up to the ceiling before making him come and cry at the same time was insanely hot, and Flynn's hands all over me the whole time hadn't hurt the situation at all either. The ease with which his friends accepted me into their little group made me feel like I belonged, not just with them, but also with Flynn.

"Trophy Doms!" Grayson stood up from his perch on Rob's lap and swirled his finger in the air. "Assemble."

"You're laughable," Dalton said, even as he stood.

"Wait, Trophy Doms?" I asked.

Grayson laughed, his posture a little wobbly from all the drinking he'd done after his little scene earlier in the night.

"The whole lot of them," he explained. "Easy on the eyes with bank accounts to match. All of them a catch except Flynn, of course."

"What the fuck, Grayson?" Flynn scoffed at the barb.

"With a couch like that."

I laughed, bringing our joined hands to my mouth and dusting a kiss across his knuckles.

"The couch is bad," I reminded him before turning toward Grayson. "But you know that you're one of them, right?"

"I am not." Grayson folded his arms across his chest like a child, which earned a quick smack on the ass from Rob, who also stood.

"You are," Owen agreed, head resting on Archie's shoulder.

The night had been fun, but long, and it was clear in everyone's body language it was time to pack it in. I didn't think last call was far off anyway, so better to get out ahead of things.

"You're kidding me."

"Your shoes are six hundred dollars," Rob said. "You're not excluded from the club just because you're new."

"What about them?" Grayson waggled his finger between Owen and me.

"We're lucky," Owen said, giving Archie's hand a tug. "And I'm about to get luckier if you could go have your identity crisis elsewhere."

"I was going to invite you back to the house, but not after that," Grayson mumbled.

Rob laughed and wrapped him in a hug, and I loved the way he dwarfed Grayson, arms coming fully around him and protecting him from the—very warranted—accusations against his character.

"I'll be taking Rose home," Flynn said, "To fuck him on that horrible couch of mine."

"Rose." Grayson untangled himself from Rob's arms. "Be sure to stain it beyond repair so he has to get a new one."

I laughed again and promised him I'd do my best, but halfway down the stairs Flynn said to me, his expression earnest and sincere, "You know if you hate it so much, I'd replace it anyway."

"It's your couch," I said, thinking back again to my conversation with Owen and Grayson earlier in the night. I had to take all of Flynn, money and bad taste included, just like had had to take all of me, even the doubt and insecurities that I didn't think I'd be able to ever fully shake.

"I want you to be comfortable in my home," he said.

We reached the bottom of the stairs. The crowd had noticeably thinned out from earlier in the evening, so finding Drake's pink hair in the middle of the dance floor was easy and also unexpected. Even more unexpected, the man he was with.

"You've got to be kidding me," I groaned, suddenly all too aware of the nakedness under my shorts, the air against my cock and balls, the tension that immediately took root in my chest.

"It's the truth," Flynn said, wholly unaware.

"Not that." I sighed, jerking my chin toward the cocktail table where my best friend and ex-boyfriend stood in heated conversation. "Him."

"Who?"

"The one with pink hair is my best friend, Drake. The other is my ex."

"The one Grayson met?"

The change in Flynn was immediate. He didn't let go of my hand, but he squared his shoulders and stood straighter. His posture was almost casual, save for the tight grip he had on my hand that gave him away.

I didn't know how long this was going to be my life for, how many times I would have to tell Cody to leave me and my friends alone. I wasn't stupid enough to think that I'd never run into him. We ran in the same circles and had some of the same friends, but Drake wasn't one of them.

Upon closer approach, I could see the anger in Drake's mouth, the tiredness around his eyes. Whatever was happening, they were arguing. Cody looked the same way he had when he came to my house with his fake apologies, like he was running out of sincerity and about to show his true colors.

By the time I realized what he was doing, Flynn had pulled me to the table, inserting himself at Cody's side and leaving me next to Drake.

"Hey," I muttered, giving Drake as much of an apologetic look as I could muster. I would have given anything for my underwear.

"I didn't know you were here," he said.

"I didn't think to invite you," I told him. "I was meeting Flynn's friends officially."

Drake's stare darted to Flynn, and an amused smile flashed across his mouth.

"You can make it up to me," he promised, stretching his hand out toward Flynn and ignoring Cody's existence. "I'm Drake. It's nice to finally meet the man who has stolen dear Rosie's heart."

Flynn returned the gesture, angling his back to Cody, who of course took it as an offense.

"I'm right here, and I was having a conversation," he snapped.

Flynn didn't even turn around. "And it's finished now."

"Says who? Says you?" Cody scoffed, balls always too big for his own good.

Flynn, for his part, looked near giddy. He took my face into his hands and pressed his lips against mine, kissing me until I moaned and opened my lips to him.

"Don't hate me for this," he whispered, turning his back on me and glaring down at Cody.

Drake grabbed my hand and pulled me back, making us both observers on the shit show that had become my life. All I wanted was for Cody to leave me in peace. He clearly didn't have any respect for me or for what our relationship had been, so I struggled to understand why he was so fixated on weaseling his way back in.

And to think, there had been a time in the not-so-distant past when I would have allowed it because I thought that was the kind of treatment I deserved. It hadn't been so long ago that I'd really believed I couldn't do better than a man like him. I found myself indescribably thankful for him and the way he'd opened my eyes.

Love exploded in my chest, and I wanted to tell him. I wanted him to know I loved him too. I needed him to understand that, in a very nondramatic way, his love had saved me from a lifetime of mediocrity. Flynn had come into my world on accident, turned it upside down with a kiss, and changed the whole course of my life.

"I'm not afraid of you," Cody said, no doubt in retaliation to whatever greeting Flynn had offered him. "I wasn't scared of the other one either."

Flynn looked over his shoulder at me and I shrugged. "Grayson?" I guessed.

Flynn nodded and looked back to Cody.

"From what I understand, you stuck your cock where it didn't belong and you're not mature enough to deal with the consequences of that," he said.

Cody stammered, unable to build a response before Flynn started back in.

"It's a hard lesson to learn," he went on. "I remember the first deal I lost. It stung, but what I didn't do was run around town making it everyone else's problem."

"You don't even know what you're talking about," Cody protested. "He's just using you to get over me. You're nothing more than a rebound. He'll be back."

"It's cute that you think that, so I won't tear that fantasy away from you just yet. But what I will do is tell you that I am exhaustingly tired of hearing your name come up, and even though I've only seen you once, I'm already tired of your face."

"Oh, my *Godddddd!*" Drake whisper-yelled in my ear, very nearly jumping up and down in place. "I tried to tell him that earlier, but he wouldn't listen."

My pulse skittered, and I held on tighter to him, worried I was going to fall. Soft material brushed up against the backs of my thighs and I looked over my shoulder, finding Grayson right behind me, with Rob behind him, and Archie and Owen to the side. Dalton filled in a gap beside Drake, arms crossed in front of his chest. All of their eyes were focused on the back of Flynn's head.

"I know you've already been told to leave Rose alone, and since you're out here harassing his best friend, I imagine you haven't taken that warning to heart. And if you don't think I have the interest or ability to *make* you, then you are sorely mistaken."

"I don't even know who you are," Cody croaked, realizing a flank of men had come to stand behind me.

To stand…for me.

With me?

"I'm the man who is reaping the benefits of your mistakes, for one. I'm also the man who is about to get you blacklisted from this club."

"Already done," Rob said.

Cody's eyes went wide and his mouth fell open like a caught fish.

"I'm also the man who knows more about you than you think possible, so if you come around here again, if you bother Rose again, or any of his friends, I'll be calling your father and letting him know that the way you treat men isn't a once-off, but a trend."

Wait.

What?

"What?" Cody repeated my thought out loud, and Flynn shook his head.

"I'm a man who does my research, Dakota, and I would much rather take Rose to bed than make that phone call, so please don't make me."

"All that from a license plate," Grayson mused.

"Are we good here?" Flynn asked, fishing his cell phone out of his pocket.

"We're good." Cody raised his hands and took a step back from the table.

"I thought so."

Flynn kept his phone out until Cody was gone, then he turned to me, almost all the bravado gone. "Please don't hate me for that," he said quietly.

"Hate you?" An unexpected laugh tumbled out of my mouth and I jumped into his arms. He caught me, stumbling back before righting himself and holding me up with his hands on the backs of my thighs. "I don't think that's anything in the realm of possibility, Mr. Galloway."

"THAT WAS REALLY FUCKING HOT," ROSE'S FRIEND DRAKE SAID, fanning himself as I lowered Rose back down to the ground. "If you weren't already spoken for—"

"He's *very* spoken for," Rose said, spinning around and smacking Drake in the face. The two of them laughed, and then Rose leaned back against me with a quiet sigh.

"Well, I think it's only fair." Drake steepled his hands together in front of him and tapped his fingers.

"What is?" I asked.

"Rose was here tonight to officially meet your friends." He gestured at the group of them who'd gathered during my talk with Rose's shitbag ex, Cody. "So now it's time for you to officially meet *me*."

"I'm tired, Drake," Rose whined, head dropped back against my chest.

"Just a burger and shakes, like we used to? Quick and dirty. Like me." Drake grinned, looking as devious as Rose had the night we met.

"I'm in," Dalton said, arching a brow.

"We are very out," Rob said, giving Grayson a pull toward the door.

"And so are we," Archie added. "But not for lack of interest. Just old and tired."

"I'm not old," Grayson protested, but he yawned and shuffled off without another protest.

"The four of us then?" Drake asked, giving Dalton a serious onceover.

"Is that fine with you?" I asked Rose.

"Yeah, but…can we talk first?" He turned and slid his arms around my waist, blinking up at me, expression still as washed in arousal as it had been when he jumped into my arms.

"Of course."

"We'll wait outside." Dalton hooked an arm around Drake's shoulders and the two of them headed toward the front of the club, leaving us alone at the table.

The house lights flipped on, and we both squinted, horrified at the sharp glare of the cool white fluorescent bulbs as they lit up the few remaining patrons.

"God, that's awful." He scrubbed a hand down his face and sighed, taking a step back and letting me get a better look at him.

"Are you upset with me?" I knew I'd acted out of turn with not just what I'd said to Cody, but what I'd done up until that point.

Grayson had written down Cody's plate, sending it my way after their first encounter in the alley. He'd had a bad feeling about Cody and in more than one way. He'd just wanted me to be aware, he'd said. I took the concern to heart, knowing from the start that nothing was going to hurt Rose as long as I was part of his life, so I'd called in a favor and run the plate to get a name. I'd found a lot more than I bargained for alongside it, including the names of his parents and sister, their legal complaints against him, a not even close to being finalized divorce decree.

"Why would I be upset with *you*?" Rose looked at me like the idea was obscene.

"Because I have more money than sense?"

A soft smile flitted across his face and his cheeks turned pink.

"I've always rather liked that about you. So, you ran his background?"

I nodded.

"Anything damning?"

"Did you know he's married?" I asked.

Rose let out a huff and shrugged. "Divorcing, he said."

"Not final."

"That…that's to be expected, I think."

"I'm not bringing it up to make you feel bad," I told him.

"I wasn't the other man."

"I never thought you were." I grabbed him and hauled him back against my chest, holding him and doing my best to protect him from the world that had been so unfair to him before we met.

And the night had started so well too.

The shower at my house, the blow jobs, the panties, the fucking. All of it had been so absolutely perfect. But more than that, Rose knew I loved him, and that hadn't scared him nearly as much as it had scared me. Even though he was in front of me again, looking as lost as he had the night he showed up and tried to break up with me.

"Don't let him ruin this," I said.

"I don't want to."

Reaching into my pocket, I pulled his most recently soiled pair of underwear out and raised them to my face where I took a long inhale of the fabric. Rose's flush deepened as I rubbed the panties across my mouth before returning them to my pocket.

"Nothing is going to take away from how gorgeous you looked tonight on your knees for me. On your back for me. Up in the air…"

He groaned and covered his cheeks, turning away. "There's something about doing this in the daylight that's really embarrassing."

"If you think I'm going to turn the lights off while I fuck you in front of the mirror later, you have another thing coming," I murmured.

"What if I want to fuck *you*?" he countered, brow arched. "You know I like being told that I'm good at giving just as much as receiving."

"You're going to make me cancel on your friend."

Rose barked out a laugh. "Oh shit, Drake. We should go."

"I'm sure Dalton has him occupied," I said, following Rose out of the church, mesmerized by the way the bottom of his ass cheeks hung out from beneath the hem of his extremely short shorts. He wasn't wearing anything underneath, and I could just reach right up and touch him if I wanted…

"You weren't kidding," Rose said, coming to a stop after finding Dalton with Drake up against the wall, hands pinned against the bricks and a thigh between his legs. "Are all of you like this? Just taking what you want?"

"Only if it's freely given."

"Always?"

"Unless there are rules in place," I said.

Rose dragged his tongue across the front of his teeth.

"Duly noted." He clapped his hands together, which was enough to startle Drake, but not Dalton. "Let's go. I'm tired and I get to have sex when I get home."

"You had sex upstairs," Drake countered, the words tapering off into a moan as Dalton drove his thigh higher between Drake's spread legs.

"I like that," I whispered into Rose's ear. "That you didn't specify it was *my* home."

"If what's mine is yours, like this cock, this ass." He wiggled said ass. "Then isn't what's yours mine?"

"All of it."

A small smile flashed across his mouth before disappearing. "Let's go. They can meet us there."

"Walking?" I asked.

"It's just a few blocks down." Rose took my hand like it was his to hold, and in every way that mattered, it very much was.

He glanced over his shoulder at the edge of the parking lot,

Dalton and Drake still flush against the building. "Dalton's a good guy, right?"

"He's a teddy bear."

"Drake has claws," Rose said.

"I think they'll be fine."

Dalton had a list of kinks a mile long, but in the years since I'd met him, I'd never seen him get in over his head, and I didn't imagine Rose's pink-haired friend was going to be the one to change that.

"Are you sure you're okay coming out with us?" Rose asked, rounding the corner away from the club.

"Why wouldn't I be?"

"It's…not like what you and your friends normally do."

"I assure you my friends and I eat often."

"None of you strike me as the greasy diner type," he said.

I dragged him to a stop, ready to put the money conversation to rest once and for all. There were a lot of things about me that I would change if I had to, if I wanted to, but my money wasn't one of them. I loved Rose, I truly knew that to be true, but I didn't want to have the money conversation with him every day.

"We have to stop doing this."

"Walking?" He played dumb, but he knew what I was talking about.

I pulled my wallet out of my back pocket and shoved it into his hands, and he pursed his lips, glaring up at me.

"My license is in there, my corporate card, my Amex, probably a thousand dollars in cash—"

He cut me off. "You carry my rent around like spending money."

"It is, Rose. For me it is. Can you be okay with that?"

Slowly, like it was a bomb, he unfolded my wallet and peered inside. The edge of his finger dragged over the thick metal of my Amex before walking over to the billfold and fanning through the hundred dollar bills and twenties I'd shoved in there the last time I went to the bank.

All of it was nothing to me. The balance on the cards, the quality of the leather, even the cash itself. I had plenty, and I had more. I had so much more than he could clean out all the cash in his hands and I wouldn't even notice the loss. And maybe that was irresponsible or stupid, or maybe I deserved a walk to the guillotine over it, but I didn't care.

I'd worked very hard for a very long time to have the things I had. To be comfortable and secure financially, to know that if my friends needed help, I could support them and not blink over it. That was what had always been important, what success looked like for me.

And for so many years I'd thought that was it. I'd considered my life good, solid, beyond compare. Even after Rob fell in love with Grayson, I didn't see any shortcomings on my side of things. Love wasn't something I'd ever chased after or pined over. Archie went next, and still I was fine.

It wasn't until I met Rose that I understood the gravity of the feelings that had taken two of my closest friends down to their knees…figuratively, of course. At least, I assumed as much. It wasn't until Rose that I'd understood the way all the things I'd done brought me right to him. And even if he wasn't ready for me, that was fine. I was stubborn and patient, and arrogant enough to wait him out.

"Do you want it?" I asked, willing to offer more than myself, more than my heart. The money was nothing compared to what I'd already given him—I wished he could see that. "Take the cash, it's yours."

"I don't want your money. I'm not a prostitute."

"That conversation is an old and tired one too. We had it. I thought we'd put it to bed," I reminded him.

"I don't need you to pay my rent." He flipped the wallet closed and shoved it back into my hands. "That's not what I want from you."

"What if I wanted to pay your rent?"

"Do you?" He cocked his head to the side.

"That wasn't what I asked."

"I don't want that from you," he said again, like he was trying to convince us both, when in reality we both knew how much easier things would be for us both if he'd let me. But I would fight that battle another day.

"You already have the most important parts of me," I told him. "This is nothing."

I put my wallet back into my pocket and folded my arms in front of my chest, waiting for his answer. Rose glared at me, ever aroused and ever defiant, always fighting against himself for no reason at all. But I'd fought the battle over being casual or serious with him and won. I fought his ex for him and won. The money battle wasn't going to be an exception to the trend.

"It's nothing for you."

"What if I *wanted* to pay your rent?" I asked. "What if it made me hard to know that you were safe and taken care of? What if I liked knowing I had an entire other house I could fuck you in if I wanted?"

"Apartment."

"What if I enjoyed it?" I pressed. "Would you deny me?"

"I'd rather you spend the money on panties and a new couch," he muttered.

I grinned, letting my arms fall. "Deal. Dalton and Drake are right behind us, so let's get to the diner. Lead the way."

Rose knew I'd bested him, but he also recognized there was no other outcome to the situation for him. I was stubborn, but never to be mean or hurtful, and he'd have to get used to it. I *wanted* him to get used to it.

"Thank you," I whispered to him, taking the victory.

"Please don't pay my rent," he said. "And please don't do something insane like buy the building I live in."

That earned a laugh and a tighter hold on his hand.

"That's rule number four of the Trophy Doms," I told him, making up the number for something that *had* been a longstanding agreement amongst the five of us. "Don't buy buildings out from under your friends."

"Oh, my GOD!" he yelled, stomping his feet on the sidewalk before smacking me on the arm. "Which one of them owns my building?"

I hooked my arm around his neck and pulled him close. He came, if not begrudgingly, sliding his arm around my waist and falling back into step beside me.

"Rob does."

"Rich asshole."

By then, Dalton and Drake had caught up to us.

"That's kind of who we are," Dalton said, and I winked at him over the top of both Rose's and Drake's heads. "It's in the name."

"I think you've done well for yourself, Rosie," Drake said, kicking Rose in the back of the knee. "This one seems like a keeper."

"He's something alright."

"What am I?" Dalton asked.

"A mistake," Drake said, laughing. "Now can we please get burgers? I'm hungry and horny, and I don't want to get mean."

QUICK BURGERS AND MILKSHAKES AT TWO TURNED INTO COLD FRENCH fries at sunrise. Stumbling over the threshold of Flynn's house just shy of six in the morning meant I had enough energy to get to his bedroom and not much else. Together, we collapsed on top of the sheets, fully dressed, his arm and leg thrown over me rather unceremoniously.

If I didn't know better, I would have thought he was trying to pin me down so I couldn't leave.

As if I would.

Spending time with him outside of what I'd always considered to be *his* natural environment had been enlightening. I was quick to realize that he was the same man, whether he was with his rich friends or me and Drake. Even when we were alone, though his mouth ran a little dirtier when we weren't in public, he was always authentically himself.

And I loved all of him.

I'd been caught off-guard when he admitted it earlier in the night, the night before, whatever the time had been, but it hadn't been a scary confession. It had felt right to me in an indescribable kind of way. Like I was me and he was him, and of course he loved me. What else was there for him to do? Thinking about it that way made me feel terribly arrogant, and I wondered if that was how he always felt.

But there was another part to the equation that I hadn't dared to admit out loud yet.

I was me and he was him. He loved me and…

I was also very much in love with him.

In the light of the late morning, I woke with the glaring heat of Flynn's body behind me and the bright rays of nearly afternoon sun streaking across the foot of the bed. At some point during my sleep, I'd taken my clothes off, or maybe Flynn had taken them off for me. He was naked too, cock half hard against the small of my back.

In that moment, I found myself desperately wishing that we'd already gotten tested because it would be so hot to just lube him up while he slept and slip him inside of me. There were times in my life when I'd risked it, but after finding out that Cody cheated on me, there was no way I'd do that to Flynn. Even as I reminded myself of that thought, the urge to feel him bare, to *take* him bare, gnawed at me.

It was Saturday afternoon, there had to be a clinic open somewhere.

But it was also Saturday afternoon and I had to work the dinner shift later that night. Because my job wasn't like Flynn's, my life wasn't like his. I loved the idea of him paying my rent, even though I would never ask for it and I would most certainly not allow it. Not having to stress about money would be a whole new chapter in life for me, and I supposed I didn't have to stress. Because even though I didn't want Flynn's money, I knew it was there if I needed it?

That felt like some kind of a concession.

Behind me, Flynn stirred, fingertips skating low across the bottom of my stomach and tangling through the golden patch of curls at the base of my shaft.

"Do you work later?" he mumbled, still half asleep as his lips sought out the angle of my shoulder blade for a kiss.

"At four."

"What time is it now?"

"No idea," I said.

"It's not very romantic…" Flynn stretched out and yawned, not letting go of the loose grip he'd fastened around my dick. "But can we go get tested today?"

My muscles went taut, and I stilled beneath his hands.

"Are you worried?"

"Worried that if I don't fuck you without a condom before the end of the day that I'm going to lose my goddamn mind."

Another kiss against my shoulder blade, this time with a slow pull down my length.

"I was just thinking the same thing," I admitted with a moan.

"Does that mean I passed the best friend test?"

Flynn had obliterated the best friend test with how much he'd passed it, but I didn't want the win to go to his head. Drake had caught me in the bathroom long after our burgers were eaten and in no uncertain terms told me if I ruined things with a man like Flynn, he would end our friendship for good. If I didn't know better, I would have thought Drake had fallen in love with Flynn overnight, but it was me. Drake loved me and I loved Flynn, and he saw the happiness in that.

"He doesn't hate you," I said with a grin.

"He doesn't hate Dalton either."

"Drake knows a good time when he sees it." Flynn was still tugging on my cock, and I dropped my head back against his chest with a sigh. "That feels so good."

He hummed thoughtfully, fumbling around behind him it sounded like before bringing his body and his attention back to me.

"I'm addicted to the way you react when I touch you."

My lashes fluttered and closed.

"How do I move?" I asked, barely louder than a breath.

Flynn moved around more behind me, and then two slippery and cold fingers made their way toward my ass, spreading and pressing inside. My back bowed and arched like a ripple wave as the sensation of being so carefully penetrated blew over me.

"Like no one has ever touched you the way I do," he whispered, keeping me close as he pushed both of his fingers all the way into my channel. His other hand continued offering it's casual attention to my cock, and maybe it was the late hour or the lack of sleep, but my brain was ready to short-circuit.

"No one has."

"Don't stop," he said with a low laugh. "You're doing wonders for my ego."

"Your ego doesn't need any he—"

A third finger seeking entrance stole my breath, but Flynn's hold on me remained steady and there was nowhere for me to go but around and against him.

"You were saying?"

"Nothing."

Flynn prepped me with his fingers until sweat broke out across my temple and my dick was leaking so much precum, it had to look like a miniature version of the Trevi fountain.

His fingers went away, and my balls throbbed at the sound of a condom wrapper opening, and then he was back and he was in, pulling me against him with both hands held firm around me. Flynn's breath shuddered in my ear as he seated himself and I hiked up one of my legs toward my chest so he could go deeper.

We'd had a lot of sex in the time we'd been together, the time we'd known each other, but something about this one felt different. Maybe it was the confession of love that hung between us or the acceptance that we were two very different people who happened to have affectionate feelings for each other. But he moved inside of me slow and with purpose, hands roaming over my body as my own scrabbled behind me to try and find purchase.

Every pump of his hips burned like his body stoked an invisible fire inside of me. One that was very close to raging out of control.

"I want to see you," I rasped, finally getting my fingers into his hair.

He shifted as best he could, managing to keep most of his cock inside as he laid me on my back and rearranged himself between my legs. I bent my knees and stretched wide to make room for him, tracing my fingertips across his cheekbones when he bottomed out.

Flynn's eyes were closed and I could barely breathe, and he moved with such a tender slowness that I knew there was no other word for what we were doing besides making love. Because he loved me. He was in love with me and I was so in love with him. The gooseflesh down my arms and the heat between my legs, it was all love for him. The fear and the insecurities that were kindling in the fire, they all loved him too, and that felt almost more important than the rest of it.

"Mr. Galloway," I whispered, petting my fingers across his cheeks and holding his face in the cradle of my hands.

He groaned at the endearment, the honorific.

"Mr. Galloway," I said again. "Look at me."

With the briefest hesitance, Flynn opened his eyes, the intensity of his dark brown eyes sucking the breath right out of my lungs. I dug my fingers into the side of his head, the soft silk of his hair like heaven against my palms.

"I'm yours," he rasped. "I'm looking."

He circled his hips, tip of his cock grazing over my prostate with the movement. I clenched my jaw, knowing my orgasm was unavoidable, but wanting to hold it off as long as possible because the weight of him, the look of him, the feel of him…it was everything. I never wanted it to end.

I knew it wouldn't be the last time we had sex, far from it, but there was something different in the air this time. Maybe it was the unspoken promise that his confession had brought around or maybe it was my willingness finally to accept all of the parts of him, even the ones that made me uncomfortable. This coupling was something big, something that was going to shoot us both well past the point of no return.

I had to know.

I had to be certain.

"I see you," he said, the pace of his thrusts quickening without turning punishing. Flynn still moved soft and slow, the wet slap of our skin when we came together the only thing louder than our breath.

"Do you?"

I was on the verge of admitting I loved him too, but his eyes went wide, nostrils flaring and his entire body went still save for the thick pulsing of his dick inside of me. Beside my head, Flynn's fingers flexed against the sheets, his mouth opening just enough to allow a sharp intake of breath.

I reached up and brushed the short strands of his dark hair off his face, smiling contentedly when he half collapsed and pressed his forehead against mine.

"That was all I wanted," he whispered.

"Hmmn?"

Even though his orgasm still trembled through his body, Flynn started to move again. Pumping in and out of me, he adjusted his angle and rose onto his knees, taking my own very hard cock into his hand.

"I wanted to see it in your eyes," he said.

"See what?"

"When you realized you loved me."

The breath in my throat turned into a laugh, and, with the quick twist of his wrist, I was coming all over him. My ass gripped and milked the last of the cum out of his cock while I painted his hand and stomach with jets of my own release. He held me down against him, making sure that even when my body twitched and seized, he stayed inside of me.

"It's not..." What even were words at that point? When Flynn was right here and all I could smell was his soap, and his sheets, and the salt of his cum.

He chuckled, and my eyes rolled back, head tipping as I bared my throat, trying to catch my breath and my thoughts.

"It's not news," I finally managed.

Flynn groaned, and I opened my eyes to see him licking my cum from his fingers, his softening cock still lodged as deep inside of me as our bodies would allow.

"Keeping secrets from me then?"

"I wanted to be sure."

His cock slipped free with an unsavory squelching noise, and we both winced at the loss. Flynn flopped onto his back beside me, rolling the condom off before tossing it onto the floor. I ached from where he'd been, but I didn't stop myself from reaching down to touch the tender puffiness from where we'd been previously joined.

"And now you are?" he asked.

I turned onto my side and quietly studied his face. He didn't say a word, but his eyes followed mine as they scanned across his features. From the faint lines around his eyes to the stubble across his jaw, and the smallest dimple in his chin, to his mouth…

His mouth.

I leaned in and slanted our mouths together, kissing the taste of my release and our sleep out of his mouth. The whole while, Flynn stroked his hands down my side, down my chest, using his body and his sounds to offer all the praise that he normally gave me with words.

I found it to be a completely different sort of experience, one that I could definitely find myself getting used to in the future. And what a surprise was that? Me getting used to a man like Flynn. To a life like this.

I kissed him until I was certain he knew the answer to the question, but the urge to say the words themselves had only been made stronger with the fire he'd tended. Even with both of us hard again, our still tired and sweaty bodies perfectly aligned, I offered the truth to the corner of his mouth, his jaw, his ear.

"I love you," I whispered. "I love you. I didn't mean to, but I love you."

Flynn grabbed me around the waist and hauled me on top of him at the same time he rolled onto his back. He took both our cocks into his fist, eyes narrowed as he tightened his fingers around our lengths.

"I love you," I said again. "I love you and I mean it."

"I love you. And please take this for what it is and not anything else, but thank you."

It could have meant a thousand different things, but I understood the intent as surely as I felt the stroke of his hand between my legs.

I'D BEEN SLACKING OFF AT WORK FOR A MONTH AND MY inattentiveness to my to-do list had finally caught up to me.

Rose and I had both received clear bills of health, but between his work schedule and the long hours I had been pulling at the office, we'd barely had time for more than a passing meal. I knew from our conversations he'd seen Grayson a couple times, Owen at least once, and Dalton more than I would have liked. But Dalton had been glued to Drake and Drake was Rose's best friend, and it was to be expected. Neither of those two had any indications that whatever had sparked between them would be real or lasting, but I couldn't fault them for having a good time.

After all, that's all I'd meant to do with Rose.

But life had a way, I supposed.

The last time I had dinner with Rose, I'd given him a key but promised not to make it weird. He wouldn't let me pay his rent, which I respected, but I wanted him to know that my house was as much his as it was mine. So Friday night, I found myself at my kitchen counter on my laptop when I heard his key in the lock. I closed the lid and stretched my arms, ready to be done even if my schedule for the day wasn't quite where I wanted it to be.

Rose had the night off, and the following day, which he hated but I loved, and I was going to take absolute advantage of the time.

I heard the familiar sound of his shoes landing on the travertine as he kicked them off and the soft pad of his socked feet as he headed inside.

"What did you do?" Rose asked, eyes immediately looking past me and into the living room.

"I bought a new couch."

I'd ordered it what felt like ages ago, the day after the first barb about my taste in interior design. The old piece was gray and sleek, more angles and lines than curves. It had matched the feel of the house, which I'd only recently come to realize was near sterile and possibly boring. The new one was different, and I knew it wouldn't suit Rose's taste, but it suited mine. Even if I was just beginning to learn what that was.

The new couch was a sectional, buttery brown leather with overstuffed cushions, the soft curve of the shape a stark contrast to the exact lines in the rest of the house. But I'd already spent many nights on it watching TV and drinking whiskey, talking to Rose on the phone as he drove home after work.

One day my home would truly be his, but until then, I could wait it out.

"When did you have time for this?" he asked, coming around the island and heading for me.

I stood and jerked my head toward the couch in question, and we both shifted direction and headed for it. The leather groaned under my weight, but wrapped around me almost like a blanket, and the decadent sound that left Rose's throat when he sat beside me was well worth the five-figure price tag.

"I ordered it a while ago," I said. "I made time, because it was important."

He shot me a knowing look, one brow raised toward the curls that hung over his forehead.

"Don't worry about it," I said. "Do you like it?"

"It's much more comfortable than the last one, but probably impossible to fuck on."

That ripped a laugh out of my throat, and I pulled him onto my lap, just happy to have him back in the same space as me. "How do you figure?"

He gave his body a little jerk, knees sinking into the cushions. "It's impossible to ride you on this thing."

"I can bend you over the back of it," I assured him, patting the back of the couch. "It would be nice and soft against your hips. Don't worry."

"There's about a thousand places in this house at hip level," he said. "I'm honestly shocked you haven't taken me over the kitchen counter yet."

"I have to save some surfaces for my housewarming present," I murmured, settling my hands against the slight swell of Rose's hips.

"Housewarming?"

"Once you live here."

"Wouldn't that be *my* housewarming present?" He started popping open the buttons on his work shirt until they were all undone and his chest was bare before me.

"What's yours is mine, remember, baby?"

I tweaked one of his nipples between my fingers and he gasped, leaning forward and bringing his chest very close to my mouth.

"I must have forgotten," he whispered.

"Then I'll have to do better at reminding you."

I moved my hands lower beneath his ass and pushed us both up from the couch to stand. Rose laughed and wrapped his arms around my neck, resting his chin on my shoulder and curling his legs around my waist. I loved how small he was. Loved the way he fit around me.

Rose laughed, his expression quickly turning somber when I carried him into my walk-in closet and set him down right in front of the full-length mirror. We were both half-dressed, him in his stained work pants and socks, me in my slacks.

I'd gone into the office earlier in the day and meant to change clothes when I got home, but I'd gotten as far as taking my shirt off before getting roped into another call and I'd spent the rest of the day with the best of intentions and not enough time.

Rose turned away from the mirror, ready to divest me of my clothes, but I grabbed him and spun him back.

"I want your clothes off." He pouted, turning his attention to his own button and zipper.

I leaned down and pressed my lips against his ear, catching his stare in the reflection of the mirror.

"Stop it," I warned.

Rose swallowed, pupils dilating and washing out the blue almost entirely.

"Sorry," he murmured.

"Sorry *who*?"

"Sorry." He let out a soft whimper. "Sorry, Mr. Galloway."

I closed the space between us and pressed my hard cock against the small of his back. "I don't think you appreciate how much it turns me on when you call me that."

"I very much appreciate it."

Reaching around to the front of him, I resumed the work he'd started on his pants, shoving them down to his ankles. He dropped his head against my chest, a practiced move by now, and leaned on me so he had the leverage to use his toes to take off his socks and kick the pants to the side.

Rose was nothing less than breathtaking, and seeing him in my closet, his cock and balls tucked away behind expensive lace and silk that I'd bought for him was enough to send a surge of owner-ship and pride up from my toes and straight to my mouth.

"I know I say it all the time, but you're gorgeous. You're perfect, Rose. You're so fucking perfect."

"For you," he whispered, lashes fluttering.

I undid my belt and made quick work of my own pants and my much less interesting underwear, pushing it all to the side and out of the way.

"Open your eyes," I said, nipping at the top of his ear.

He groaned, but obliged, again seeking out my stare in the reflection of the mirror.

"Don't look away," I told him.

"Don't embarrass me."

I tutted my tongue against the roof of my mouth and shook my head. "Don't be embarrassed."

He sighed, but held my gaze just the same. His cock was half hard, and he moved like he wanted to touch it, but that wasn't part of my plan for the night. At least, not yet. I pinned his wrists together at the small of his back, my fingers splayed around the small and knobby bones. The position arched his back and pushed his chest out, putting him on display in a way that made me absolutely ravenous.

And still he kept his eyes on me.

Slowly, I went to my knees behind him.

With his wrists still in my hand, the shift arched his back more, spreading his legs and bringing me eye level with the part of him I was after.

"My mouth is about to be very full," I said, sinking my teeth into the meat of his ass, leaving a wet mouthprint against his underwear. "So I'm going to need you to talk me through it."

"Are you fucking kidding me?" he gasped.

"Not in the slightest."

With my free hand, I tugged his panties down to his knees, bringing his legs back together. I realized that I wouldn't be able to keep my hold on him, but I was so close to his ass and so hungry for him, something had to give.

"Put your hands on the mirror and don't look away," I demanded.

"If you look away or if you quit talking, I stop."

That was the last warning I gave him before spreading his ass apart and sealing my lips around his gorgeous, pink rim. Rose groaned, but didn't say a word, so I stopped.

"Fuck," he cursed under his breath and slapped his palm against the corner of the mirror. "I don't know what to say."

I figured that would be the case. In fact, I'd planned on it. This was an idea that had been brewing in my head for a considerable amount of time because while Rose was learning to take what he wanted from me, he was far from believing that he deserved those things.

I wanted both.

"Start by asking for what you want," I suggested.

"I want you to eat my ass," he said quickly, pressing back and chasing after my mouth.

I delivered a quick swat against his backside, which earned me a high-pitched and surprised-sounding squeal. It made my cock leak, so I did it again.

"Do better," I said, licking him from his balls up to his hole.

"I want you to kiss my hole," he said, barely a whisper.

I glanced around his hip to catch his reflection in the mirror, and instead of looking at himself, he was staring down at me, which felt allowable in that moment. His cheeks, his throat, his chest, the whole front of him was flushed a violent shade of hot pink, and I knew how hard it had been for him to face himself and make the admission.

I dropped a very quick and very chaste peck against his hole and peered back around him. "What now?"

"With tongue," he said, chest heaving.

"How?" I asked him again. "My job is to please you, baby. It's your job to make sure I'm doing it right."

"You're going to kill me." He thumped his head against the mirror and closed his eyes, taking one deep breath after another.

I dragged my hands up and down the outside of his legs, hoping the touch would calm him. "Do you hate this?" I asked.

He shook his head.

"Does it make you uncomfortable?"

He nodded.

"Why?"

Rose groaned, banging his head against the mirror again. I already knew the answer, but it was important for *him* to know the answer. And it was important to me that he be able to understand it and verbalize it. I had no problem taking the lead and driving things in the bedroom. In fact, I very much preferred it. But it was important to me that my partner knew what they wanted and weren't scared to ask for it. It was so easy for me to sometimes get lost in my own world, in my own head. I knew how to get myself off, knew how to get him off, but I wanted it to be more than that. I wanted the depths of the exploration that could come with love and trust and respect, because if we didn't have that, what was the point of being in a relationship?

"I don't feel like I have a right," he finally confessed.

"Do you not have rights to everything here? With me? Is my body not yours to command however you want?"

"I thought you were the Dom," he said, opening his eyes and seeking me out in the mirror. "Thought you did the directing here."

"My job is to serve," I reminded him.

"There's no way around this, is there?" Rose groaned again, but even with the resistance, his cock was still long and thick, leaking precum from the tip and smearing it across the mirror.

"If you want me to stop, we can stop."

"That feels less fun," he grumbled.

Laughing, I pressed a kiss against the sharp jut of his hip bone and worked my way back between his legs.

"You're not wrong," I agreed.

Rose inhaled a deep breath and let it out, flexing his toes against the floor and shifting his weight from foot to foot. With my face squarely behind his ass, I felt the change in his posture when he reared back enough to keep his own face in focus. Another series of deep breaths and a few beads of sweat that trickled down the small of his back, and then he was ready.

"Mr. Galloway," Rose whimpered and I hummed an approving sound in the back of my throat.

"Yes, baby?"

"Lick my asshole, and then…then kiss it with…"

I licked him like he asked, then sealed my mouth around his rim with a sloppy and wet kiss.

"Like that, yeah. Oh, fuck."

Rose let out a slew of curses under his breath and I kissed him until my jaw ached, open-mouthed with a tease of my tongue around the rim of his hole.

"With tongue," he pleaded. "Wet like that with tongue and… oh…"

I swirled my tongue around his hole and them pressed past the tight muscle to get inside of him that way. With my hands still bracketed around his slim waist, fingers almost touching beneath his navel, I speared my tongue into him, kissing and licking him until his thighs began to shake and his words had devolved into moans and sighs.

Even though they were the prettiest noises I'd ever heard, that hadn't been our deal.

I pulled back and withdrew my tongue, ghosting my breath over all the wetness I'd left behind while I waited for him to give me my next instruction.

"Are you going to fuck me?" he asked.

"With what?"

"Anything." Rose laughed, weak and shaky. "Your mouth, your cock."

"All of the above," I promised.

"Cock now."

He didn't ask, he told me, and I was on my feet so quickly that I almost sent him headfirst into the mirror. Rose glanced up at me over his shoulder, cheeks still flushed, but a very happy smile on his face. I'd already brought lube into the closet earlier in the day, but no condoms since our test results had proved we didn't need them.

I flipped the tube open and squirted far too much onto my hand, a glob of it landing on the floor with a very undignified plop. Rose laughed, watching the whole scene behind him play out in the mirror, and I loved the way he'd followed instruction. He'd kept his eyes on me or himself the whole time, and he'd talked me through what he wanted until he wanted something more.

"I love that you're not afraid to ask me for what you want," I praised, holding him still with one hand as I lined my cock up with his spit-soaked hole.

"I'm terrified to ask for what I want," he said, swallowing audibly. I watched his Adam's apple bob in the mirror, and I pressed my forehead against the back of his shoulder. He was so much shorter than me I had to drop into a squat, but sliding into him came with the ease of straightening my knees.

"I love that you do it anyway," I said, pushing my cock into him. "I love that you know you're safe here with me."

"Oh, God," Rose wailed, rising up onto his toes as I seated myself all the way inside of him.

I wrapped one of my arms around his chest and held him steady, adjusting my height so he wasn't forced to scramble against the floor.

"Look at you," I whispered into his ear, mouthing against him with wet kisses while I waited for him to do it. "Look how good you look with my cock inside of you."

He held my stare in the reflection, eyes wide. "I'll come if I look down."

I slid one of my hands down his chest toward the bottom of his stomach, withdrawing and pushing back into him slowly.

"Feel it then," I said, lifting my hand.

Nervously, Rose settled his hand against himself and I covered his with my own, repeating the movement of my hips. It wasn't a huge shift, but as I buried my cock inside of him, his body swelled from the intrusion.

"You take my cock like you were made for it," I went on, setting a slow but hard pace. The pressure of our hands through his body was entirely new to me and was enough to bring me close to my own edge much sooner than I had planned.

"I love how you feel inside of me," he rasped. "When it hurts a little bit because you're so deep."

"I love that too."

"I want to feel you come inside of me." Rose's breathing stuttered and he tore his hand away from his stomach, slamming it against the mirror and screwing his eyes closed.

I went still, waiting for another reaction from him before I made another move. "Are you okay?"

"I don't want to come yet, and my body feels like it's on fire." He huffed and blinked me back into focus, the burn in his eyes sparking me toward the same infernal end.

"Don't come yet," I warned. "I'm nowhere near done with you."

"I don't think I have much control ov—"

The sharp snap of my hips shut him up and I grunted, changing the pace to something that would get me off before him. My intent wasn't to deprive him, though my motivation could have been considered selfish.

"If you don't want me to come, you can't fuck me like that," he protested between gasping breaths.

"I want you to come inside of me, baby." Rose's eyes rolled back in his head. "You can hold out for that, can't you?"

"I fucking hope so."

I redoubled my efforts, focused on filling him up so I could get onto my knees and take him in return.

Everything about Rose was an aphrodisiac for me. The feel of his sweaty skin against mine, the sounds he made when he was close to coming, the loud breaths when he slept after a long day of work. More than that, though, the way he made me feel. The way he made me want to be more myself for him.

Maybe he'd been onto something the very first night we'd met, but I was glad of my own arrogance. Too proud to see room for change when back then I was a man who didn't know myself at all. With my pre-ordered furniture and a severe lack of midnight milkshakes in my diet, I'd built a life around expectation and accomplishment.

I hadn't truly known a thing about myself until I walked into Rose's life on a dare and he'd shown me who I was meant to be.

"I'm gonna come," I choked out, fucking into him so deeply, I moved him off the floor entirely. Rose gasped and whimpered, his entire face glitching from pleasure when I set him back onto his feet. And the whole time, he watched me.

He *saw* me.

When I eased myself out of him, Rose was quick to reach behind himself and press his fingers against his still gaping hole. Cum trickled out of him, though I knew it wasn't a loss and there was plenty to be found much deeper inside of him. He brought his hand around front of him and smeared my cum up the length of his cock.

Something dangerous and heady flashed in his eyes, but neither of us looked away, even as my stare flickered between his face and the masterful way he covered his cock with my cum.

"Get on your knees now, Mr. Galloway," he said, chest heaving. "It's my turn."

Even on his hands and knees in the middle of his closet that was very nearly the size of my apartment, Flynn looked like a predator. He was six feet of long and lean muscle wrapped in tanned skin with a dick to die for and an ass like a statue's. And his eyes followed me around the room like he was ready to strike, or fuck me again if I didn't hurry up.

I wasn't worried about him changing his mind, but it had been so long since I'd gotten him beneath me. I was already perilously close to coming, a truth my body reminded me every inch I moved. My muscles ached from how thoroughly he'd just taken me and my chest matched the feeling…on account of the whole mirror thing. But there was absolutely no way I was going to come anywhere besides as deep inside Flynn as our bodies allowed.

"Hurry up then," he grunted, dropping his forehead against the carpet.

It caused his back to arch into a deeper angle, spreading his ass apart and showing me the exact place I wanted to be.

Flynn had dropped the lube onto the floor, and I snatched it up, pouring a liberal amount all over my shaft and my fingers. With one hand splayed against his lower back, I made quick work of shoving my fingers into him. The sounds he made from the penetration went straight to my cock and I prepped him as quickly as felt fair. Once he started fucking back onto my fingers, I pulled out, lining my cock up and pushing into him.

He cursed under his breath, his exhale turning into something that sounded a lot like my name, and I had to go still after bottoming out so I didn't fill him on the first thrust.

"Look at yourself," he choked out, face still pressed against the carpet.

I should have known better than to think my little encounter with the mirror was finished just because we flipped. But I didn't want to look at myself. Flynn was almost out of the reflection entirely and it was one thing to look at myself with him there behind me, it was another entirely to have those moments almost alone.

"I want to look at you," I said, tightening my fingers around his hips so I could fuck into him harder.

"Do as you're told, Rose."

My jaw clenched, but heat raced up my spine at the command. Not for the first time, I wondered if there was something to be said about the whole Dom/sub thing that Flynn loved so much. I'd bought into it to some degree, only really coming into it recently in a way that felt right. But when the instruction landed on my ears, my brain almost went haywire.

The juxtaposition of being on top while being told what to do was enough to wipe my mind clear of anything beside the things Flynn said and the things I felt. I supposed that was the point.

"Fine," I grumbled, angling my chin to the left so I could see my face in the mirror.

"Describe it to me," he said. "Tell me what you see."

I withdrew until the flared head of my cock teased and pulled against his rim, then slowly pressed my way back in, setting a pace that gave me the ability to keep speaking before I worried about answering him. Flynn gave me time to get my pace and my bearings, but he rolled his cheek against the floor so I could see the side of his face and I knew I was out of time.

"I love how you look when you bottom," I started saying.

"You're so much bigger than me, so much more dominant. When you get on your back, on your knees, the sight alone is almost enough to make me come."

"Then why aren't you?" He snickered.

I slammed as deep into him as my cock would reach, and he whimpered.

Flynn *whimpered*.

"Because I feel powerful like this," I admitted. "I feel like I'm in control when my cock is in your ass."

"You're always in control," he said. "Even when you're on your knees."

I trailed one of my hands around the front of him, reaching to see if his cock had gotten hard for a second time.

"I never went soft," he said, like he knew what I'd been after.

"Can you come again?"

"Can you make me?"

The tease reminded me of our first night together, and immediately I was dedicated to the idea of him being the one who came so many times that he was boneless. A vision of Flynn crawling back to the bed, spent from all the sex sent a jolt though my balls, and I clenched my teeth together, trying to push myself away from the edge.

"What else do you see?" he asked.

"Me," I whispered, admittedly softer than the rest.

"How do you look when you fuck me?"

Flushed.

I looked flushed because the talking was hot, but the describing was…well, the describing was hot, but it was also uncomfortable. Especially with him out of the frame.

"Like I was made to do it," I answered.

"Are your nipples hard?"

"Yes."

"Pinch them." With his eyes on me, Flynn watched as I tweaked my nipple, gasping from the wet coldness of my fingers.

He growled, turning his face back toward the floor. "You're so unbelievably gorgeous."

I chuckled, bracing one hand against his waist and the other around his shoulder so I could find better leverage.

"If you can still manage a five syllable word, I'm not doing too good back here," I murmured.

"Then do better."

"As you say, Mr. Galloway."

I stopped talking, then.

We both stopped talking until my name was on lips and his cum was across his fingers. When Flynn came, all of those muscles I'd been admiring earlier when tense and taut, gripping my cock and milking the cum from me whether I was ready for it or not. My orgasm crashed through me and I fell forward, my weight taking Flynn's arms out and sending his chest against the floor. My hips moved on their own, heat searing over me as I pumped my release into him.

Gasping, I rolled off of him, landing on top of a Tom Ford shoebox and the bottle of lube. Flynn's legs collapsed under him and he landed on his stomach, the hand he'd been using to jerk off still sandwiched between him and the floor. He turned his head to the side, toward me, but he kept his eyes closed.

Flynn was handsome.

He always had been, and not just in a traditionally attractive way. He was chiseled and respectable with his dark hair and dark eyes, and those big hands of his. But Flynn was always the one to compliment me, to say the kind praise to me. I tried to remember the last time I'd told him how hot he was or how kind he was, and found myself coming up woefully short. More than anything, I'd spent our time together telling Flynn he was too dominant, too arrogant, too rich, just…too much.

"I love you," I said quickly, finding the strength to scramble into a sitting position.

With a groan, he rolled onto his side and opened his eyes. "I love you too."

"You're…" There had to be a better word than handsome, better than gorgeous, better than pretty. "You're breathtaking, Flynn."

Those olive-toned cheeks of his turned red and the corner of his mouth pulled up into a tired but pleased smile.

"Thank you, Rose."

"I mean it." I didn't know if it was the dopamine crash after the orgasm or all the time I'd spent staring at myself in the mirror and saying nice things to myself, but I wanted him to know I felt the same for him. That he deserved all of that praise and more. "I know I've been kind of hard to love, and I—"

"Don't." He cut me off, pressing his cum-stained fingers against my mouth to silence me. Instead, I licked the taste of him from his fingertips and went on.

"I've been argumentative."

"I told you I don't mind a challenge."

"Love should be easy," I said.

"And it is." He set another fingertip against my mouth, pinching my lips to stop me from talking. "Loving you is the easiest thing I've ever done, and I will not have you sit here with my cum up your ass and on your tongue while you try to tell me otherwise."

He let his hand fall away, but only to shift onto his hands and knees, and then onto his ass. We were still barely level, considering how short I was, but he stared down at me with as serious of an expression as he always had.

"I won't hear any more of this slander," he said. "Don't even start on it. Not after all the truths you told us both in front of that mirror."

I swallowed back any remaining protests that would have dared slip out, because Flynn was right.

"I'm sorry. It's…it's an old habit."

"I have some of those myself," he said, reaching for my hands and accidentally pulling me across the closet and onto his lap. "They're nothing to apologize for."

"I love you," I told him again. "I really do. I love you so much."

"I love you so much," he repeated. "I also love that your cum is so deep inside of me that it's probably still going to be there in the morning."

"Oh, my God." I buried my face against his shoulder, and he laughed, rearranging me on his lap so he could stand with me wrapped around him.

"The only thing that feels better than your cock inside my ass is mine inside yours," he said, carrying me toward the bedroom. "And even then, it's a *very* close second."

"Then I'll have to try harder next time."

Flynn dropped me onto the comforter, and I kicked it out of the way, sheets included, to make room for us. He crawled in with me and reached for the fireplace remote, turning it on high before stretching out one of his arms to make room for me against his chest.

With my cheek pressed against his sternum, I could tell his heart hadn't slowed from earlier. It hammered out a steady and quick pace against my ear. I rested one of my hands against my own chest, curious if the beats matched. They were close, but not in time, instead beating out a near constant vibration through my body from one side or the other.

We lay like that for what felt like hours, but couldn't have been more than a few minutes. Across the room, the fire crackled, and the sweat on our skin dried until our bodies warmed up from the contact and the sheets. Flynn folded his arm in and worked his fingers through my hair, then bent to kiss the top of my head.

"Tomorrow morning I want to make you breakfast," he murmured.

"I think we can arrange that."

"Then I want to bend you over the back of my very new and un-sexed couch and fuck you until you can't see straight."

Even though my balls were absolutely, one hundred percent, completely and fully drained, my cock twitched at the promise, poking against Flynn's thigh. He laughed and took my hand, pressing it against his dick, which had done the same.

"And then what?" I asked, smiling against him.

His cock was hot and smooth in my hand, and I was happy just to hold him there, another part of his body against mine. Another piece of him that belonged to me.

"Admittedly, Rose." I could hear the smile in voice, followed by a short yawn. "I have no idea."

I closed my eyes, using my toes to grab the sheet and pull it up until I could get my hand around it, then I tugged it higher and tucked us both in.

I found it somehow reassuring that Flynn didn't know what came next. I knew he wasn't speaking so much to what the rest of our Saturday was going to look like, but more of an uncertainty about our future together. Not meaning that there was any possibility of being without him, because now that I'd allowed myself to get used to him, there was no chance in hell of me giving him up without a fight. But more to mean that he didn't know what the next step was, the next goal post.

We were both in this together and we were both new to so many things about what it meant to be with each other. There was compromise, sure, but there was happiness, and love, and obviously really great sex.

"I hope that you dream about me tonight," Flynn whispered.

I wiggled against him until our faces were close enough for me to steal a kiss, and then I gave him a truth. I hoped he would take it for the compliment—for the praise—it was. Flynn had come in like a cyclone and turned my world upside down, and considering our relationship had started as a kiss on a dare and turned into something bigger than us both, I knew I was the luckiest fool on the planet.

"I've dreamed about you my whole life. I don't think I'll stop now."

CHAPTER 33
FLYNN

IT HAD BEEN SIX LONG MONTHS AND A HANDFUL OF ROUNDS OF SEX IN the closet, and the bathroom, and even the foyer, but I still hadn't convinced Rose to move in with me. I'd taken him to his knees and on his knees, I'd had him with my feet up around my ears and then later on with his legs tied to the posters on the bed. I'd asked him over breakfast and dinner, and I'd even resorted to having Grayson and Owen try to find out why he kept telling me no. I knew Rose was as stubborn as I was, but his denials were something entirely different.

"Will you stop asking me if I say yes?" he countered one morning, standing at the foot of the bed in nothing but his work pants and an amused smile.

"Obviously."

"Come and ask me out here." He jerked his head and disappeared out of the bedroom.

I flung the covers back and chased after him, catching up to him in the living room. He stood behind the couch, his waist pressed against the back and his eyes focused on the hallway. His stare followed me across the living room until I came to stand behind him, covering his body with my own. With one hand braced on either side of the couch, I dipped my head down and sucked the crook of his neck until he moaned.

"Will you move in with me?" I asked, licking my way up to his hear.

"I can't," he whispered, back arching as he bent halfway over the couch.

"You're killing me."

"I can't possibly move in with you until I know if your new couch is good for sex or not."

The breath left my lungs in a whoosh, and I had his pants around his ankles before the sound of his laughter reached my ears.

"Are you shitting me?"

Even though he hadn't moved in with me, Rose spent enough time over at my house that I'd taken to stashing lube somewhere in every room. The living room was no exception and I tore myself away from him long enough to grab the bottle out of the decorative box on the side table.

I shoved my pajamas down and kicked free of them, slathering my quickly hardening cock with more lube than the little brat deserved. He kept laughing even as I bent him in half, pressing his face into the cushions and using my other hand to guide my dick between his cheeks.

"The other one was ugly as sin, but it wo—"

I pushed into him, cutting off the rest of his retort.

"But it what?" I asked, burying myself to the hilt.

I fucked into Rose so hard, his laughs turned into breathy moans, and the moans turned into pants and then he was babbling my name and singing hymns and cursing me all at once.

I lifted him enough that I could get his cock into my hand, because for as much money as I had and as happy as I was to be fucking Rose over the back of the couch I'd bought specifically for him, I didn't know what cum would do the leather and I didn't want to replace it so soon. Curling my hand around his cock, I began to stroke him in time with my thrusts, getting harder every time his teeth snapped together from the force of it.

"Is it good?" I asked, tightening my fingers. "Is it good for fucking, Rose?"

He answered me with an orgasm, shooting jets of cum against my hand. He cried out, thrashing against me and the couch as his release spurted out of his dick. He was hot against my fingers, and I smeared them across his open mouth, groaning when he sealed his lips around me and sucked.

"That's it, baby." My cock slammed into him, skin loud and wet from the lube as I slid my fingers toward his throat. Sometimes I wished he gagged when he had his mouth full, but I didn't hate the way he took me into his throat and I would never complain. "Suck them clean so we don't make a mess of the couch that means so much to you."

"Don't...don't care," he mumbled around my fingers, and I withdrew them, blindly scooping the cum I'd streaked across his chin and cheeks onto his waiting tongue.

Rose writhed against me, hips circling as he humped his still coming cock into the leather. Fuck the stains. Fuck all of it. I'd buy a new couch every day if he wanted to ruin them over and over. None of it mattered.

Nothing mattered besides him and me and these moments.

The way he felt so good beside me, inside of me, beneath me. The way he loved me and let me love him. The trust, the responsibility. I'd spent years avoiding all of the things I'd wanted the most, and maybe that was for the better. Because having them for the first time with Rose made me appreciate them so much more than I ever thought possible.

"Flynn." He gasped, reaching back and digging his nails into the outside of my thigh. "Don't stop. Don't stop. Fuck."

I wanted to give him everything he wanted, but I was only a man and he was a dream come true.

"I fucking love you." I bit his ear, hips stuttering. "I fucking love how you take me. How you beg me for what you need."

"Close again... oh, God," he wailed, grip loosening on my leg. He slapped the outside of my thigh like he was in pain, whispering curses under his breath as I chased after my own release. I'd already started to sweat, moisture beading in the center of my chest and racing down my stomach, mixing with the lube. I'd fuck every possible bodily fluid he'd allow into him—spit, sweat, cum, tears. I'd give that man anything he asked for, and I only wanted one more thing.

Well, at least one more thing besides everything.

"Move in with me," I choked the words out as my own orgasm slammed into me. The urgency of them as bright and loud in my brain as if it was a siren calling attention to the obvious lack in my life.

I lost control of my body after the last demand, fucking into him so rough that he was half over the couch with his toes dangling in the air before I'd emptied myself fully inside of him. He whined and moved against me, then gasped and stilled. His entire body trembled, and I knew without looking that he'd come a second time...all over the leather.

"Move in with me, baby." I kissed the back of his neck, lifted him, and lowered his feet to the floor.

Over his shoulder, I could see the sweat stains on the back of the couch, the sticky white smears of cum from where he'd spilled a second time. I swiped the mess up with my fingers and eased half out of him, smothering my cock with his cum and pushing back in. I was so sensitive, every nerve in my body on fire, and we both stuttered and gasped as my softening dick filled him again.

"Mr. Galloway." He let loose a trembling exhale, dropping his head against my chest and revealing the soft curve of a tired and sated smile. "I thought you'd never ask."

I didn't waste any time getting him packed up and shuffled across town. We'd spent the night at his apartment a handful of times before the move, and I knew Rose was self-conscious about the space, but I loved it. His apartment was small and comfortable. It smelled like him, and eventually it smelled like both of us together. Now my house smelled like the two of us, the crisp pine of his preferred soap and the ever-present undercurrent of sweat, thanks to all the sex.

I had no complaints.

While we'd barely started to integrate our things, our lives were already intertwined. And that was how I found myself out on Thursday night with my friends, while Rose caught the turtle races across town with Owen, Grayson, and Grayson's friend Wesley. Drake might have been with them too, or he could have been tied to a bed somewhere waiting for Dalton to get done.

It was anybody's guess.

It had made me happier than I'd ever admit out loud when Grayson and Owen were so quick to take Rose under their wings. He was younger than both of them and a thousand times more temperamental, but I knew they'd be a good support system for him while he adjusted to this new part of his life. Hell, it was an adjustment for me too, but nowhere near the change Rose was dealing with. Watching how he'd taken everything about being with me in stride just made me love him more.

He occupied the main part of my brain almost all of the time. If I wasn't with him, I was looking forward to seeing him. If we were together, I was looking forward to getting him naked. If he was naked, I couldn't wait for the quiet moments when he whispered secrets to me and touched my skin with the sharp edges of his fingernails. There was always something to look forward to with him, and I loved that change and what it meant for my life.

For our life.

Rose had taken something I thought I understood, dominance and praise and responsibility and trust, and shown me that I'd really only ever scratched the surface. Without even trying to, he'd pushed me out of my own comfort zones, forcing me to really examine what all of those things meant for me. And what I wanted them to mean for somebody else. He'd unintentionally shown me how to better myself, even when I hadn't seen room for improvement.

I loved him so fucking much, and I couldn't wait for him to get home so I could tell him that.

"You're mooning," Rob observed, jingling the ice in his empty glass.

I took a sip of my whiskey and gave him the finger. "That can't be a real figure of speech."

"You're distracted," Archie said.

"Is that what mooning means?" Dalton asked.

"Wait. *Mooning*?" Archie scrunched his nose.

"Mooning."

"I thought it was *mooing*."

"I'm not a fucking cow." I finished the rest of my drink and raised the empty glass in the air, catching our waiter's attention.

Rob rolled his eyes and pulled his phone out of his pocket, tapping away at the screen before giving all of us a self-satisfied smirk.

"Mooning," he said, poking at his phone. "Behaving in a listless manner."

"I'm hardly listless," I argued.

"About being here you are," Archie countered.

I let out a tired breath, shaking my head. "I look forward to our Thursday nights."

"We're going to have to change the plan soon," Rob said, returning his phone to his pocket.

He was the one to say what I know I'd been thinking. Our standing drink night was one thing when the five of us were single, but with Rob, Archie, and me all partnered up and monogamous—as far as I could tell, at least—it was time to renegotiate what our nights looked like.

"You can't cancel our friendship just because the lot of you have fucking boyfriends," Dalton argued, folding his arms in front of him and looking more put off than I'd ever seen him.

"That's not what they said," Barclay assured him with a pat against his elbow.

"This place is too small for eight of us is all I'm saying. We'd be too loud and annoying," Rob explained.

"We're already that." Archie laughed, accepting a drink from the waiter, who had appeared with five fresh glasses. He collected the empties and again left us to our conversation.

"You know what I mean."

"What do you propose?" I asked.

"Sex party at Rob's house," Dalton suggested with a cocky grin.

"Just because I allow Grayson to tag team touch-starved men with you doesn't mean he's allowed to run amuck on the general population," Rob drawled with a half shrug.

"Wait." I raised a hand to stop him. "You let Grayson what?"

"It's not nearly as exciting as he's making out." Dalton shook his head, the earlier grin turning into a pretend frown. "He lets Grayson play with rope and then steals him away. If I want more than that, it's all on Barclay."

"Don't sound so excited about the prospect," Barclay deadpanned.

"I just mean you and I go back."

"Don't we just," he mused.

"My house is an option," Rob said, cutting off Barclay and Dalton's back and forth. "So is yours."

"Mine?" I asked.

"With that nice new couch of yours," Archie teased.

I sighed, rubbing the bridge of my nose while I entertained the idea.

Now that Rose lived with me, I did enjoy being home more than I had before. Having a comfortable couch was a cherry on top of the cake that looked a lot like him running around mostly naked in barely there underthings. At the end of the day, with the expansive open floor plan, my house had been designed for entertaining, even though I rarely used it for that. Rose had invited Drake over more times than Rob had been over in the past year, and I wondered if I was a bad friend, if not just a distracted one.

"We could try my house," I offered.

Dalton chuckled. "I still vote Rob's."

"We could also just go to the turtle races with the other menfolk," Archie suggested.

"How is that bar any different than our bar?" Barclay asked.

"It's a lot louder, for one." Archie raised a finger, then added a second. "And the drinks are cheaper."

"Since when have you cared about how much a drink costs?" I asked.

"Since Owen."

The answer came quick and easy, and it was enough to drown any retort in the back of my throat before the words had a chance to come together.

Since Owen for Archie, and since Rose for me.

It was one of those things between us that even though my taste in liquor wasn't something he'd ever poked at, I knew it was one of the expenditures that had always sat uncomfortably with him. Undoubtedly as a result of the time he'd spent in the service industry. Even living with me, he'd kept his job, which I knew better than to complain about. Without the rent to pay, though, he'd started buying things for himself, which ended up also being treats for me, and I would never complain about that.

One of his most recent splurges was monthly manicures, sometimes with colored polish and sometimes without. There was definitely something to be said for his finely cleaned cuticles and smooth palms wrapping around my cock at the end of a long day.

"Rob's kitchen whiskey costs more than the shit here," I reminded Archie.

He turned to me with the corner of his mouth quirked up into a grin. "Your house it is then. Next week."

"And we're inviting Grayson, Owen, and Rose?" Rob asked.

Dalton took a long swallow of his whiskey, smacking his lips. "I'm just letting everyone know I love your men, but I hate the idea of this."

"Not every week," I promised, but he gave me a doubtful look. "I swear."

"We'll see."

"What about Val?" Barclay asked, leaning back in his seat and stretching out his legs.

That was the question, wasn't it?

What *about* Val?

Val, who had been Barclay's most loyal partner for well over a year. Val, who had been the one to nurse Barclay through the engagement and marriage of his first love, Dennis. Val, who was definitely not a boyfriend, but something far more than a casual partner, even if neither of them wanted to admit it out loud.

"Are you going to admit you're in love with him?" Archie asked, bringing up his ongoing taunt about their relationship.

"Val can come," I said before Barclay could mutter a curse. "Of course he can come. He's always welcome."

"Again." Dalton gave a little wave. "I hate this."

"Aren't you fucking Rose's best friend anyway?" Archie asked, looking smug at the question.

Dalton was, in fact, sleeping with Rose's best friend. I knew that because I'd heard it from Dalton himself, and also from Rose, and even from Drake on the occasions he'd been over and talking entirely too loudly about it. But I also knew that Drake and Dalton were so casual that it made Val and Barclay look like they'd been married for decades.

"Drake is just a bit of fun," Dalton said. "And he knows it. He's not on the Christmas card list."

"You send Christmas cards?" Archie asked with a laugh.

"I think I'm ready to go." Dalton poured the rest of his whiskey down his throat and stood, smoothing his hands down the front of his slacks.

I grabbed for his hand, catching his wrist instead. He looked down at me, lips pulled taut and expression looking tired. He could handle the teasing, I knew, but the shift in our friend group wasn't sitting right with him. I needed to make a point to spend time with him one on one, with or without the rest of them. Dalton had always been an amazing friend to me, and I didn't want him feeling growing pains over the changes in the rest of our lives. "They're just teasing, D."

He gave a small nod and shook me off. "I know."

"Excuse me?" A soft voice from behind me had all of us turning our heads toward a petite, middle-aged woman in a very plain-looking business suit. She had a manila envelope in her hand, a stern expression on her face, and she looked absolutely out of place at the bar.

"Yes?" Rob asked, stare dragging from her sensible shoes up to the blunt cut of her mousy brown bob.

"I'm looking for Dalton Fox."

"That's me." Dalton shifted toward her, just as she shoved the manila envelope against his chest. His hands came up, instinctively trying to catch the envelope before it fell. "What's this?"

She gave him a casual shrug and took a step back, swiping her hands together like she was washing them off.

"Mr. Fox, you've been served."

ALSO BY KATE HAWTHORNE

Trophy Doms Social Club

Humbled

Edged

Praised

Bound

Shared

Giving Consent

Worth the Risk

Worth the Wait

Worth the Fight

Worth the Chance

All in Good Time

Necessary Space

Necessary Time

Duality

Dual Destruction

Dual Surrender

Dual Defiance

Two Truths and a Lie

A Real Good Lie

A Cold Hard Truth

A Matter of Fact

Room for Love

Reckless

Heartless

Faultless

Fearless

Limitless

A Very Messy Motel Brothers Wedding

Relentless

Secrets in Edgewood

A Taste of Sin

The Cost of Desire

A Love Made Whole

Secrets in Edgewood: The Complete Series

The Lonely Hearts Stories

His Kind of Love

The Colors Between Us

Love Comes After

Until You Say Otherwise

STANDALONES

Rebound

One for the Road

Daybreak - Vino & Veritas

Unfettered

Dreams

A Thousand Lifetimes

<u>**COLLABORATIONS**</u>

With E.M. Denning

Irreplaceable

Future Fake Husband

Future Gay Boyfriend

Future Ex Enemy

With J.R. Gray

May the Best Man Win

ABOUT KATE HAWTHORNE

Kate Hawthorne is a writer and author educator with over three dozen published romance novels spread across two successful and award winning pen names.

Known for stories that pack a figurative (and sometimes literal) punch, Kate has built a recognizable brand that consistently delivers emotionally charged and character driven happy endings for everyone.

Visit her website
http://www.katehawthornebooks.com

Sign up for Kate's newsletter
http://www.katehawthornebooks.com/extra

facebook.com/authorkatehawthorne

x.com/katewriteswords

instagram.com/kate.hawthorne

patreon.com/katehawthorne

www.ingramcontent.com/pod-product-compliance
Lightning Source LLC
Chambersburg PA
CBHW030129010826
48973CB00002B/486